*For all the "cowboys"
who defend our lives and liberty.*

Praise for *Slow Hand*

"Could hardly put it down…I highly recommend *Slow Hand* as an enjoyable romantic story with some comedy, some drama, and lots of scorching sex."

—*USA Today Happy Ever After*

"The rich story line and vibrant characterizations serve to make *Slow Hand* an intense and satisfying read. There are several twists along the way to keep the reader guessing… A quite gratifying read; enjoyable and highly recommended."

—*Fresh Fiction*

"A sizzling beginning in her Hot Cowboy Nights series. A great story and even greater characters make this a must-read."

—*Romance at Random*

"For erotic passion and one-liners, the first book in Vane's new series will satisfy… Vane's latest gets a big yee-haw."

—*RT Book Reviews*

"[A] red-hot cowboy tale… Well-paced, scorching scenes and witty banter move the story along while setting the stage for Wade's war-hero brother to find his own true love in the next installment."

—*Publishers Weekly*

"Pull the fire alarm and stock up on fire extinguishers for this steamy romance!"

—*Avon Romance*

Chapter 1

Casper, Wyoming

Seated on the top rail above the bull pen, Janice watched with growing impatience as the final riders finished. Unlike most of the girls she'd grown up with, she'd never had much interest in can chasing. Sure there was good money in it, but she just didn't see the challenge in running circles around barrels.

Bulls, on the other hand — massively muscled, notoriously unpredictable, and dangerously aggressive — were her passion. She'd been raised with cattle and had fed bawling calves from the earliest time she could remember, but bucking bulls provided her family's real living.

While the final scores were announced and the barrels cleared from the arena, Janice hopped down from her perch. Time to get back to work. Although she could have used some help tonight, there was none to be had. Ready or not, she was Combes' Bucking Bulls' new chute boss. Janice walked the length of the pens, inspecting the animals and watching for any sign of trouble as the other stock hands prodded and loaded their animals into their respective chutes.

There were at least two dozen riders already surrounding the bull pens. Some were shooting the shit, and others were immersed in their preparations. Janice looked casually over the group for the one cowboy who made her pulse race. He was one of the early draws, but Dirk Knowlton hadn't made his appearance yet.

Although he'd never looked sideways at her, Janice had followed Dirk's rodeo career since high school, when they'd competed on the same team. He'd ridden rough stock while she'd competed in breakaway roping. She'd always enjoyed working with ropes and livestock. Roping required speed, skill, and near-perfect coordination between horse and rider—practical skills that were invaluable on a working ranch—and Janice was nothing if not practical. She'd been real good at it too. Probably could have gotten a scholarship or even gone pro if her family's needs hadn't kept her tied to the ranch.

In the end, she'd gone to work full-time for her father, and Dirk had won a full scholarship to Montana State. She'd run into him on occasion since then, mainly during branding season when all the ranches helped each other out, but he'd never taken notice of her then either. He'd been too wrapped up in Rachel Carson. Along with half the boys at Twin Bridges High, he'd only had eyes for Rachel. Gangly Janice had never stood a chance against the pert and pretty, blue-eyed blond.

Since graduation she'd rarely run into Dirk, usually no more than a hat-tipping at the ranching co-op or the stock sale, but now that she was working the rodeos, their paths had once more crossed—not that it made any difference. Little had changed. Rachel was still the rodeo queen, leading the grand entry glittering with rhinestones, while Janice looked on from the rough stock chutes, mired ankle-deep in manure and smelling like the livestock.

Even now that she'd finally filled out in all the right

places, she was either completely tongue-tied or jabbered like an idiot whenever Dirk came around, which was every day for the past week. It wasn't just his rugged good looks that made her palms sweat—there was something about Dirk, besides his long and lanky physique, that put him head and shoulders above the rest.

With her heart lurching into her throat, Janice watched as the cowboy of her dreams swaggered up to the holding pens. Clad in ass-hugging denim with leather chaps flapping, a white Stetson shadowing his ice-blue eyes, and a rigging bag slung over one broad shoulder, he threw his rope over the corral panel in preparation for his ride.

Now or never, Janice. He'll be called up any minute.

With her heart hammering, she inhaled for courage and licked her lips with a tongue that suddenly felt as dry as sandpaper. "I watched you on Outlaw Josie Wales in the second go 'round yesterday," she blurted.

"Why thank you, ma'am." Dirk tipped his hat with a mile wide grin.

"You about spurred his head off," she continued. "It was one of the best rides I ever did see."

Grady Garrison leaned over from his perch on the adjoining pen and spat a wad of dip. "Good thing Pretty Boy scored so high on the broncs, 'cause he sure as shit won't make the cut on the bulls."

"That so?" Dirk paused in prepping his rope, his eyes meeting Grady's for only a second. "Funny, as I recall it, just last week in Red Lodge I made the whistle while your ass hit the dirt." He went back to work, crushing the lump of rosin and wrapping his gloved hand around the bull rope.

Grady jumped down from the pen with narrowed, steel-colored eyes. "I'm still going into the short round with the high score. You're delusional as shit if you think to beat me." His shoulders were thrown back and his thumbs hooked in his belt loops—the ones that supported the huge Collegiate Champion Bull Rider buckle.

Any stranger who didn't know them as longtime rodeo buddies would surely think fists were about to fly, but Janice suspected it was just pre-ride posturing. Cowboys, as a rule, were ridiculously competitive. Still, she bit her lip at the tension of rising testosterone.

"Maybe you're right, Grady, but a closed mouth gathers no boots."

"What're you sayin'? You think I'm all talk?"

Dirk shrugged. "I think a lotta rodeo legends are made by a flannelmouth on a bar stool. So maybe you'll wanna put your money where that big fat mouth is?"

She wondered how far they'd want to take this pissing contest. Dirk was a decent bull rider, but the smaller and wiry Grady was one of the best. Unfortunately, like a lot of cowboys, he too often let his mouth run off, and his ego get in the way of his good sense.

"All right, Pretty Boy. How 'bout the lowest score on the next ride buys the drinks tonight? And none of that cheap shit either."

Dirk stood up straight, rolled his neck and shoulders, and then extended his hand. "You're on."

Grady accepted it with a laugh. Janice breathed a sigh of relief. The announcer gave the final scores on the barrel racing and then broadcast the imminent start of the bull riding.

Grady puffed up like a fighting cock as soon as audience attention swiveled to their end of the arena. "Now the *real* rodeo begins."

"Plenty of people watch the other events too," Janice protested. "The broncs are my personal favorite." She darted a glance to Dirk. "Classier than the bull riding."

"Bullshit," Grady scoffed. "You know as well as I do that the bulls are what eighty percent of these people come for. No one really gives a rip about all the warm-up acts, though team ropin's probably the worst." He looked to Janice with an air of expectancy.

"Don't ask why, Janice," Dirk warned. "It's his worst joke—and the one he always uses when he's itching for a bar fight."

"Oh yeah?" Janice couldn't stifle her grin. "Why's that, Grady?"

Grady smirked. "Because team ropin's a lot like jacking off, Sweet Cheeks—kinda fun to do, but no one wants to watch it."

Dirk rolled his eyes and Janice shook her head with a derisive snort. Grabbing her flank ropes and hook, she methodically moved down the row of massively muscled, shifting, snorting bovines. Janice spoke in low, calm tones as she handled each animal. She knew every bull in the circuit by name and endeavored to treat each one with the care and respect they deserved. To her annoyance, Grady followed her, jabbering on about nothing, while she flanked her bulls. It was damned irritating how the cocky SOB refused to be ignored.

After finishing with Sudden Impact, Janice double-checked the bulls in the pens. When she returned, Dirk was standing on the platform above Magnum

Force, armored with his Kevlar vest. "You the gunner?" she asked.

"Yup." Dirk nodded. "Drew this big bastard. New one, isn't he?" He jerked his head toward the massive Brahma shifting restlessly in his pen.

"Yeah. He's new all right."

"What happened to that ol' sonofabitch, The Enforcer? Did you retire him?"

"Hell no. Daddy sold him. Pocketed a big chunk of change and still had enough left to buy two replacements that he found down at this shithole farm in Arkansas. Mag here is one of 'em." She nodded to the bull.

While her father had made a respectable name in stock contracting, she'd always felt his methods were a bit hit-or-miss. He'd struck it lucky enough times to stay in the business, but would never make it to the top because he was too quick to sell his best bulls for cash in hand. To Janice's frustration, he'd never focused on the business of breeding his own stock. They had the land and the know-how, so it seemed a wasted opportunity.

Janice, on the other hand, saw a future in bucking bulls. While traditional rodeo was dying out, struggling just to break even, the new bull-riding associations were packing 'em in, even in the big cities. It was the new "extreme" sport. Breeding the rankest bulls for the toughest cowboys was her dream—what she was secretly working toward. She just needed the right foundation bull. She'd already wondered if Mag might be the one. If he made it big on this circuit, she was determined to buy him out for breeding—no matter the cost.

"I detect a pattern here. *Outlaw Josie Wales?*

Magnum Force?" Dirk chuckled. "Your ol' man's a real Clint Eastwood fan, isn't he?"

"Yeah. He's always named his rough stock after favorite movies but the primest of the lot are called after Clint Eastwood flicks. Be careful with this one, Dirk. I think Mag just might be the rankest bull we've ever had. He's no chute fighter, but once that gate flies open, he's unpredictable as hell."

"Oh yeah? If you've got any other secrets to share, I'm all ears."

Grady snorted and spat another black wad of dip. "You so scared of eatin' dirt that you're asking the stock hands for lessons?"

"Damned straight, Grady. Her father owns the bull and I'm one ride away from winning the overall."

"Shit. If you're so hard up for teachin', you shoulda just watched me ride that badass." He jerked his head at Texas Tornado, the notorious bull he'd ridden for a high score of eighty-six points.

"Your style wouldn't cut it with Mag, Grady," Janice interjected.

"Oh yeah?" Grady pulled out another chuck of wintergreen Skoal and stuffed it under his lower lip. "There ain't a bull in the world that can't be rode, sweetheart—"

"Or a cowboy that can't be thrown," Janice finished with a smirk of her own. Although one of the top contenders, Grady needed to be taken down a peg or two and Janice hoped Dirk would be the one to do it.

"And just how many bulls have *you* rode now, sweet pants?"

"None," she shot back. "But that doesn't mean I'm ignorant. Maybe you forgot I grew up with these animals. I know when I load 'em what kinda mood they're in and most times how they're gonna act."

"That may be, but all bets are off once you're actually forking the SOB with the flank rope on."

Janice shrugged. "I'm just sayin' look out if you ever draw this one, Grady. Usually the bulls clue you in on what they're thinking, but not this one. When you assume he's gonna spin into your hand, he blows, or he looks like he's fading right and then ducks off left, or maybe takes a sudden nosedive and snaps his head like ol' Bodacious did. He's smart as hell and he'll set you up for a big hurt in a heartbeat. This bull's gonna rearrange a lot of cowboy faces in his new career."

"Then it's too bad Grady didn't draw him this go round," Dirk taunted his buddy. "Rearranging *his* ugly mug could only be an improvement."

Grady grabbed his crotch. "It ain't my face the buckle bunnies are after, Pretty Boy."

Janice ignored the vulgar exchange. "Mag's an ornery bastard if you yank a foot on him. Ride him too aggressive and I promise he'll eat you up. If you don't want to be the first one to kiss that bull, Dirk, you'd do well to spare the spurs."

Dirk attached the bell to the rope and gave her a crooked smile that revealed a deep left-side dimple. "I hear you loud and clear."

Every bucking horse and bull presented its own challenge, and Mag was new and an unknown entity. A savvy rider studied his draw before his ride and talked to the stock hands. She was glad Dirk was willing to listen.

"Why all this concern about *that* dink?" Grady muttered, jerking his head in Dirk's direction.

"Maybe 'cause he actually asked my advice."

"How 'bout I give *you* some advice, Sweet Cheeks? Don't waste yourself waitin' around on Dirk. Everyone knows he has it bad for Rachel. They've been playing it hot and heavy for years. 'Sides, there's better cowboys willing to keep company with a sweet thing like you."

"Better cowboys?" She let her gaze flicker over Grady for a fraction of a second. "Like who?"

Grady grinned big, broad, and bad. "Why, yours truly, of course."

"Really?" She cracked a smile despite herself. "Does anyone besides you and your mama share this grandiose opinion of Grady Garrison?"

"Oh yeah, baby doll. Ask any buckle bunny from here to Houston."

"That so?" Her smile instantly faded. "Then I ain't interested."

"Maybe I just need the right woman to make me wanna settle down."

Janice snorted outright. "What a crock! Does that line of bull really work for you?"

He grinned shamelessly. "More times than I could count."

"You're the one who's wasting your breath, Grady. I don't sleep around, especially not with horndog cowboys."

Ignoring her racing pulse, Janice double-checked the flank while Grady hooked Dirk's rope around the animal's massive barrel. A moment later, Dirk climbed up and over the chute, then quietly lowered himself onto the bull's back. He warmed the rosin-coated rope before tightening it around his bull and then tied himself on.

He'd passed on a protective helmet to keep his white Stetson instead.

"Who said anything about mattress dancing?" Grady smirked. "I'm only offering you a drink after the rodeo—Dirk will be buying of course."

"I wouldn't be so sure."

"Then how 'bout another wager? One just between you and me?"

"What kind of wager?" She knew better than to commit to anything Grady came up with without hearing all the details first.

"If I beat his ride, you'll go to the party with me after the rodeo."

"Isn't it a private event, only for the team members?"

"Yeah," he replied. "But I'm on the team and I'm inviting you."

"I'll think about it, Grady." Janice eyed the bull, hoping to hide the sudden flush in her face. Mag appeared deceptively docile, but there was a dangerous fire blazing in his eyes. Her gut told her the bull was gonna blow.

As the daughter of a stock contractor, she'd seen more rodeos than she could remember and more wrecks than she could ever forget, but no matter how hard she tried, she'd never become desensitized to the gory aftermath of any bull ride gone bad—usually resulting in lots of blood and mangled bones twisted at unnatural angles.

Up to this point, the finals had been surprisingly free of injuries, but the bull riding was where most of them happened. The last seconds in the chute never failed to send Janice's heart into her throat. She'd kept a close tally of Dirk's points and knew just covering this bull was all he needed. She hoped he wouldn't slough off her advice about spurring. Her fingers closed tightly around the cold steel of the chute panel as Dirk raised his right arm and nodded at the gateman.

Chapter 2

STRADDLING THE RAILS ABOVE THE BULL, DIRK focused solely on his routine. Releasing one foot at a time from the steel rail, he stepped lightly onto the bull's back, testing Mag's reaction and then easing himself into position behind the animal's massive shoulders. The bull snorted, pawed, and then tensed, a dangerous shiver of awareness rippling through the three-quarter-ton beast.

Using his gloved hand, Dirk gave a few swift jerks up and down the sticky, rosin-coated rope and then pulled it through his hand in a suicide wrap. He then sidled his hips up closer to his hand and pounded his closed fist to cement his hold.

Although he'd spent plenty of time backing broncs, nothing on earth compared to the addictive rush of a bull ride. The sensation of backing a bull was a heady shot of pure adrenaline that coursed through his body, exciting every nerve. Just like a junkie seeking the next fix, bull riders risked life and limb grasping for that elusive eight-second high.

It was balls to the wall every time the chute opened.

He inhaled deeply and then slowly emptied his lungs. In these final seconds his senses were hyperaware. Everything seemed magnified—his own heartbeat, the sensation of his blood pulsing through his veins, the noise of the crowd buzzing in his ears, the familiar smells of dirt, sweat, and manure.

Dirk shut his eyes and closed his mind to everything but the snorting mass of muscle and sinew under him. "Fuck Grady," he murmured. "This is between you and me, Mag. It's just us."

Dirk opened his eyes and raised his right arm, acutely aware of the metallic click of the gate latch echoing in his ears as he gave the nod to the chute man.

The gate swung free to the last gong of AC/DC's "Hells Bells," and Mag exploded out of it like a derailed freight train. With his jaw set in fierce concentration, Dirk countered the frenetic and frenzied fits of jumps, kicks, dives, and spins in the battle of domination with the bull.

With his body jerking in all directions at once, Dirk reached for that precarious sweet spot of equilibrium, rising into his riding hand on each kick and pushing his fist deep into the bull's shoulder on every rear, following the bull's lead in the deadly dance. Hell-bent on hurling him through the air, the bull snorted and grunted with the jarring force of each buck and kick.

Heeding Janice's advice, Dirk held off plying his heel—at least for the first five or six seconds—but with only a second or two remaining, he raked his spurs upward into the bull's hide, hoping to score extra points. Just as Janice had warned, Mag gave a furious toss of his horned head that narrowly missed Dirk's face. Undeterred, he dropped his heels back into position for another go—but the buzzer sounded.

Dirk fisted the air to proclaim his victory, then grabbed the rope tail to release himself. In that instant, the bull dropped his head and ducked off into a hard right that threw his body hard left. In the blink of an eye, he was cast into the middle of a slow-motion nightmare.

Mag bucked, leaped, and jackknifed in midair, only to land in a clockwise spin that pitched Dirk over the bull's right side—into the well of the spin. He struggled to keep his wits about him and his feet on the ground long enough to free himself, but the bull had other ideas, hooking him with his horns and tossing him into the air and onto the other side…now the outside of the spin. Time seemed suspended as Dirk flailed—completely at the mercy of a raging bull.

White-hot pain seared through his arm and shoulder while Mag spun with enough momentum to turn Dirk into a horizontal propeller blade. Twisted the wrong way in the bullrope, his left hand had gone completely numb, while his right arm, which he needed to free it, jerked helplessly in the air in rhythm with the bucking bull.

The first bullfighter appeared in the periphery of Dirk's vision, but with his feet dragging and scrambling for purchase, he was powerless to help himself. Mag's attention now turned to the bullfighter. Whipping around the other way, the bull harrowed the fighter across the arena like a supercharged John Deere.

Horses, ropes, and two more blurry bodies appeared, but true to his name, Mag was a force to be reckoned with—bucking, charging, and dragging Dirk helplessly along with his body flailing like a rag doll. Dirk's chest was heaving, and sweat poured off his body in his effort to prevent his complete mutilation, but he was losing it fast.

"Hang on, cowboy! Stay on your goddamn feet until we shut this motherfucker down!" Grady's voice was the last thing Dirk heard before the bull's horns struck again, slamming into his head and then ramming his rib cage. Pain, blinding and deafening, exploded inside him, wiping his mind and sucking him down into its black void.

———

"Fucked that one up but good, din't ya, cowboy?" Grady's face came slowly into focus.

"Made the whistle, didn't I?" Dirk grunted back through the racking spasms in his rib cage. His head pounded like hell and it hurt like a sonofabitch just to breathe. He spat a mouthful of blood and then searched with his tongue for any missing teeth. Satisfied they were still intact, he performed a tactile survey of his face, squinting at fingers that came away smeared with blood. "Holy shit! How bad is it?"

"Coulda been a lot worse. Looks like the cocksucker only broke your nose. Don't sweat it though, Pretty Boy. It's an improvement." Grady grinned. "'Sides, chicks dig scars."

"Not Rachel," Dirk groaned. "She's gonna be pissed." That was for damn sure. They were supposed to have photos taken together at the after-party for her Miss Rodeo America campaign.

"Talk about pussy-whipped," Grady mumbled with a head shake.

"How many points?" Dirk asked, eager to know. It had been a hell of a ride. Roughest ever, but at least he'd covered the bull. The hang-up afterward wouldn't count against him.

"Eighty-eight," his buddy answered with a scowl. "But that motherfucking bull did all the work. He scored forty-nine of it."

A grin broke over Dirk's blood- and muck-smeared face. "Beat your last ride by two points, didn't I? Looks like you're gonna be buying the drinks."

"I still have another go, but even if I don't outride you on the next one, you owe drinks to the whole damned team for that dinked-up performance."

"A bet's a bet, Grady." Dirk tried to sit up and hissed with pain.

"Hold on there, cowboy." A hand landed firmly on Dirk's shoulder. "Gotta check you out first."

"Says who?" Dirk tried to look up but a foam cervical collar restricted his movement.

"Says me. I'm Josh, the chief medic here. It's good that you've revived so quickly, but a loss of consciousness suggests a concussion. How do you feel?"

Pretty fucked-up. "Fine, except my shoulder," Dirk lied. He knew for a fact *that* was screwed up, but the bone-jarring pain that jolted him with every breath told him he'd probably busted a couple of ribs too. He hoped he hadn't punctured a lung but wasn't about to volunteer anything that might put him in an ambulance.

Josh palpated his left shoulder.

"Sonofabitch," Dirk groaned.

"Looks like you've got an anterior dislocation. Have you ever had one before?"

"Yeah. Once. Long time ago."

"That makes repositioning the bone back into the joint a lot easier."

Dirk gritted his teeth. "Just do it, all right?"

"A few questions and we'll take care of it. What's your full name?"

"Justin Dirk Knowlton."

"What's the date?"

"June..." *What day was it anyway?* Dirk squeezed his eyes shut. It was right on the tip of his tongue. "Thirteen...*shit, no*...fourteen."

Josh's mouth tightened. "Where are we?"

Dirk gazed up at the stands again, blinking several times to force his vision back into focus. This one was easier. "The rodeo."

"Which one?"

"What the hell does it matter? They all look the same from down here." He grimaced. "They smell the same too."

The medic frowned and scribbled some notes. Grady squatted beside him with a muffled cough that sounded a lot like "Casper."

"We're at the Finals," Dirk blurted. "In Casper. Will you *please* put this damn shoulder back in now?" Dirk looked up into the stands where spectators leaned over the rails for a better look. He despised being on display all sprawled out in the dirt.

Janice had now joined Grady and a number of others crowded behind her to gawk.

"C'mon," Dirk insisted. "Don't make me lie here like a jackass."

"Please, Dirk," Janice pleaded. "Just let him check you out and make sure you're OK."

"Look," Dirk protested, "my brain's not scrambled. I just need my shoulder put back in." He raised his right arm and ripped off the Velcro collar. "If you won't do it for me," he challenged the medic, "Grady will."

"It'd be my pleasure." Grady grinned.

Dirk reached a hand up to Grady who hauled him

back to his feet, actions that incited a wave of specta-
tor applause, whistles, and cheers. "Where's my hat?"
Dirk demanded.

"Here." Janice handed him the dirt-covered Stetson
with a look of mixed concern and disapproval. "Are you
sure you should be on your feet already?"

"I'm standin', ain't I?" Dirk placed the hat solidly
back on his head. "I've held up this show long enough."

"All right. All right," the medic grumbled in defeat.
"We'll finish this up back in the med trailer."

Leaning heavily on Grady, Dirk staggered out to
the mobile triage unit. Moments later, he was lying
on the paper-covered exam table, bracing himself for
the inevitable.

"Relax your left arm and don't fight me," Josh said.
"This is gonna hurt pretty bad for a minute or two, but
then it'll feel a whole lot better."

Dirk dropped his left arm by his side as instructed,
grinding his teeth as the medic raised, rotated, and then
jammed the bone back into place with an audible pop.

"It'll hurt much worse tomorrow. You'll need to wear
a supportive sling for a few days. No drinking or riding
of any kind for at least a couple of weeks."

"Weeks? Yeah. Right." Dirk laughed and then winced
in pain. His left hand was swelling up like a friggin'
balloon. He couldn't make a fist and hoped it wasn't
destroyed. His ribs were probably cracked, but there was
nothing to be done for that and he wasn't about to stand for
any more poking around when Grady was about to ride.

"I mean that about the drinking, Dirk. Especially
tonight. The body responds unpredictably to alcohol
following any kind of head trauma. The injury lowers

tolerance and reduces cognitive function, not to mention impairing the brain's healing abilities." Josh's gaze met Dirk's and held. "It could even trigger a seizure."

"Right. No drinking. Heard ya the first time," Dirk replied.

Favoring his left side, he pushed up into a sitting position and then slowly stood, pausing only long enough for the world to stop spinning. He rolled his shoulder forward and then backward, finding his agony had been almost completely alleviated. "Thanks." He tipped his hat and made for the door.

"Hold on, cowboy," Josh protested. "I'm not finished."

"Then you'll have to continue without me. Gotta go now," Dirk shot over his shoulder. "My buddy's up next."

Dirk emerged from the med trailer on his own, albeit a little unsteady. Janice watched him out of the corner of her eye as she flanked the next two bulls. With his arms over his chest and one booted ankle crossed over the other, he leaned against the chute to watch the last two rides. It was a deceptively casual pose that might have fooled anyone who didn't know him, but she could tell by his pallor and shallow breathing that he hurt far more than he was willing to show. A moment later, the medic brought him a sling, but he didn't put it on.

"C'mon, Dirk," she cajoled. "Don't be a dumb-ass. Let me help you with that."

"Don't need it," he growled.

"Then why are you favoring the arm?"

He released it instantly from his chest with a scowl.

"Please," she cajoled. "No one's gonna think less of you for wearing the sling. Everyone saw how that bull freight-trained you."

"Need both arms. I promised Rachel I'd dance with her tonight."

"Then she'll need to make do with a one-armed two-step."

"No good. She's Miss Rodeo Montana and I've just won the All-Around. The sling'll screw up the pictures. She's already gonna be pissed enough about my face."

"That's ridiculous!" Janice snorted but then grimaced at the truth of it. His face really was a mess with a split lip and a nose swollen to half again its normal size.

Dirk shrugged. "The whole PR thing is her gig. I won't ruin it for her."

"Then just take it off for the pictures."

His mouth compressed. "Thanks for the concern, Janice, but just let it be, will you? I already have a mother."

"Sorry...I just...well, you know..."

He cocked a brow. "No. I *don't* know."

"I thought maybe we'd become friends is all."

"A man can never be *friends* with a woman, Janice. Unless she's a troll, there always reaches a point when the guy starts thinking about gettin' into her jeans. It's just how it is. You ain't no troll, and I got a thing going with Rachel."

Janice looked away, hoping he wouldn't notice the flames heating her face. "That's not what I...but you'd never..." She stammered at the idea that he'd ever think of her in *that* way.

"No?" His gaze tracked slowly over her and his

mouth kicked up in one corner. "Think again, sweetheart. By the way, I've noticed Grady sniffin' around you. Be careful with him, Janice. He rides damn close to the edge sometimes."

"What do you mean?"

His mouth moved, but the announcer's blaring voice drowned out his reply.

"Next up is last year's CNFR champion bull rider, Grady Garrison of Three Forks, Montana, coming into the short round on Rio Bravo."

Janice grinned. "Speak of the devil…"

"Yeah," he said. "And he's about as much trouble."

Janice grimaced. "Look, Dirk, I've been around long enough to recognize his type. Grady blows about as much hot air as a Chinook."

His gaze narrowed. "Don't be fooled. He does blow a lot of smoke, but his bad boy *act* isn't an act, and he doesn't know how to keep his mouth shut either."

Her temper flared. If Dirk didn't want her, why shouldn't she go out with Grady? A drink or two was no big deal. "You didn't take my advice about the bull, why should I take yours?"

"Because you're a *nice* girl, Janice," he replied. "I'd hate for him to change that."

On those parting words, Dirk tipped his hat and limped away to join some teammates, leaving a dull ache in Janice's chest. "That may be," she whispered to his back, "but it seems nice girls always finish last."

―∾―

Grady's ride was the final event of the rodeo. He'd pronounced with his perpetual smirk that it was because they saved the best for last. Although Janice would like to have seen him pulled down a notch, he finished with another strong performance, riding and spurring his bull all the way to the whistle, and then dismounting with exaggerated panache for a score of eighty-eight points.

With the final scores called, the spectators slowly dispersed from the arena. While the rough stock contenders packed up their gear, Janice fell back into the dirty and mundane routine of sorting and penning her bulls for the next haul. Dirk had joined the others behind the pens where the cowboys exchanged good-natured ribbing and swapped stories about their respective rides.

"So you coming or not?" Grady surprised Janice from behind.

"Where?" she asked.

"To the party."

"Oh, that. I said I'd think about it if you *beat* Dirk. You didn't. You tied."

"That may be but I damn sure rode better than him, and you know it. Hell, it was the bull that made *his* ride. I had to spur the shit out of the dink I drew to get anything out of him."

Janice grudgingly acknowledged that Grady had milked the most out of his ride. Rio was a highly respected bucking bull, but he was approaching retirement.

"Let me on *that* badass motherfucker"—he nodded to Mag—"and you'll see a *real* ride."

"If you're going to Thermopolis, you might get your chance."

"Is that where you're headed next?"

"Yup," she said. "My ol' man scored a contract with a bigger outfit. We're to supply a dozen bulls for the

summer circuit. I'll be hauling them down the road—
Thermopolis this week, then Sheridan, Cody, and
Cheyenne for Frontier Days. After that, we'll be back in
Montana from Cowboy Christmas till the finals."

"Then you're in luck, Sweet Cheeks. I'm heading
to Thermopolis too. I need to rack up some points and
paychecks if I want to get into the pro bull circuit."

"You planning on ridin' bulls full-time now?"

"Yeah. Unlike Pretty Boy there, with his ranch to fall
back on, I got nothing else. I gotta earn my own bread and
ridin' bulls is what I was meant to do. I'm hoping that by
summer's end I'll qualify for the new Rough and Rank
circuit out in Vegas. That's where the real money is."

"And bulls no one can ride," she countered.

"Hell, they're all just some cow's calf, ain't they?
'Sides, some cowboy's gotta ride 'em."

"And you think that's you?"

He smirked. "All the way to Vegas, baby."

"What about Dirk? Is he going to Thermopolis too?"

"Nah. Says he has other plans."

"But I thought you were traveling buddies."

"We were. We've been rodeoin' together 'bout four
years, but I'm bent on doing only bulls and he ain't no pro
bull rider. Too big for it. He only rode this year to qualify
for the All-Around, so it looks like we'll be parting ways."

"What's he going to do?"

He shrugged. "Hell if I know. Probably a bunch of
that PR fundraising shit with Rachel. Says he'll probably
meet up with me for Cowboy Christmas though. We've
always done that circuit together. The situation really
sucks for me since we've always shared expenses."

"Guess you'll be looking for a new buddy?"

He considered her for a moment and grinned. "Think I already found one."

"Who?" she asked.

"You, Sweet Cheeks. Given you and me's goin' in the same direction, I'll be ridin' with you now."

"*With me?* Funny, I don't recall inviting you, Grady."

"We'll split the expenses. Only makes sense to share a ride. Whadaya say we talk about it over those drinks you promised to have with me."

"I never promised anything. Besides, I can't drink if I'm driving, especially not while hauling stock."

"It's only two hours to Thermopolis," he said. "We can party tonight and head out first thing in the morning."

"But I don't have any decent clothes," she protested. "I can't exactly show up at the Plaza with shit-covered boots."

"Who you lookin' to impress? You already got *m*y attention."

She snorted. "Am I s'posed to be flattered by that?"

He considered the question. "Maybe flattered ain't quite what I had in mind."

"No? Then what am I supposed to feel?"

"This." Grady's mouth came down on hers in a confident, almost aggressive kiss that tasted vaguely of wintergreen tobacco. Taking advantage of her surprise he plunged his tongue into her mouth. Warm, wet, and slick, it tangled with hers. Caught off guard, Janice softened involuntarily. Shutting her eyes she imagined for a moment that it was Dirk kissing her and Dirk's arms around her. Grady deepened the kiss, cupping her ass, and hauling her against him. He was growing hard and his mouth more insistent.

Realizing where this was headed, Janice panicked,

shoving hard against his chest to break the kiss. "I didn't invite that, Grady."

"Liked it though, didn't ya? Seems to me you took your sweet time deciding when to quit."

She flushed, furious with him, but even more with herself. "I told you I'd have a drink with you, and a drink is all I meant."

"C'mon, Janice," he cajoled. "I only want to show you a good time. Sweet thing like you shouldn't spend the evening alone."

His words weren't without effect. She'd spent countless nights alone watching her portable TV and staring at the ceiling of her stock trailer.

"What makes you think I'm looking for that?" she retorted.

He grasped her shoulders, his fingers firm and his gaze hard. "You seein' someone?"

She hesitated, her gaze darting to Dirk who lingered in the background. His eyes met hers in a scowl that made her bristle. "No. I'm not."

"That's good news, Sweet Cheeks." Grady brushed a thumb over her lips. "'Cause the way I see it, we might as well get to know each other better—being that we'll be doing the circuit together and all."

"Can't you take a hint, Grady? I'm not attracted to you that way."

"Yeah you are." He grinned. "Your body already told me so. Your head just don't know it yet."

Janice stared at him dumbfounded. "You are the cockiest damned cowboy I've ever met."

She'd never known a man as full of himself as Grady Garrison. While her attraction to him was nothing compared to what she felt for Dirk, she wasn't completely immune to his confident charm. He'd also made his interest in her as clear as Dirk had made his indifference. If Dirk didn't want her, why shouldn't she flirt a little with Grady?

He flashed his big, bad grin. "It ain't cocky, sweetheart, when you *are* the best."

—ᴠᴠ—

Dirk watched Grady and Janice with a vague feeling of irritation. Hadn't he warned her about him? He'd traveled with Grady long enough to know exactly how he operated. Grady might not be the biggest or best-looking guy on the circuit, but his bad-boy attitude never failed to attract female attention. Like his bull riding, he scored far more often than not, and just like the bulls, once he'd conquered one, he was always looking for the next challenge—and that was all Janice was to him.

Dirk had known her since high school where she'd proven a real hand with a rope. In the past year of working the rodeos with her ol' man, she'd proven herself again, winning all the cowboys' respect. It was no small feat and he hated to see that hard-earned regard destroyed—but it would be, once Grady started running his mouth off about her.

He told himself it was none of his business, but still felt a compulsion to break his buddy's face when Grady made his move. He forced himself to look away. He'd hoped she wouldn't make that mistake, but now it was out of his hands. Turning his back to the couple, he grabbed his rigging bag. "You comin' or not, Grady?"

He threw the question over his shoulder. "Rachel's waiting on me."

"Go on without me," Grady replied. "I'm hitching a ride with Janice. I'm gonna help her finish up here and then we'll head on out."

Dirk turned back asking Janice, "Need an extra hand?"

Grady gave him a look that said "back off" in no uncertain terms. "I got her covered. 'Sides, you won't be any help anyway with only one good arm and a busted-up hand. Go on ahead, and we'll catch up with you. We'll be done directly."

"You sure about that?" Dirk sought Janice's confirmation, hoping she'd change her mind.

"Yeah. You can go on, Dirk. Grady's agreed to help me out in return for a lift to Thermopolis. Until you two get back together on the circuit, I'm his new ride."

"His new ride, huh?" *More than you know, sweetheart.* Dirk bit back the retort that hung on his tongue.

"Oh yeah," Grady replied with a coyote grin. "It's gonna work out real good."

The two men stared one another down until Dirk reminded himself it was no skin off his hide what they did. He still couldn't figure out why he felt so protective about a girl he hardly knew but then shrugged it off, wincing at the reminder of his injury before tossing his bag over his *good* shoulder.

—◦◦◦—

Janice looked after Dirk wondering if she'd misjudged him, if somehow she'd made a mistake. It was like he said one thing but really meant another. Only an hour ago he'd insisted he was involved exclusively with

Rachel, but his whole demeanor had changed when she'd mentioned traveling with Grady. He'd seemed almost pissed off about it.

Why should he care if they traveled together? Was it just a fraternal kind of concern? If so, he was acting damned hypocritical. He'd accused her of acting like his mother only to turn around and take a similar posture — one she didn't want or need. She certainly didn't need any head games. At least Grady made clear what he was after. She assured herself she could handle him. She was used to looking out for herself.

Dirk had ruffled her feathers, but she shook it off to concentrate on work. Twenty minutes later she pulled off her leather gloves and brushed the dirt from her jeans.

"Can you give me a few minutes to shower and change?" she asked Grady. "I've got some clean clothes in my trailer. I'm not about to go to a fancy party reeking of the stock pens."

"Sure thing," he replied. "I'm going to hit the locker room and grab a quick shower myself. Don't make me wait too long." Grady placed a callused hand on the small of her back. "I've got a real thirst tonight for a whiskey..." He raked a hungry gaze slowly over her five-foot-eight-inch frame. "And a tall drink of water."

Chapter 3

AFTER A QUICK SHOWER, DIRK THREW ON SOME FRESH Wranglers, toweled his head with his good arm, and then scowled at the fifty-dollar button-down from the George Strait collection laid out on the bed for him—the one Rachel had purchased at the Wrangler Fashion Show. She'd presented it as a gift, and expected him to wear it tonight. He felt a surge of resentment at the subtle ways she'd begun controlling him.

It seemed everyone had expectations of him these days.

Big. Expectations.

Although they'd not actually talked about it, with his graduation and now the rodeo win, they'd all be anticipating a move on his part, most likely tonight, but the idea of hobbling himself at age twenty-two, even to Rachel, galled him to no end.

They'd been together off and on since high school. She was the girl every guy had wet dreams about. Gorgeous, bright, and bubbly, she'd won Miss Teen Rodeo in high school and now wore the crown for the state of Montana. On top of all that, her parents were loaded. Rachel's ol' man flew her around on his Beechcraft Baron twin-engine during her queen campaign and tonight his money paid for a fully catered shindig for family and friends.

Dirk had sensed their disapproval of him from the

get-go, but after four years, her parents had grudgingly accepted him. But the feeling that they expected him to be grateful about it irked the hell out of him. Although his family wasn't stinking rich like hers, they were still highly respected fourth-generation ranchers with a decent spread and a fairly profitable operation—by current ranching standards anyway.

He considered the expensive dress shirt, weighing the ire he'd incur from Rachel if he didn't wear it. In the end, he threw down his towel, pulled a black tee out of his bag, sniffed it, and then grunted through the pain of pulling it on over his head. He knew he'd draw some severe looks by not dressing up, but he had a point to make. Like a hardmouthed mule, he wasn't about to cave to the pressure. There would be no proposal. No engagement announcement tonight. Eventually. Maybe. But damn sure not tonight.

―∿―

Janice brushed out her hair, applied a bit of blush and mascara, and then eyed herself in the mirror with a feeling of dismay. She wore her favorite pearl-button Western shirt with clean, if faded, jeans. Her only adornment, proudly worn, was the gold-buckled belt she'd won for breakaway roping at the high school rodeo. She'd polished up her ropers and dusted off a hat that was in bad need of reshaping. She wished now that she'd brought her "town" hat. Deciding she'd do better to go without, she cast the hat aside.

She hadn't expected the party invitation and wished she'd brought nicer clothes, but she really didn't have anything suitable at home anyhow. The only dress she owned was the one she'd worn to the senior prom three years ago, but she'd filled out so much since then that it probably didn't fit anymore. She wondered what the other girls would be wearing, then told herself it didn't matter. No one would be looking at her. She'd just fade into the background, stay for one quick drink, and then make a quiet departure. Alone.

Although Grady hadn't called it that, Janice realized with a pang that this was her first real date since that same senior prom—a blind date set up by her best friend, Kelly. It had turned into the longest night of her life, spent fighting off her date's sloppy kisses and groping hands in the backseat, while Kelly and Tom made out in the front. Danny, or maybe it was Donny, had called her a few times afterward, but she'd made enough excuses that he'd eventually given up.

After graduation she'd been too busy on the ranch even to think about guys. That was not to say any had ever given much thought to her, even though she'd dealt with dozens of cowboys since she'd begun helping her ol' man. Sure, she'd exchanged playful banter while loading and flanking the stock, but it had never progressed beyond light flirtation. It had always been business.

Janice Lee Combes, twenty-one years old and barely kissed—least until now.

Grady had certainly kissed her like he meant business but her instincts told her he wasn't one to invest his time and effort without expectation of a return. She had a sinking feeling she'd have a big decision to make before the night was out.

She wasn't sure how she felt about that—or how

prepared she really was to deal with it. She'd be lying to herself if she denied being flattered. She'd blown plenty of smoke earlier too. It was nice to have some attention, to be thought of as a girl, for once.

On cue, Grady rapped on her trailer door. "You ready yet, Sweet Cheeks?"

"Yeah. Be right there."

She didn't know why she'd allowed him to continue calling her that. "Sweet Cheeks" was annoying as hell—but mildly gratifying too. Maybe it was just the novelty, the fuzzy feeling of actually having a pet name. Even her parents had never called her anything but Janice or Janice Lee.

She fluffed her hair, applied a bit of lip gloss, then grabbed the new tooled-leather purse she'd bought earlier at the vendor booths. Taking a deep breath, she forced a smile and opened her trailer door. "I'm ready."

"You look good enough to eat." Grady flashed that coyote grin again—the one that made him look like a predator who indeed planned to make a meal of her. For the second time Janice wondered if she might actually be in over her head. She'd be wise to listen to that little voice.

One drink, she repeated, and then she'd leave the party. Alone.

Dirk paused at the entrance to the Plaza ballroom. There were a couple hundred guests, but he only recognized a handful of them. The collegiate bigwigs and all the rodeo officials had made an appearance, as well as members of the local press. Other than a handful of

Dirk's rodeo buddies, the rest were the kind of people who never got their hands dirty — the highbrow, hobby-ranch society types that he didn't know…or much care to. Although it was a post-rodeo celebration, he guessed most of the people had never seen the inside of a live-stock arena. They were the kind who watched it on their wall-mounted ultrahigh-def TVs — like the one that now played a slo-mo loop of his earlier hang-up.

Shit.

With a mix of annoyance and embarrassment, Dirk pulled his hat over his eyes and dug his hands deep into his pockets, hoping to slink past the group surrounding the TV. Was it only an hour ago he'd been lying in the arena splattered with his own blood? Now the sounds of jangling spurs were replaced by the clink of crystal, and the noise of lowing cattle with the buzz of conversation punctuated with ripples of laughter.

He scanned the crowd for Rachel, locating her across the room with her mother and a group of expensively dressed women he didn't recognize. A photographer was snapping pictures as they sipped champagne. Rachel flashed her rodeo queen smile for the camera.

He stopped in his tracks. God, she was gorgeous.

The sight of her always stole Dirk's breath, but tonight she was particularly hot in a body-hugging red and white leather dress. A white felt Stetson topped her head and her hair fell in a sexy blond cascade over her shoulders. His gaze lingered in appreciation of a sight he thought he'd never tire of — and one he longed to get a whole lot more of in private. His imagination took hold, conjuring a vision of her wearing only the hat, the boots, and the smile — a smile that instantly froze when she noticed him.

Her gaze raked him head to toe. She broke from the group and rushed toward him. "My God!" she whispered. "What happened to your face?"

"A bull named Magnum Force *happened*." He jerked his head to the TV. "Hard to believe you missed it."

She looked chagrined. "I got here late and only saw the replay after the ride was over. Of course I was concerned, but Wade said you were fine." Her forehead wrinkled. "By the look of you, he lied."

"I've been a helluva lot better, but I'll survive."

"Poor baby." Her lips formed a sexy pout. "Maybe there's something I can do to make it all better?"

"Oh yeah, Sunshine. I can think of all kinds of things."

He leaned down to kiss her mouth but she turned her cheek instead.

"Remember Mama and Daddy," she hissed under her breath.

"You don't think they know we kiss? We've only been dating four years."

"Almost five," she corrected. "And of course they do, but I have to take my reputation very seriously. You know how people like to gossip. As the new queen I have to be ultracareful. Speaking of which…" She stepped back, eyeing him with a downward turn of her mouth. "I can't believe you walked in here in a T-shirt! Where's the new button-down I bought you?"

"This is fine," he said. "It's clean."

"No it's not, Dirk, and you know it! Maybe you don't realize how important this is to me. That photographer over there is doing a spread on all the state rodeo queens for *American Rodeo Today*. He's been waiting to get shots of us together. Why don't you just be a sweetheart and run back upstairs and change."

"Why don't you just let me have a beer or two first, Sunshine. I could use one after getting mauled tonight."

"It was only a matter of time," she retorted. "You know how I hate the bulls. I wish you would quit the rough stock."

"You never minded before," he said. "As I recall, it's how I caught your eye to begin with. You *used to* even come out and watch me."

"All the girls watched you, Dirk. You were the hottest thing out there—you still are. You wanted to ride bulls this year and you did. You even won thc overall. Now you can move on to other things while you're still on top."

"Who says I *want* to move on?"

Her gaze locked with his. "Don't you?" She twincd her left arm around his neck and ran an indcx finger gently over his broken nose. "Maybe this time it wasn't serious, but you can't afford to take these kinds of risks anymore."

"Says who?"

"*Says me*," she insisted. "If you won't give it up for your own good, then do it for me. I don't want you getting hurt again."

Although he hadn't planned to ride any more bulls in the summer circuit, he bristled at her attempt to manipulate him, to use his dick to control him—not that his dick had ever gotten its full reward for his compliance.

"I could get hit by a truck crossing the street. I could get struck by lightning walking across my front yard. Point is, I'm not going to live my life in fear of what *might* happen to me."

She withdrew her arms. "I'm not asking you to, but why tempt fate? That bull could have killed you tonight, Dirk! He might have gored you to death. Do you want to end up like Lane Frost?"

He waved his good hand in annoyance. "You worry too much."

Her brows met in a frown. "I'm talking to a brick wall, aren't I?"

"Don't you think this conversation is a mite bit hypocritical coming from someone who aspires to be the face and voice of American rodeo?"

"Maybe so, but you have no idea what it feels like to have the one you love risk his life for an eight-second ride. Besides, you know how people tend to judge by association—birds of a feather and all that. You should think about that now."

His gaze narrowed. "What do you mean?"

"Just that the rough stock cowboys are so...so..." She made a face.

"So *what*, Sunshine?"

She sighed. "Do I really have to spell it out?"

"Guess so."

"Coarse. Crude."

He winced, a gesture that made his face hurt but her words made his head pound even worse. "Is that how I rate with you, Sunshine? Coarse and crude? If that's the case, I wonder why you'd lower yourself to be with me."

"Of course, I don't mean *you*!" she protested. "It was just a generalization about the bull riders. If you still want to rodeo, why don't you switch to roping? You and your brother could team rope together. It attracts a much better class of people. Besides, if you roped Daddy could get you endorsements. He has a lot of connections and even golfs with the CEO of Lariat Ropes."

Grady's roping joke came to mind. Dirk couldn't suppress a smirk.

"What's so funny?"

"Something Grady said, but I doubt you'd appreciate the humor."

"Grady?" she scoffed. "I'll bet. And that's precisely what I mean. He's too vulgar and rough. Continued association with him will only drag you down."

"Now you're concerned about my association with a *champion* bull rider?" Grady was a bit rough around the edges, but most cowboys were.

"He may be a champion today, but what's he going to be tomorrow? Ten years down the road he'll have nothing to show for it but scars, broken bones, and a stupid belt buckle."

"It's more than the buckle and you know it."

"But there's more to life than the thrill of the ride, Dirk."

"Is this you or your father talking now, Sunshine?"

She gnawed her lower lip. "You can't make a living at rodeo—not a decent one anyway."

"Don't need to. My truck's paid for and I've got a roof over my head as long as I want it."

"But what about us? Don't you care what I want?"

He felt a pang of conscience. His voice and posture softened. He cupped her cheek. "I do care, but I'm just not ready to think that far ahead yet, Sunshine. Maybe I will be soon, but not right now."

"But we've both graduated. Isn't it time to think about the future?"

The future? Shit. By the looks of things "the future" was suddenly now. Damned if the sneaky bitch hadn't crept up from behind and caught him with his pants down.

Part of him couldn't blame Rachel. She'd never hedged about her expectations, but he hadn't anticipated it all happening so soon. But pressuring him about it, especially tonight, only got his back up.

"A bottle of Coors," Dirk quipped. "That's in my future—the immediate one anyway."

"But what about the pictures? The photographer's been waiting all this time on you. Please Dirk." She gave him a beseeching look. "If you don't want to go upstairs and change, maybe you could just borrow Daddy's jacket."

"Your father's jacket?" Dirk shook his head with a derisive chuckle. "I'm sorry, Sunshine, but your Daddy's jacket won't fit me any better than his shoes."

"What's that supposed to mean?"

"You'll figure it out. I'm going to the bar now. You want anything?"

"No. Thank you," she snapped.

When he moved to kiss her cheek, she jerked away.

"I'm not waiting on you anymore, Justin Dirk Knowlton."

"C'mon. A few more minutes won't make any difference."

"That's *not* what I meant. You've taken me for granted long enough." Standing as tall and defiant as her petite frame would allow, she anchored her hands on her slim hips. "I think it's decision time for us."

She was telling him in no uncertain terms to ante up.

He opened his mouth and then closed it again, biting

back the apology that had sprung to his lips only seconds ago. He wasn't about to kowtow to someone else's
expectations and desires—even Rachel's. It was *his* life,
damn it! He was only twenty-two. He needed to live a
little before settling down.

When he failed to respond, her pretty mouth molded
into a mutinous expression. "I mean it, Dirk. I'm done
with waiting…I'm done *with you*." With an angry toss
of her blond head, she spun on her boot heel, leaving
him staring after her.

She'd issued her ultimatum. He'd balked. And now
she'd broken it off. This entire night had turned to pure
shit! First the bull ripped his arm out of the socket and
tried to impale him and now his girl dumped him?
Maybe he'd gone too far, but he still couldn't regret his
actions. He refused to be led by his nose—or any other
body part.

She'd strung him along for four years with promises
that made him salivate. That wasn't to say he hadn't had
a taste of her. He had, and she was a fine dish indeed, but
the appetizer had only made him all the hungrier for the
main course. He doubted he could have held out much
longer if she hadn't reciprocated in kind. Although she'd
compromised her vow of purity to keep his interest,
she'd also made it abundantly clear that anything more
would require a multifaceted, two-carat emerald-shaped
promise on his part.

He knew what she needed now, sure enough, what he
could do to make things right at least for a little while.
Ten minutes in a janitor's closet with his face buried in
her snatch would have her purring like a kitten again.
Only problem was there were too damn many people

around for them to disappear together, especially with a
magazine photographer in the house. He wouldn't take
that risk. She was right about her reputation. He could
just imagine what kind of photo spread would hit the
newsstands if Miss Rodeo Montana got caught with his
tongue up her twat—one far better suited for *Hustler*
than *American Rodeo Magazine.*

In no mood to go chasing after her, he told himself a
little distance wouldn't hurt either of them—at least until
he figured some things out. He really needed that beer.

Although Grady had invited her, Janice still felt like an
interloper at the party. She was neither family nor friend
to the Carsons, but just a lowly stock hand. Entering
the Plaza ballroom, she felt completely outclassed. She
wasn't the only girl wearing jeans, but hers weren't
accessorized with eighteen-hundred-dollar, hand-tooled,
Swarovski-crystal-covered boots. Her hair wasn't
impeccably coiffed and crowned by a rhinestone tiara
over a Resistol beaver hat.

But it wasn't just their pricey designer clothes. The
snide sidelong looks from the counterfeit cowgirls told
her she didn't belong. Janice felt the same way. With her
self-confidence in shreds, she made an excuse to Grady
and a quick detour to the ladies' room from which she
planned to make a quick and painless exit.

All of that went out the window, however, when she
came face-to-face with a teary-eyed, mascara-stained
Rachel the rodeo queen, surrounded by her buckskin-
fringed court. Greeted with dagger looks, Janice froze
in her boots. Feeling like an intruder into a private

melodrama, she was half tempted to back her way out the door but then they all turned back to Rachel. It was as if Janice had become suddenly invisible. More likely, they'd just decided she was beneath their notice.

"That bastard!" a brunette indignantly declared. "I can't believe he'd string you along like that! It's past time you kicked that cowboy to the curb, Rae."

"Yeah," a strawberry blond chimed in. "You've wasted enough time on him. There's plenty of hot guys just dying to go out with you—ones who would show you the kind of respect you deserve."

Respect? What was up with that? They couldn't be talking about Dirk. Janice had never seen Dirk disrespectful to anyone who didn't deserve it—especially not to a woman.

"I hate him," Rachel sobbed. "No," she amended through gritted teeth, "I positively *loathe* him."

Janice closed the stall door, latching it shut behind her.

"Assholes like him always treat a woman like shit once they've gotten what they want."

"I guess you'd know best, Mary Jane," Janice heard the brunette mumble.

"But I didn't...we haven't..." Rachel protested.

"What?" exclaimed the cowgirl choir.

Janice felt her own jaw drop. Although her conscience told her to tune them out, she found herself holding her breath while she emptied her bladder.

"Let me get this straight," said Strawberry. "In almost five years, you still haven't done the dirty?"

"No..." Rachel replied. "Not *technically* speaking..."

"How *technical* are we talking, sugar?" the voice belonging to Mary Jane eagerly inquired.

"It's vulgar to kiss and tell, Mary Jane," Strawberry chided. "Didn't your mama teach you anything?"

"Yeah, how not to get knocked up." Mary Jane giggled. "I just can't believe Rae took that ninth-grade purity vow for real. I think mine barely lasted through my sophomore year."

"*We know*," said the brunette. "The whole school knew. It's probably why you never wore a Miss Teen Rodeo crown."

"Fuck off, Miss Holier-Than-Thou."

The girls had their claws fully exposed, and Janice half expected to see dark locks of hair and leather fringe flying over the stall door.

"Cut the bullshit, you two," said the third voice. "This is about Rachel and Dirk. And it seems to me she made the right decision to hold out. He's toed the line until now, hasn't he? How many of you can say that?"

"Sorry, Rae," Strawberry said. "She's right, but if he's taking you for granted, maybe it's time to shake things up."

"What do you mean?" Rachel sniffed.

"There's a whole room full of hot cowboys just outside that door. You only need to waltz your little moneymaker out there and take your pick."

"But that's just it," Rachel wailed. "I don't want any of them. You can't understand how it is between him and me. It's always been Dirk. It's *only* been him."

Janice watched through the crack as three sets of arms enfolded her, muffling her sobs.

"What about Wade?" one of them suggested. "He's pretty damned hot."

"I wouldn't mind a piece of that myself," said Mary Jane.

"Exactly," replied the voice Janice recognized as Strawberry. "What better way to make that SOB pay than to play up to his little brother?"

"Little?" Mary Jane said. "He's gotta be six foot three at least, and you know what they say about the tall ones. Or maybe it was boot size? Anyone get a good look at his feet?"

"He's perfect, Rae!" Strawberry intoned with another annoying giggle.

Yeah, perfect if you're a nasty, conniving, and manipulative bitch, thought Janice. Hadn't any of them grown up yet? This whole scene was like junior high all over again. She'd heard more than enough. Janice rose and flushed. She was thankful they were gone by the time she opened the door.

Although Rachel knew Dirk far better than she did, Janice couldn't imagine him putting up with this kind of childish crap. He wasn't an adolescent boy to play those games with. Half of her hoped Rachel wouldn't take such inane advice—but the other half couldn't help hoping something else altogether.

Dirk was nursing a longneck and mulling over his next move when he spotted Don Carson at the end of the bar. Given that Carson was both Rachel's father and the host of the bash, he figured it best to man up now about the tiff, rather than dealing with awkward repercussions later.

Seeking a bit of liquid courage, Dirk emptied his beer and ordered a second, but by the time he turned around again, Carson was engaged in conversation with Jack Evans, a prominent Bozeman attorney. He made his way closer to the pair, pulling on his beer and waiting for a lull.

"Who's that young man with Rachel?" Evans asked Carson.

"I believe that's Justin Knowlton's younger son, Wade," Carson replied.

Dirk's gaze followed theirs across the room to find his brother—the smooth, schmoozing bastard—posing for pictures with his arm around Rachel's waist.

Wade was only a year younger than Dirk and a former classmate of Rachel's. He'd had the hots for her for years, but she'd blown him off in favor of Dirk. Now it seemed she'd set out to make him jealous, and Wade appeared more than willing to conspire with her.

"Low crawlin' sonofabitch," Dirk mumbled and took another long pull on his beer. Although he was only halfway through his second drink, Evans's and Carson's voices had taken on a buzz-like quality that made his inner ears itch.

"Isn't Rachel seeing the older one, the bull rider who wrecked tonight? Did you catch the replay of that?" Evans visibly shuddered. "I'm surprised he lived to walk away from it."

"Yes. I saw it, and needless to say, I've serious qualms about my daughter tying herself to a rodeo cowboy. I like the boy well enough, I s'pose, and I'll allow he *might* be the exception, but as a rule they're a good-for-nothing lot. I don't have to tell you I wouldn't mind if she switched her interest to Wade over there. I hear he plans to study law."

"Does he now?" Evans assessed Wade while Dirk ground his teeth. "I could use another clerk this summer. Why not introduce the boy."

"Sure. Why not? C'mon, Jack. I want to get a few photos with my gal anyway."

Dirk tracked their progress across the room with a scowl hanging over his eyes. Rachel chose that moment to look in his direction. Their eyes met just long enough for her to see that he'd noticed her, before she turned back to Wade, laying a hand on his arm and flashing him a brilliant smile.

"Fuck it. If that's what you want, go for it, Sunshine. I ain't playin' that game."

Turning his back to her, he upended his bottle, drained it dry in three swallows, slammed it down, and ordered another. He was on his third when Grady entered the ballroom. Catching Dirk's eye, he made a beeline to the bar. Dirk acknowledged him with a silent nod.

"What's up your ass?" Grady demanded.

"Nothin'," Dirk snapped.

"Bullshit. Why are you over here drinkin' alone when there's a party going on?"

"Where's Janice? I thought she was coming with you."

"That'll happen later," Grady smirked. "It's only proper to buy her a drink first."

"Asshole. That's not what I meant."

"She's in the john. I told her to meet me here." He signaled the bartender and ordered a double shot of Pendleton.

Dirk's gaze riveted back to Rachel and Wade. His brother was leading her out to the dance floor with the photographer still snapping. The band had switched to a slow dance, a mediocre cover of George Strait's "Marina Del Rey." Dirk silently dared his brother to move his hands an inch closer to Rachel's ass. She pulled Wade's head down to hers almost as if to kiss him. Dirk saw red. He was poised to bolt out of his chair when she looked straight at Dirk and whispered in Wade's ear.

"Wanna tell me what the fuck's goin' on?" Grady asked.

"Not really." Dirk took another brooding swig of his beer, his gaze never leaving the dancers. When the song ended, he spun back around before Rachel could catch him staring. The band followed up with another George Strait number, "She'll Leave You with a Smile."

When Dirk looked out on the dancers again she was doing exactly that, staring adoringly into his brother's face. He wondered if she'd requested that song just to rub salt in the wound.

"Ah." Grady nodded. "I get it now. Fuck that shit. You can have all the rodeo queens, Pretty Boy. The maintenance is too high for my blood. 'Sides"—he grinned—"I'm hankering for a piece of that." He inclined his head toward a tall redheaded cowgirl approaching the bar.

Dirk's hackles rose to see that he meant Janice. He didn't understand why Grady'd set his sights on her when there was any number of women present that he could have taken straight up to his room, probably without even buying them a drink.

"What's your poison, Sweet Cheeks?" Grady asked.

"Just a beer for me. Whatever's on tap is fine," Janice replied.

Grady signaled the bartender, ordering Janice's drink and another shot.

Dirk called for another beer.

Janice frowned. "Are you sure you should be drinking tonight?"

"It's only beer," Dirk protested.

"You think that doesn't count? You've done rodeo long enough to know it's a bad idea to drink anything after getting knocked out."

"I wasn't knocked out."

"Sure looked that way to the couple thousand people watching," she argued.

"Told you I already have a mother, Janice," Dirk snarled.

"Fine. Be an idiot." She snatched up her beer.

"Don't mind him, Janice. He's having a bad night. Rachel just dumped him and his brother's already moving in."

"With her father's blessing," Dirk muttered. "Doesn't like her slumming with rough stock riders. Thinks we're a bunch of lowlifes."

"That so?" Grady spun around on his stool. "What else did the dickwad have to say?"

"He thinks Rachel would be better off with Wade. That about sums it up." He jerked his head toward the couple on the dance floor. "And if I wasn't all busted up I'd be kicking Wade's ass about now." He was pissed as hell and would love to knock his brother's lights out, but he was in no shape to take Wade on tonight. Tomorrow, however, was a new day. He'd be feeling more up to it then.

The dancers broke up a few minutes later when the band started up a piss-poor cover of "Cowboy Up" by

Chris LeDoux. Dirk caught Rachel searching the room for him. This time he turned his back.

"Her ol' man called us lowlifes, huh?" Grady downed his second shot with a thoughtful look—the one that usually meant trouble. "Guess we can't kick *his* ass."

"No." Dirk gave Grady a warning look. "*We can't.*"

After a Garth Brooks number, the band announced a twenty-minute break.

"This is Carson's party, ain't it?" Grady asked.

"Yeah. It's all on his dime," Dirk replied. "Money's no object when it comes to Rachel. He wants her picture in all the magazines and big papers. Uppity sonofabitch thrives on the spotlight."

"That so?" Grady rose from his bar stool. "If it's attention he wants, why don't we help him out?"

Janice laid a hand on his arm. "Where you going?"

Grady gave them a wicked grin that boded no good. "I just got an idea to shake things up a bit. I'll be back directly, Sweet Cheeks."

Dirk watched his buddy wend his way through the crowd to the stage where he tipped his hat to the DJ filling in during the band's break. The burly Charlie Daniels look-alike offered his ear then gave a vehement head shake. Further persuasion ensued in the form of cash. The encounter ended with a hand clasp.

Grady swaggered back to the bar with an even bigger grin stretching his mouth.

"You know him?" Janice asked.

"Yeah. He's an ol' buddy of mine," Grady replied. "I greased him up to do me a favor. At first he was afraid of losing the gig, but who can hold him responsible for a request, right?"

Janice's gaze narrowed. "I s'pose it would depend on the kind of request."

"What do you think a low-life cowboy would ask him to play?"

"Dunno." Janice shrugged. "Maybe 'The Rodeo Song' by Gary Lee and the Showdown?"

"Close but not raunchy enough. Ever heard of Rehab?"

Janice's brow wrinkled. "No. I don't think I have."

"The DJ has an old copy of their original album, before they went and cleaned up the songs. He's gonna play 'Sittin' at a Bar.'"

Dirk nearly choked on his beer. "Carson'll shit a brick."

"Least I didn't ask him for Chinga Chavin's 'Cum Stains on My Pillow.' He had that one too." Grady laughed and downed another shot. "If you really wanna stick him in the craw, you and me could go out there and make it a karaoke version."

"You know if we do this, we're gonna get tossed out of here on our asses," Dirk said, but he was too pissed off at the world to care much about repercussions.

Grady shrugged. "Won't be the first time...and I doubt it'll be the last. 'Sides, do you really want to stay here after what that asshole said?"

Dirk shook his head. "Hell no."

"You remember the lyrics?" he asked.

"Yeah, I remember," Dirk said. "All right, Grady, I'm in." He rose too quickly, or maybe it was the effects of four beers. In either case, he had to steady himself on the bar.

"Care to make it a trio, Sweet Cheeks?" Grady asked Janice. "You can sing backup."

"I don't think so. I don't even know the song."

"Doesn't matter," Grady said. "You can just lip-synch."

She looked from Grady to Dirk and back again. "Sorry. You two can make jackasses of yourselves all you like, but this is too much for me."

"You're bailing on us?"

"Damned straight." She grabbed her purse and rose.

Grady grabbed her by the arm. "I don't think so. You came with me. You'll leave with me."

"Let go of me, Grady." She tried to shake his hand off, but he held her. She looked to Dirk.

"Let loose, Grady," he said quietly. "She doesn't want to stay."

"Keep out of this, Pretty Boy." Grady's gaze narrowed, his threat clear. "She's with *me*."

Maybe it was the whiskey, but Grady seemed to be itching for a brawl. He was unpredictable on a good day—add alcohol to the mix and he became volatile as hell—friendship be damned. On any other night Dirk might have indulged the impulse to mix it up but tonight he was in no shape for it.

"Dirk's right," Janice replied, tight-lipped. "I don't want to stay. I promised I'd have one drink with you and I did. That's as far as it goes. Thanks for the drink." She jerked her arm free and made a swift exit.

For a second or two Grady looked as if he'd go after her, but then he visibly relaxed. He took up his drink, raising it to his lips with a shrug. "I'm not likely to get any from her tonight, so why waste the effort?"

Dirk breathed a sigh of relief that Grady had abandoned his designs on her. But by the look of things, he'd either get his brawl, or just pass out shit-faced before the night was out. Seconds later, a third option presented itself in the form of a brunette Dirk recognized as Rachel's friend, Mary Jane.

She edged up to the bar, eyeing Grady up and down until her gaze rested on his crotch, her red lips curving into a seductive smile. "Impressive...buckle."

"Mary Jane." Grady tipped his hat with a wolfish grin. "Been a long time."

"It has." She acknowledged Dirk with barely a nod and then took up Janice's vacated seat. "I'm thinkin' maybe too long. Buy me a drink, cowboy?"

Grady's smile widened. "Sure thing."

"I watched you tonight." Gazing up through lowered lashes, Mary Jane scored a painted fingernail up his forearm. "Do you always ride so hard?"

"Depends on what I'm ridin', sweetheart...and how much they can tolerate. Some can take a whole lot more of me than others." He placed his hand on the small of her back.

"Oh yeah?" Her brows arched. "Lotsa cowboys *talk* a good ride, but put to the test, most of 'em ain't worth their salt."

"Then you've been hanging with the wrong cowboy. Whatcha havin'?"

"I dunno." She pursed her lips and then one side of her mouth curved up. "Think maybe I'm in the mood for a Suck Bang and Blow."

Grady's brows shot up. He slid his hand down to her ass, his fingers reaching into the gap of her waistband to stroke the bare skin. "Maybe you'd like to chase that down with a Multiple Screaming Orgasm?"

"That's a real tall order, cowboy."

"I can fill it."

"That so?" She reached into her purse for her card key and slipped it into his hand. "Number two twenty. Just give me fifteen minutes to get rid of my pain-in-the-ass roommate." She slid off the stool with a wink. "Guess I don't need the drink after all."

Grady stuck the card key in his shirt pocket and watched her walk away, his eyes glued to her denim-clad ass. "As I recall, back in high school MJ gave a helluva BJ. Wonder what other tricks she's learned?" A moment later, the DJ gave them a nod and began playing "Sittin' at a Bar" by Rehab.

Shit! Dirk had forgotten all about Grady's request, but the music had started. It was too late to back down now.

Grady threw his head back with a guffaw. "Showtime, cowboy."

With drinks in hand, Dirk and Grady made their way a bit unsteadily toward the stage where Grady picked up the mic to join the song mid verse, "'I'm sittin' at a bar on the inside, waitin' for my ride on the outside. She broke my heart in the trailer park, so I jacked the keys to her fuckin' car. Crashed that piece of shit and then stepped away…'"

They barely made it through the chorus before the speakers went dead. Seconds later, the deafening silence was broken by a chorus of boos and hisses from a handful of drunken cowboys.

Wade appeared at Dirk's elbow, hissing under his breath, "What the fuck was *that* performance?"

"Long story that begins with your own performance with Rachel," Dirk slurred.

"Look, you ungrateful asshole, I was helping you out."

"Helping me?" Dirk repeated. "How the hell do you figure that?"

"She said you wanted me to stand in for you. Told me you weren't up to all the PR stuff since you got busted up."

"The hell she did!"

"Whatever." Wade shrugged. "I'm not going to argue with a drunk." He looked to Grady who eyed him back with close-fisted belligerence. "And I'm sure as hell not going to pick a fight with one. Start anything with me, Grady, and I guarantee you'll spend tonight in the county jail. 'Course you might be sleeping there anyway, since Carson's asked you both to leave the hotel. *Now*. If you go quietly you'll be saved the embarrassment of an escort by hotel security."

"Rachel wouldn't let him do that," Dirk argued.

"Oh yes she would," Wade said. "Given it was her idea."

"Shit!" Dirk groaned.

"Oh yeah. You've fucked it up real good tonight, big brother. If you broke her heart there's a whole lotta guys willing to help her put it back together... And I don't mind sayin' I'll be first in line."

—◦◦◦—

Janice glanced twice over her shoulder as she darted toward the exit, but to her relief Grady hadn't followed. She'd watched the interplay between Dirk and Grady in the last few minutes with growing tension. She suspected there would be a fight before the night was over and knew she'd made the right decision to cut out.

Cowboys, especially the rough stock variety, always exuded an excess of testosterone and frequently needed to blow off steam—especially after an event. She'd heard enough to know that rough sex and bar fights were the preferred means.

She'd never understand how guys could beat the shit out of one another one minute and then share a beer in the next, slate wiped clean—usually with blood. Sometimes she envied a man's freedom to live for the moment and act out physical impulses without thought of repercussions.

Maybe the male way was better.

Women were vindictive, often carrying grudges for years without achieving any kind of resolution. She wondered what life would be like without overthinking every little detail—less complicated for sure—which brought back the whole scene in the ladies' room. She wondered what had actually transpired between Dirk and Rachel, who seemed to be the rodeo world's most perfect couple. They hadn't spoken to each other from the time she and Grady had arrived and seemed to be purposely avoiding one another, except for the exchange of baleful looks. On top of that, Rachel had been flirting outrageously with Dirk's brother, Wade.

Janice shook her head. What a stupid move that was. Wade might be taller and maybe even better looking in the conventional sense, but he wasn't Dirk. Janice didn't know a guy around who could hold a candle to Dirk—at least not in her estimation. He just seemed to personify everything a man should be—strong, honest, loyal. Dirk had integrity. He didn't cheat. He'd never stepped out on Rachel, to her knowledge, and Janice was in a position to hear. Cowboys weren't above gossip—especially concerning who's banging who.

Rachel's revelation that they hadn't slept together had come as a shock, but now only reinforced Dirk's strength of character in Janice's eyes. How many other guys would have waited all this time?

If only… She sighed.

Dirk and Rachel might be "off" at the moment, but they'd be back "on" again soon enough. They'd probably announce their engagement within the month. Maybe that would be better anyway. If they were engaged, if he took that definitive step, she could maybe give up this ridiculous hope.

Hope of what? Get real, Janice. Do you think he's gonna suddenly fall at your feet and beg you to bear his children? She gave a derisive snort. *Not likely!*

She thought about Grady with a grimace. He was the kind of guy she'd probably end up with—a swearing, swaggering, smoking, drinking, cheater—a man just like her own father, or at least like he used to be before he gave up bull riding. Her mother had simply accepted the drinking and whoring as part and parcel of the cowboy package.

It wasn't what Janice wanted, but what other kind of man was she ever going to be exposed to? Her life outside of home was spent with livestock and cowboys.

Still contemplating her dissatisfaction with her lot in life, Janice returned to the Events Center. After changing into sleep shorts and a cami, she crawled up into the gooseneck of her trailer. It had only the most rudimentary living quarters, and she hated sleeping in it while on the road, but she hadn't thought to book a motel room until it was too late to get one. With the rodeo finals there were none available in Casper. She figured she might as well get used to it anyway, as she'd be camped out at a different venue every week for the rest of the summer. The trailer saved her money. Every penny she didn't spend was more money in her pocket—money she'd need if she ever wanted to go anywhere or do anything with her life.

Problem was, she didn't have a clue what she wanted—besides a certain cowboy who seemed as far out of her reach as the moon.

Chapter 4

JANICE AWOKE TO THE FLASH OF LIGHTNING, PELTING rain, and a trailer-shaking rumble of thunder. It was storming fiercely. She rolled over and pulled the covers over her head with a groan, but couldn't muffle the noise. Following the next window-rattling clap, she thought she heard someone calling her name.

Confused and alarmed, she sat up, rubbing her bleary eyes and holding her breath.

There it was again—a thump and a voice coming from the other side of the door. "Janice? You awake?"

"Shit!" She slid down from the gooseneck, almost missing the step in her haste. What had happened? A wreck with the livestock? Bad news at home?

With her mind racing, she flipped on the light and flung open the door.

Clothes plastered to his body and water pouring down from the brim of his hat, Dirk stood shivering in the narrow doorway.

"Dirk?" She gasped. "What are you doing here?" She looked at her watch. It was almost one a.m. "What's happened?"

He gave a dry laugh. "You might say '*shit happened*.'"

"I'm guessing the karaoke routine didn't go over so well?"

"You guessed that right. We were 'asked' to leave, but Grady'd already had a few too many and wasn't in any mood to cooperate."

"No. I don't suppose he would have been," she said. "It seemed he was itchin' for any excuse to brawl tonight." She stepped closer, noting that Dirk had added a black eye to his prior battle scars. "Guess you weren't so willing to go quietly either?"

He flashed a shameless grin. "It's a cruel world. We low-life cowboys have to stick together."

Janice couldn't stifle a chuckle. "So where's Grady now? Is he with you?" She looked over his shoulder but saw no one.

"Nope. He found other accommodations." Dirk didn't elaborate so she didn't press. "Mind if I get out of the rain?"

"Sure. Sorry." She stepped back, allowing him to enter the tiny confines of her living quarters.

He doffed his hat with a nod. "Nice digs."

"Yeah, right," she snorted. "Mind telling me why you're here?"

He heaved a sigh that made him wince. "Had nowhere else to go."

Janice flinched in sympathy. "Shoulder botherin' you?" He still wasn't wearing the sling.

"S'alright."

"How about that hand?"

His left hand was wrapped but his exposed fingers looked like purple sausages.

"Not so bad." He shrugged. "I mighta broke a coupla fingers but I don't think it's anything that won't mend. It's mostly my head now…and the damned ribs."

"Your ribs? You didn't mention those to the medic."

He shrugged. "My lung didn't perf, so there's nothing he could have done anyway. I think they're only bruised."

"So what happened after I left?"

He dragged a hand through his dripping hair. "It was all a big to-do 'bout nothin' really."

"Oh, really?" She raised her brow in disbelief.

"Yeah. We barely got through the first verse when they cut the music and gave us the boot."

"And then what?"

He looked abashed. "We didn't just have to leave the party, we got kicked out of the hotel too."

"Evicted from your room?"

"Yup. And there aren't any others available in all of Casper."

"I know," she said. "It's why I'm camped out here." She paused to digest what he'd left unsaid. "So you and Rachel?"

He shook his head with a scowl. "We're done now. Quits."

"You're kidding."

"Nope. History. Case closed."

"It'll blow over."

"Don't think so. It was her idea to boot us. Said she didn't give a shit if I had a room tonight or not. Then I couldn't even try finding anything outside of town because my asshole brother took my keys so I wouldn't drive. My next move was to pilfer a blanket and pillow and camp out under the stars in my truck bed, but then it started pouring on me."

"So you came here. How'd you do that with no wheels?"

"Walked."

"Three miles in the pouring rain? No wonder you look like something the cat dragged in."

"Can I crash for a coupla hours? Maybe just camp out in the backseat of your dually? All I need is to get warm and dry again."

Janice's mouth went dry as sawdust. Dirk Knowlton. Cold. Wet. Here. Now. Wanting a bed? She'd give her right arm to warm him up. *Heck yeah*.

Misreading her silence he mumbled a curse. "Sorry, Janice. It's my damned head. I'm not thinkin' right. It's still throbbing like hell. Haven't been myself all night. M'pologies for being such a dumb-ass and imposing on you—" He turned to the door.

"No! Wait. It's not that." She grabbed his sleeve. "I was just thinking of your injuries. You don't need to make matters worse by sleeping all cramped up in the truck." She gnawed her lower lip and then blurted. "Y-you wanna just stay here instead?"

"Here? That's mighty generous but there isn't a whole lot of room for both of us." He glanced up at the gooseneck with a frown. "If you'll just gimme a blanket, I'll take the floor."

"You don't need to do that," she said. "The bench here flips down over the table and converts into a single. It's really narrow and not very comfortable, but still better than the truck. Warmer anyway. Besides you need to get dry."

"You sure about this?" he asked.

"Yeah." She smiled. "What are friends for? I'm sure I've got a shirt for you too."

"Thanks, Red. That would be great."

Red? The single syllable rippled warm and tingly, all the way to her toes. He followed up with a lopsided grin that stopped her in her tracks. She turned to the small cabinet that served a dual function as dresser and closet and shut her eyes on a sigh—but the same air stuck in her throat the minute she turned back around.

He'd shed the denim jacket. And the black tee. His bare torso with well-developed pecs and a mouthwatering six-pack greeted her. He was drying his face with his discarded shirt. Janice tore her gaze away and cleared her throat. "Here." She thrust an extra-large Dixie Chicks T-shirt into his hands, a souvenir from their Top of the World Tour. "I—I can get you a towel too."

He eyed the shirt skeptically. "No thanks."

"What? You don't like female musicians?"

"Don't like their politics. Natalie should just shut up and sing."

"Ah." She nodded slowly. The shirt was from the tour that caused the "incident." A lot of her friends had since thrown out their Dixie Chicks CDs, but Janice still loved their music. "I Can Love You Better" was her favorite. The lyrics—"she's got you wrapped up in her satin and lace. Tied around her little finger…but I can love you better"—perfectly summed up all the heartbreak and frustrations of unrequited love; all her secret feelings for Dirk. She only wished she could show him now that he was here. In the flesh. A big, strong, blue-lipped, and teeth-chattering fantasy come true.

"You're shivering," she argued. "It's a silly time for political statements."

"Sorry," he said. "But I never compromise my core principles. I support the war. Wholeheartedly. Somebody's gotta make those sons of bitches pay for what they did. If we don't defend our country, our freedom, who will?"

"There's other ways than war," she argued. "Like the UN—"

He made a choking sound. "Don't get me started there, Red."

"But—"

He raised a hand. "Look, it's already clear we don't see eye to eye, and nothing you say can change my views, so don't you think the conversation is kinda pointless?"

"All right," she conceded. "I suppose we can just agree to disagree."

He gave her a curt nod. "I'd say that's fair enough."

Janice pulled out another shirt and offered it to him with a twinge of embarrassment. "How 'bout SpongeBob? Is he politically safe?"

"SpongeBob's my man." He chuckled and took the shirt. Their fingers brushed. Their eyes met. She shivered. His gaze drifted southward. "You cold too?" he asked.

She tracked the direction of his eyes and swiftly crossed her arms over her chest to hide her hardening nipples. "Yeah, I must be cold." She turned away, briskly chafing her arms. "I don't have any jeans that will fit you, but maybe some sweatpants?

"Would you be offended to see me in my boxers?" he asked.

Janice pursed her mouth and shook her head, unable to form a coherent response.

Hell no, her brain screamed. "Offended" was the very last word that came to mind.

"Damn!" Dirk toed off his boots with a mumbled curse. "Is there anything worse than trying to peel off wet jeans?" His clothes were stuck to him and his bum left hand and shoulder didn't make it any easier.

"Here, let me help you."

Before he could protest, Janice had squatted down in front of him. She went right to work tugging the bottom half of his pant legs—a position that put her face level with his crotch.

Instinctively, Dirk's gaze drifted to her mouth. It was a pretty mouth, maybe not as full and overtly sensual as Rachel's, but nicely shaped. It was also too damned close to his dick. *Down boy!* She glanced up at him wide-eyed, which only made matters worse.

Far worse.

He shut his eyes on a muffled groan trying to banish his lewd thoughts and will away the stirrings his imagination had invoked, but he was getting a hard-on, and there was not a damn thing he could do about it. Panic set in.

Fearing she'd notice, or worse yet, his dick would poke her in the eye, he tried to back away. With wet jeans tangled around his ankles, he lost his balance, and crashed backward, striking his head on the table before hitting the floor. "Goddamn sonofabitch!"

"Dirk!" Janice cried. "Are you OK?" She knelt beside him, pulling his head onto her lap to palpate his scalp. "There's no blood. Thank God. Does it hurt?"

The pain in his head was blinding. "Hell yeah. It hurts!"

She bit her lip. "Is it worse on the inside or the outside?"

"Both," he snapped. "It was mostly on the inside until this last dumb-ass maneuver. I'm wondering if

I've developed some kind of subliminal death wish. Got a sledgehammer?"

"What for?" she asked.

"To finish the job and put me out of my misery."

She shook her head with a sympathetic smile. "I don't but maybe I can make it better?"

"You sure as hell can't make it any worse," he said.

"Hang on." She softly lowered his head to the floor, then stood up to grab a pillow from the gooseneck. She then wet a dish towel at the sink and returned to sit cross-legged beside him with the pillow on her lap. "Head. Here." She patted the pillow.

Dirk complied without protest, easing his head into the marshmallow softness. She folded the wet dish towel and placed it over his eyes. "Trust me and try to relax. I do this for Mama whenever she gets migraines," she explained in a voice as soft and soothing as her touch.

She had magical fingers, he decided, after only a few seconds of her temple massage. She didn't smell half bad either. His nose was badly swollen but he could still detect the subtle scent of vanilla. Vanilla was unfairly maligned in his estimation. He particularly liked vanilla. He breathed it in.

Though his eyes were covered, he could see through a small gap alongside his nose. A gap that gave a very fine view of her breasts. They weren't overly large, but perfectly shaped—nicely rounded and full. They jiggled slightly with the movements of her arms. He also noticed her nipples were still hard, much like his prick. His boxers were loose, but couldn't camouflage his hard-on if she looked. He hoped she wouldn't.

A moment later, the abrupt pause of her fingers and sharp intake of breath told him she likely had. He held his own breath, waiting. Would she think him a complete perv, drop his head to the floor, and kick his ass out the door? To his relief, the scalp massage continued.

"Feeling any better?" she asked after a bit.

"Yeah," he said. "You've got great hands, Red. Feel free to put them on my body anytime."

"Yeah?" Pause. "How's the shoulder?"

"Real stiff." *Like my dick*. His early words of warning to Janice came back to haunt him with an erection-sustaining vengeance. Soft, warm, and vanilla smelling Janice sure as hell wasn't a troll.

"Oh?" He detected the smile in her voice. "Want me to try and work the kinks out for you?"

She took the cloth away and their eyes met. He'd never given Janice's eyes a good look before. Couldn't even have said what color they were—until now. Warm brown with tiny flecks of gold. Her cheeks colored. They had tiny flecks too. Freckles. Sun kisses, his grandma used to call them.

She broke eye contact first. "Can you sit up?"

"Yeah, I can sit," he replied.

She opened her legs and crooked her fingers, gesturing that he should position himself between them. He hesitated, wondering if it was a good idea to put his ass that close to her soft, bare thighs.

She regarded him with a wrinkled brow. "Do you want me to try that shoulder? Or not?"

"Yeah." He moved into position, figuring the case would be a lot worse if she positioned *her* ass between his thighs, but changed his mind a minute later. No matter whose ass or thighs went where, the position was pretty damned intimate.

Her hands began at his neck, her thumbs circling firm but gentle over his spine. He let his head drop to his chest with a groan. *Holy shit, that felt good. Damned good.*

She slid her hands a bit lower, her fingers probing deeper into his shoulder muscles. Her hands were strong, and confident, delivering a medicinal mix of pleasure and pain. He'd never had anyone touch him like this—not even Rachel. And his body responded to it.

"You'd better stop that now, Red." Standing up would only make his condition more evident so he scooted forward, away from her reach.

"Did I hurt you?" she asked.

"No," he replied tightly. "I just don't want it to end up the other way around."

"What do you mean?"

"I told you, a man and woman can't be friends. Sooner or later he'll want to get into her jeans. Maybe you didn't mean to, but you got me achin' to do just that."

"Aching?" she repeated dumbly.

"Yeah, Red…as in blue balls." He shifted in growing discomfort knowing he'd get no relief tonight. "Maybe you should climb up into that gooseneck now."

"Is that what you *want* me to do?"

"What I want?" He gave a deprecating laugh. "You shouldn't ask questions like that, sweetheart. You'll never get the truth out of a man with a hard-on." He spread his hands in a helpless gesture. "I can hardly deny what's staring you right in the face."

Her gaze dropped. Her brown eyes widened.

He covered his face and blew out a long breath. Maybe it was the injury that had his head all screwed up, or the alcohol he shouldn't have drunk. Or more likely, it was pent-up frustration from long-term abstinence. Whatever it was, his resistance was crumbling to dust with vanilla-scented Janice staring at his dick.

"Shit, Janice. You're not making this easy on me. I'm trying my damnedest to act like a gentleman."

"What do you mean?" she asked, her gaze flickering back to his face. "What did I do?"

"Hell, you don't have to *do* anything when you're looking at me that way."

"What way?" she asked, her soft brown eyes searching his.

Her whole demeanor was a provocative mix of earthy innocence. Her hands were strong and gentle. Her eyes, honest, and guileless. Everything about Janice felt so warm and inviting, in stark contrast to Rachel who ran hot and cold with nothing in between. For almost five years Rachel had strung him along, teasing with promises and vacillations. Now here was Janice—warm, welcoming, and smelling good enough to eat. His gaze dropped to her mouth, to lips that softly parted. Her unspoken invitation was the straw that broke the cowboy's back.

Janice knew what she was doing—at least she told herself she did. She'd never dreamed of anyone but Dirk. It seemed like she'd waited half her life hoping he'd notice her—and now here he was—and he'd definitely noticed.

Maybe she was taking unfair advantage of the situation. He was on the rebound. Though he'd never admit it, he was hurting bad and not just on the outside. She knew he and Rachel would eventually patch things up. Her eyes were open on that score, but right here, right now, none of that mattered. This was Dirk.

Her breath came in rapid puffs. She shut her eyes in anticipation, waiting and willing him to commit himself.

His fingers cupped her chin, firm and gentle at the same time. Her body tensed and stomach tightened as inch by devastating inch he lowered his head toward hers until his mouth hovered only a hair's breadth from hers.

Her heartbeat accelerated, her lips parted.

His warm breath caressed her face, teasing her with its scent while the yearned for kiss hung between them—a sweet promise suspended in time.

Please. She sent a silent supplication to the heavens.

A heartbeat later, her prayer was answered as his lips brushed over hers—soft, warm, sweet. The stuff of her girlhood fantasies. She wanted to melt into him, to throw her whole being into her response, but he stiffened and drew back, as if ready to abort what they'd started.

Her breathing stilled. Her eyes opened. Her heart squeezed with the fear of rejection, but rejection wasn't what she saw reflected back at her in pools of crystal blue. His gaze was searching hers as if silently seeking confirmation that *she* wanted what *he* wanted.

Now or never, Janice. Time to cowgirl up.

She took a breath, and then the dive. Stepping into him, she snaked her arms around his neck, until they stood chest to chest, thigh to thigh, separated by only thin layers of cotton. His erection surged between them, pressing hot and hard against her lower belly. Threading her trembling fingers through the hair at his nape, she pulled his head back down to hers for another kiss.

Like the flip of a switch, everything shifted. Transformed.

His hands tightened on her face as he claimed her mouth again, but this kiss wasn't soft and tender. It was hungry. Fierce. His mouth melded with hers with an urgency that made her chest tighten. He licked across the seam of her mouth and she parted her lips on a soft moan, welcoming his exploration, and the slick, swirling strokes of his tongue.

His hands dropped to her shoulders and his mouth to her neck. Sucking, licking, gently biting. Her mind emptied of everything but Dirk. It was him. Only him. His mouth. His hands. His soft words murmured against her skin. The deliciously abrasive bristle of his whisker stubble. His fingers pushing her camisole strap aside. His mouth replacing it, moving over her shoulder in a hot wet trail across her collar bone.

The sensations of his mouth, his hands, and hot tongue robbed her of breath. Her nipples were swollen, almost painfully erect. Her breasts ached for his touch. She clutched his hair with a soft sound—a plea for relief that he didn't ignore. *Yes. Sweet Jesus. Yes.*

His mouth came down, kissing, gently biting, and then suckling her breasts. He teased, strummed, and plucked her nipples, inducing a sudden surge of wetness between her thighs and transferring the ache to a different place.

She slid her hands down his neck, over his broad shoulders, to the wide, smooth plane of his back. He brought his hands lower too. Her body rippled under his fingers tracing gently down her spine until they rested on the small of her back. His callused thumbs located the hollowed dimples. Circling, stroking. Every touch, kiss, breath, and heartbeat wrested a response, ramping her need to a fever pitch. She'd never felt like this before, on fire and burning up with want. She whimpered and ground herself against him. The friction of his erection created a blinding rush of pleasure. He ran a hand up her thigh, reaching inside the leg of her shorts to stroke his fingers through her damp curls. He kissed her again. Slow and deep. He also probed further. Deeper.

She clutched him tighter, her body quivering.

"You nervous, Red?"

"Well, yeah," she confessed.

"It's all right," he soothed. "I won't be rough and I'll take care of you first."

Before she realized what he meant by that, he'd dropped to his knees. Caressing the length of her legs, his mouth trailed up the wake of gooseflesh created by his hands. He nuzzled her through her shorts. She gasped at the mind-reeling jolt of pleasure.

His gaze shot up to hers. "You like that?"

"I—I—I don't know," she answered back. "I think so."

"What're you saying, Red? No one's ever gone down on you before?"

A flood of heat invaded her face. Her gaze dropped from his. "Ah...well...ah...no."

He grinned. "Hell, sweetheart, I consider it an honor to be the first."

Her body tensed with apprehension. She squeezed

her thighs tightly together. "Y-you really don't have to do *that*."

"Yeah, I do." He laughed. "Maybe you aren't certain about it, but I promise you I am. You just gotta trust me on this one, Red. I swear you'll like it…a lot."

Before she could protest again, he smoothed his hands up to her hips. Anchoring them there, he buried his face fully into her, licking and nibbling through her shorts. She bucked against him but he held her firm and strong against his mouth until she swayed drunkenly on her feet.

He gazed back up at her with a smug grin. "That was just a sample, darlin'. Wanna let me peel those shorts off now?"

———

She was hot and wet and willing, but too tense and too tight. *Not ready*. But oral was one thing Dirk prided himself on—and it was no chore to do it.

He didn't wait for her answer but braced her hands on his shoulders and then dragged her shorts down over her hips and those sleek mile-long legs. Her musky perfume surrounded him, filled him. He pulled a deep breath inward, wishing to inhale her into his lungs. *Holy shit!* The essence of an aroused woman always made his cock swell and his balls ache. He wished he could bottle it.

The second she stepped out of the shorts, he dove in, sweeping through her slickened folds with long hungry swipes of his tongue. Hands on her hips, he feasted on her, stoking, probing, licking, swirling, drinking her juices, and fucking her with his tongue until he was nearly out of his mind with lust.

She whimpered and writhed, clawing his scalp and pulling his hair. Hell, she was almost there. He applied his mouth to her clit, circling and sucking the swollen nub until her knees buckled and her body convulsed in a climax against his mouth. Holding her upright, Dirk nuzzled and kissed her belly until she came back to earth.

"Good for you, Red?" he asked with a self-satisfied smirk.

"What did you do? I never—" She gazed back at him, looking flushed. Bewildered. Beautiful.

He'd never thought of Janice that way before, but shit yeah. She was hot as hell right now. He rose and kissed her again. Slow. Deep. Using his tongue to restoke the fire. She melted into him all soft, warm, wet woman. His need for relief was approaching desperation. She was as ready as she was gonna get and he was miles past ready.

He scanned the cramped quarters. His gaze shot up to the mattress in the gooseneck. Even if he could make the climb there'd be no room at all to maneuver up there. He sure as hell didn't need to smack his head again tonight.

Shit.

There wasn't even a chair, just a tiny table with a built in bench seat. She said it flipped down into a cot but it was way too narrow. He regarded the table skeptically. He doubted it would hold any weight. He didn't want to shove her up against the door. He'd waited too friggin' long to do it quick and dirty like that. Not the first time anyway. It just seemed fundamentally…wrong. He wanted to savor the experience of feeling himself finally wrapped in a hot wet pussy—as long as he was gonna be able to savor it anyway. As excited as he was, he doubted he'd last very long once he was snugly gloved inside her hot, sweet flesh.

His frustration rising, he clawed a hand through his hair. It wasn't what he'd really wanted but he guessed her mouth would have to do—not that he didn't love a blow job. Hell, what man didn't?

"Any chance you wanna return the favor?"

She glanced down at his crotch where his prick strained rigid as rebar against his shorts. Uncertainty flickered in her eyes. "You mean..."

His breathing suspended. Was she unwilling? *Shit!* He hadn't even considered *that* possibility. "I won't come in your mouth, Janice. I swear it." He was almost pleading but if she agreed to blow him, he'd hold back his release if it fucking killed him.

"It's not that. It's just...I don't...I haven't ever..." She shook her head with an embarrassed look.

"You've never done that *either*?"

"No, Dirk. I haven't had much experience. With all the work, I've never had time for dating."

He held back a chuckle. "Giving a guy a BJ is hardly dating, Red."

"Don't tease me," she snapped. "I already feel inadequate enough."

Inadequate? He could hardly wrap his mind around that one. He stroked his thumb over her lips. "I assure you, sweetheart, you are *more* than adequate."

Her gaze softened. "I don't know what to do...what you like."

"If you just wrap those pretty lips around me I promise I'll like it just fine."

She still looked tentative. Unsure. "Will you tell me if I do it wrong?"

He was throbbing for release and all this talking about it only made his balls ache worse, but he knew he had to be patient. "You can wipe that thought out of your mind, sweetheart. There's no right or wrong—only what feels good."

"Then you'll tell me what feels good?" she asked.

"Yeah, Red. If that's what you want. You can start like this."

He brought her hand down between them, wrapping her fingers around him. His cock twitched in her hand. Her gaze widened. He closed his hand firmly over hers and moved it up and down. She followed his lead, stroking him awkwardly at first, until she found a rhythm.

"That's it. Just keep it right along these lines," he coaxed her low and husky.

Ignoring the sting of his split lip, he crushed his mouth to hers, kissing, nipping at her lips, then sucking her tongue into his mouth. She reciprocated eagerly, throwing herself hungrily into the kiss, as she continued to pump him. Their moans mingled. His need grew more urgent.

As if reading his mind, she broke from his mouth to work her way down his body. Touching, licking, kissing his neck and torso, tonguing and then sucking his nipples, she incited surges of sensation deep in his groin. He backed up to the table, giving her more room.

She hit her knees, her breath fanning hot and moist against his belly. She gazed up at him shyly, wetting her lips. His pulse accelerated. His body tensed…his cock throbbed for release.

She drew his boxers down.

He exhaled the breath he didn't realize he'd been holding.

He sprang free into her hand.

He shut his eyes and began slowly counting, tamping down the urge to thrust himself into her mouth. Much like working a skittish colt, he had to let her figure it out for herself. It wasn't long…maybe only twenty seconds or so before he felt the first smooth brush of her lips over the head of his prick. She followed with the first velvety swipe of her tongue that sent a ripple of sensation deep into his balls. "Jesus. That's good, Red. Just like that."

She responded to his encouragement with longer licks over the head of his glans, and then down his shaft. Coming back up again with wicked little flicks and darts of her tongue, then slowly circling the corona. She was a quick study, his shy little Janice. He palmed her head with a moan. "You're killing me, sweetheart," he groaned. "Take me in," he urged. "I need to feel your lips wrapped around me." He thought he'd lose his mind if she didn't do it soon.

She opened her mouth and shut her eyes, using one hand to guide him over her velvety tongue and into the warm, wet cavern of her mouth. His head reeled with sensation. He tangled both hands in her hair with a guttural sound, fighting back the urge to thrust. Instead, he gently rocked his hips. Taking his cue, she drew him further, deeper into her wet heat, then slowly released with a steady, mind-blowing suction. Her hands roamed over his abs and hips to rest on his buttocks, squeezing his ass as she worked him with her mouth.

"That's good, sweetheart," he groaned. "Really good. Take me all the way." He sychronized her movements with shallow thrusts and lost himself in deep, drugging pleasure.

Dirk's eyes were squeezed shut, his mouth slightly parted and his head thrown back. She was enthralled by the look of intense concentration on his face, the ragged rise and fall of his chest, his heavy breaths filling the air. She was almost dizzy with disbelief that she could affect him this way.

She'd heard plenty of talk about blow jobs, mostly filthy stuff from cowboys who'd either forgotten she was around, or maybe had just forgotten she was female. She'd known it was at the top of every guy's list, but the idea of some guy sticking his dick in her mouth had always seemed repulsive—until now.

She'd never considered how different it could be with someone she cared about. Rather than aversion, she was deeply aroused—more turned on than she'd ever been in her life. She loved the silky sensation of his hot flesh between her lips, the salty tang of him on her tongue, his hard ass flexing beneath her hands. She was becoming drunk on *his* pleasure. In this moment, she understood. This was about giving him the same kind of devastating, earthshaking pleasure he'd given her. He'd put his needs aside to rock her world and now she wanted to blow his off its axis.

She gently fondled his sac, felt it tighten beneath her touch, drawing up close to his body. She knew even before he spoke that he was closing in fast on the point of no return.

"You gotta stop now." His jaw was clenched, his voice tight. "I'm about to blow like Old Faithful."

He withdrew from her mouth with a guttural sound. Janice watched in dismay as he fisted himself to finish. She didn't want it to end like this. It felt too much like rejection. She'd already made the decision to give herself to him and ached to have him inside her. Body joined to body. Filling her.

She rested her hand on his. "Please, Dirk. Not like that. Can't we still…" She rose and backed up to the table and hoisted herself on top of it. It was too small to lie on…and shaky…and hard as hell under her ass, but Janice didn't care about any of that.

He gave it a dubious look. "I'd like nothing better than to oblige you, but I'm not too sure about that table."

"Please. I want to feel you inside me. Just this once."

"Hell, since you asked so sweet…" He grinned. "Gimme just a minute." He turned away to root through their discarded heap of clothes for his jeans, fishing a foil packet out of his wallet. "Been there so long the damn thing's probably expired," he mumbled, then tore it open with his teeth. He came back to her, nudging her knees apart and stepping between her thighs, his coarse hair abraded her skin. Her legs trembled uncontrollably.

"You seem a bit jittery there, Red."

"Only a little," she answered with a tremulous laugh.

His blue eyes met hers once more searching. "You having second thoughts? Do you really want this?" He gestured between them. "You…me?"

She bit her lip, but her gaze never wavered from his. "Yes," she whispered back through swollen lips.

He held out the condom. "You wanna do the honors?"

"No." She shook her head briskly. "You go ahead this time."

This time? She'd spoken as if this was actually the beginning of something, when she knew deep down it wasn't. Not that it mattered. She didn't care if it was only once. Only tonight. In this moment it was warm. It was real. Dirk wanted her and she'd never wanted anyone else.

He gloved himself.

She propped back on her elbows, a position that allowed her to watch. And she wanted to watch. This was her rite of passage to full-fledged womanhood and she wanted to savor it with all of her senses.

He positioned himself between her legs and wrapped hers around his flanks. He probed her entrance. She tensed and inhaled a gasp, then bit her lips, hoping he hadn't noticed.

But he had.

He froze. Withdrawing far enough to meet her gaze, he voiced the dreaded question. "You haven't done this before?"

She had to look away. "Well, no. I told you I didn't have much experience."

"Shit, Red! Not *much* experience? That statement was a tad misleading, don't you think? I expected you were green, but now you tell me you've never even been backed?"

"Nope. But it's OK," she blurted. "I really want this. I'm twenty-one. Isn't it past time?"

He stepped back with a groan. "Look, Red. Age has nothing to do with it. If that's your motivation, we're doing this for all the wrong reasons."

"No!" she protested. "That's not what I meant."

He scrubbed a hand over his jaw. "I don't know what you want from me, but what *I* want is the truth. Why tonight? Why me?"

She swallowed hard, but the lump in her throat didn't budge. It was indeed the moment of truth. "B-because I want *you*," she whispered. "I wanted you the minute you showed your face at my door. Nope, scratch that. I've wanted you ever since the day I saw you on the high school rodeo team, only I was too young even to understand what it was I wanted. But now I do. Understand. And I'm not sixteen anymore."

His brows came together and his mouth hardened. "I don't get it. *Why* me?"

"I don't know. You're just different from the others. I knew it would be better with you than with anyone else."

He shook his head slowly. "I sure don't know what to make of that."

"What about you?" she asked. "Why did you come here tonight? There must have been someone else you could have called."

"I don't know," he said. "It's been a shitty night. I was feelin' pretty low. I just started walkin' and then I found myself here... Maybe I was hoping I'd be welcome at your door."

"Maybe you were right... So where does that leave us?"

"I don't know, Red. This is new territory."

"Have you changed your mind because I don't know what I'm doing?" she asked.

"Hell, no. That's not it. It's just you and me. I didn't expect this."

"Neither did I…but that doesn't mean I didn't hope for the right time…the right one."

"And you think that's me?"

"Yeah." She nodded. "I know it is. I've *always* wanted it to be you. Now I've told you everything." With her heart in her throat she gazed up into his face. His expression was harsh and unreadable. She swallowed hard and whispered, "Do you still want to? Want me?"

He stepped into her, murmuring only inches from her mouth, "If we just take this nice and slow, I think we'll figure it out." Cupping her nape, he kissed her again. Long and deep, his tongue tangling with hers, sending ripples low into her belly. He withdrew from the kiss and brought his fingers to her lips. "Open. Get me wet."

She sucked his fingers into her mouth. When she released him, he urged her legs farther apart and slid his hand up her thigh. "Shut your eyes," he commanded.

She closed her lids on a shudder of pleasure, basking in the sensation of his mouth on her breasts and his wet fingers circling her entrance. He probed inside her. "That hurt?"

"No. It feels…good." She shifted her hips, urging him deeper.

He added another finger and moved it inside, sliding in and out with ease. The hair of his thighs abraded her as he positioned himself once more between her thighs. "Open up. Wider." He urged her legs apart. "Try to relax now. I promise I'll go slow."

Janice willed her body to relax and her passage to open. Dirk hovered over her, his brows contracted, his face drawn taut as he penetrated her in a slow and steady push that simultaneously stretched and filled her.

The pressure continued, as he advanced inch by inch until he was seated with his sex pulsing, hot and hard, deep inside hers. There was a little discomfort but not the pain she'd expected. For long seconds, they remained perfectly still, the silence filled only with her own heartbeat.

"You OK?" Dirk asked at last. He wore a look of fierce concentration. Veins stood out in his neck and arms, and sweat beaded his brow.

She released the breath she'd been holding. "Yes." She'd barely voiced her reply when he began moving inside her. "Sweet heaven," she moaned. It was surreal. It was sublime. Her inner muscles clenched and contracted around him. She angled her hips to take him deeper.

He exhaled a hiss. "Sweetheart, if you do that again, I'm not gonna last thirty seconds."

She grinned up at him. "But I thought cowboys only went for eight anyway."

His body suddenly trembled, shaking the rickety table beneath her. It was a moment before she realized the tremors and low rumble was laughter. She joined in the tension-breaking burst of mirth until tears streamed both down their cheeks. They were still tightly joined when Dirk wiped a hand across his eyes.

"Maybe I can do better than that if I try real hard."

"You think so?" she challenged.

"I think it'll all depend on how badly you wanna buck me off."

"Maybe I don't wanna buck you off, cowboy." Janice dug her heels into his flanks urging him deeper. When he moved again inside her, all humor died away, supplanted by sensations that stole her breath. "Please. Don't stop. I don't want this to end," she whispered.

Ever remained unspoken.

———

Janice never closed her eyes all night, too afraid to wake up and find him gone. Instead, she lay beside him on the mattress in the gooseneck, under the faint glow of her night-light, simply watching him sleep. She'd never had an opportunity to study him at such close quarters before, and, damn, if he wasn't worth the study—even bruised and busted up as he was. Her gaze shifted to his face, both manly and boyish with thick lashes casting shadows above his chiseled and bruised cheekbones. His mouth was slightly parted and he snored softly. His nose was probably broken, but she suspected that would only add to his appeal—not that he needed any help in that department. He was already devastating as far as she was concerned.

He'd flung the covers aside and lay sprawled on his back, arms outstretched, taking up most of the space on the mattress—not that she minded. Janice sidled up snugly against him, her shoulder set in the hollow of his shoulder, her head resting on his chest where she lay hypnotized by the slow and steady drumbeat of his heart. She'd never felt so warm, comfortable, and safe as she did with Dirk. He was everything she'd wanted— everything she'd dreamed of. He'd been patient and tender, making her first time a memory she'd cling to forever, and now she wondered if any other man would ever measure up.

It wasn't just a physical attraction, but what she'd

seen on the inside too. Dirk was strong, self-assured, and confident in his own skin—a man who took life by the horns. He was also honest and forthright and caring to those he loved. She couldn't fathom how Rachel could have been so mistaken to think she could manipulate him. He wasn't the type to put up with those kinds of games. Maybe she'd succeeded for a while…and maybe he'd go back to her…for a while…but she'd never be able to keep him—not like that.

Yeah right, Janice, you're quite an expert on men.

Nevertheless, her instincts had been right. Dirk had balked. She still marveled at the events that had brought him dripping wet to her door, but like the stroke of midnight for Cinderella, the rising sun meant the end of the magic—and the hours were ticking away.

This whole night seemed so unreal to her now. She'd given him her virginity without a second thought. Although she didn't have a clue what the morning would bring, she couldn't regret any of it. No, she wouldn't take it back for anything. Tomorrow he might belong to Rachel again, but she refused to dwell on that. For now he was all *hers*.

Chapter 5

DIRK STARTED AWAKE TO A BLAST OF MUSIC. BOLTING upright, he smacked his head on the thinly insulated trailer ceiling and then shut his eyes, cursing a blue streak. His head already felt like it was going to explode, and his body ached like he'd suffered the rack.

The music continued… "Cowboy take me away, fly this girl as high as you can, into the wild blue. Set me free, oh I pray, closer to heaven above and closer to you."

"Cowboy Take Me Away"? The Dixie Chicks? He hated that song. Clutching his throbbing skull, he consigned the Dixie Chicks to a very special place in hell.

Once the pain subsided to a dull throb, he slowly cracked his lids open and looked around, disoriented and confused. Where the hell was he?

The throbbing increased again with the brief flashes he recalled of the night before.

The bull ride gone south. The party. Rachel's teary eyes. Grady singing karaoke. Getting kicked out. The storm. Janice.

Shit! What the hell had he done? Had he and Janice really…as if on cue, she burst out of the bathroom to shut off her alarm. Her gaze met his and she froze, her teeth sinking deep into her lower lip.

The towel wrapped around her did little to cover all that creamy white flesh. She looked like a French pastry—good enough to eat. His dick twitched at the sight. Oh yeah. Last night was very real.

"Mornin', Red—" His gaze never left hers as he slid down from the gooseneck and grabbed his jeans and shirt. "I gotta get you some different CDs."

"I got some Chris LeDoux if you prefer," she said.

"About last night—" Their voices collided in a disharmonious duet.

He inclined his head. "Ladies first."

"I'm surprised you're here," she ventured shyly.

"Why?"

"I dunno. Just thought you'd probably be gone."

That supposition definitely didn't set right with him. "Is that what you wanted?"

"No! That's not what I meant. I just thought—"

He scowled. "That I'd slink off without even buying you breakfast?"

"You don't need to feel obligated to me."

His mouth compressed. "Whadaya mean, Red?"

"I just want you to know I don't expect anything," she said. "Sometimes things just happen. I'm not naive about that. I know last night doesn't *mean* anything."

"Sure it does. It *means* I was right about men and women being friends."

"Maybe you were," she confessed. "But we can at least try, can't we? Please, Dirk. I don't want things to be awkward between us now."

"Women." He pulled his shirt on with a mumbled curse.

She frowned at him. "What *about* women?"

"You think too damned much!" He stomped into one boot and then the other. "You have to overanalyze every little thing."

"It wasn't a *little* thing! It was a very *big* thing—well, for me anyway," she murmured.

He chuckled. "I'll take that as a compliment, sweetheart."

Her head snapped up, her brown eyes narrowing as if she wanted to slug him. "That's *not* how I meant it."

He shrugged. "If the boot fits…"

She grabbed one of hers and threw it at him. Dirk barely dodged the manure-covered missile. "Hold on there, Red." He raised his hands, laughing in surrender. "Can we call a truce? I'm awful hungry."

"What time is it?" she asked.

Dirk glanced at his watch. "Six fifteen. Go ahead and get dressed. I'll take you to breakfast. You got plenty of time."

She regarded him with uncertainty. "But I need to head out to Thermopolis soon, and Grady'll be here any minute. He's riding with me."

"Doubt that. He's more'n likely passed out. He was pretty wasted last night."

"You never said where he went. Weren't you both kicked out of the hotel?"

"He crashed with a friend," Dirk said carefully.

"A friend, eh?" She cocked a brow. "And there wasn't room for you too?"

"It would have been a bit crowded," he replied.

She opened her mouth again and he raised a staying hand.

"Look, Red. There's no point in giving me the third degree. I don't pry into Grady's personal business, and he don't pry into mine. You want pancakes or eggs?"

Janice's stomach gave a loud growl and she colored as deep as her hair.

He laughed. "Pancakes it is."

"Make it a full stack." She grinned back. "I'm starving."

"Let's go then. There's a decent diner just a little ways down the road. Do you mind driving? I don't have my truck. I'll give Wade a ring and see if he'll meet us there so I can get it back."

"No, I don't mind driving."

"Good, then I'll just go ahead and unhook the trailer while you dress."

He'd just grabbed his hat and shoved it on his head when a knock sounded on the door.

"Grady!" Janice cast a panicked look at the door and then back to Dirk.

"It's all right, Red. I'll handle it," Dirk said smoothly. He grabbed her discarded clothes and stuffed them into her arms. "Just step back into the bathroom and get dressed, and no one'll be the wiser."

"But. How will you explain—"

He propelled her firmly toward the bathroom door. "Said I'd handle it."

The knocking grew more insistent. "Janice? You there?"

Dirk flung the door open. "Mornin', Grady."

Grady's mouth dropped open "What the fuck you doin' here?"

Dirk shrugged. "Lookin' for you."

Grady's bloodshot eyes narrowed. He shoved past Dirk. "Oh yeah? Then where's Janice?"

"Getting ready. Since you weren't here yet, I offered to buy her breakfast. Wanna come? Looks like you need coffee." His gaze raked over Grady, taking in all the evidence of last night's dissipation. "Lotsa coffee."

"You ain't lookin' so hot yourself, Pretty Boy," Grady growled.

He looked around the room, his eyes lingering on the unmade bed. Dirk tracked his gaze, hoping they'd left no evidence from the night before. He suddenly thought of the condom. *Shit*. He hoped he'd disposed of the thing. He had no recollection.

"Did you fuck her?" Grady demanded.

"Have a little respect, asshole. This is Janice you're talking about."

"Respect?" he persisted. "All right, did you fuck Miss Janice Combes?"

"No, I didn't fuck her," Dirk lied through his teeth. "I told you I just got here."

"How? I didn't see that piece of shit white Ford."

"'Cause Wade still has my keys. I couldn't get him on the phone, so I walked."

"You walked."

"Yeah. I got two good legs last time I looked, and it's only a coupla miles."

Dirk hoped Grady wouldn't ask where he'd slept last night. He was damned if he could come up with anything plausible. But then again, Grady'd drunk so much the night before he probably wasn't even aware of the storm.

"Why'd you come?" Grady continued his interrogation. "What did you want me for?"

Dirk's mind scrambled for another answer. "I've had a change of plans."

That one was true enough. Lots of things had changed overnight. He'd *planned* on spending the summer campaigning with Rachel, but now that was shot to hell—along with the entire relationship. He still didn't know what to think of that. Hadn't even had enough time to properly digest it. Last night he was pissed as hell, but now in the light of day he only felt strong resentment coupled with vague confusion.

He still didn't know what had compelled him to Janice's door—he'd just found himself here. He couldn't deny that sleeping with her had been a much needed balm after getting dumped, but it was a lot more than that. He liked Janice. A lot.

She was so different from Rachel, so easy to be with. She didn't place demands on him—even after what happened last night. He *really* didn't know what to think about that yet. By the way she'd avoided his gaze, she didn't either. He needed time to get it all sorted out—to get his head straight. Maybe she understood that too.

"I'm not dropping out of the circuit," Dirk suddenly declared, wondering if the head injury had scrambled his brains after all. But the notion of Janice traveling alone with Grady stuck in his craw. "You still need a buddy, don't you?" he asked.

"Told you last night, I got one."

"You mean Janice? She might be able to give you a lift as long as you're headed in the same direction, but that won't last long if you plan to do Cowboy Christmas. 'Sides, she can't share your room expenses."

Grady passed an assessing look over the trailer. "Who says I plan to have any?"

Dirk fought the urge to grind his teeth. "Don't you think you should clear that with her first?"

"What with who?" Janice emerged from the tiny

bathroom. She nodded to Dirk. "Sorry for keeping you waiting so long."

She was dressed but he'd forgotten to give her her boots. She played it cool, nonchalantly grabbing a pair of socks from a drawer, sitting down, and then dragging them on along with her boots.

"Just talking about the rodeo schedule, Sweet Cheeks," Grady dissembled.

Dirk noticed her slight grimace at the pet name. It annoyed her, but he guessed she was either too shy or too polite to say so.

"Great. We can talk about all that over breakfast." Janice stood with a bright smile. "Let's go. I'm starved."

The diner was only a couple of miles down the road. As they drove, Janice and Grady carried on some small talk while Dirk was lost in his thoughts. He didn't know why he'd made the decision to rodeo all summer. He'd actually looked forward to a break from it. He'd never planned to go pro and make a career of it as Grady wanted to do, but he also wasn't ready to settle down to full-time ranching yet either.

They pulled into the diner with his mind still racing. Dirk ordered his breakfast without even looking at the menu and a minute later excused himself to make a call. He stepped outside, scowled at his phone, and dialed his brother.

"'Bout time," Wade answered. "Was wonderin' when I'd hear from you."

"Now," Dirk replied. "I need my truck back, asshole."

"Look, Dirk. Wanna lay off now? You know you

were in no shape to drive last night. I was only looking out for you the same way I *hope* you'd look after me."

Guilt hit him between the eyes like a two-by-four. His brother was right. He shouldn't have driven last night. "All right," Dirk conceded. "I'm the asshole. Happy now, li'l bro?"

"Is that an apology?" Wade asked.

"It's as close as you're gonna get."

"I can live with that." Wade laughed. "You were getting damned tiresome, you know. Did you call home yet? Mama's about out of her mind with worry after what happened to you last night. I told her you were OK, but it'd be best if she heard it straight from you."

"I'll call. You didn't mention anything 'bout me and Rachel, did you?"

"Didn't have to. Rae had already called to cry on her shoulder."

"Shit." Dirk kicked a boot toe into the dirt. "That's all I need."

"You gonna try to make it up to her?"

"Hell no," Dirk said. "I'm letting sleeping dogs lie till I get everything figured out."

Figured out? That was a tall order, Dirk thought dryly. It wasn't that he didn't want Rachel anymore. He did—or at least he'd *thought* he did. Hell, after last night he wasn't sure about anything anymore. Which now brought things back around to Janice. He scrubbed his face. What the hell had he been thinking last night?

"You better not take too long deciding," Wade warned. "You can't keep stringing Rachel along. I told you last night there's plenty of guys ready and able to take your place."

"Let it go," Dirk growled. "I'll deal with it when I'm ready…and I'm *not* ready."

Silence. "She's too good for you."

"Fuck you. And when you're done, bring me the truck, will ya? I'm at Casper's Good Cookin.' Gonna have breakfast and then head out for Thermopolis with Grady." He decided it would be better to make no mention of Janice. Things were already tangled enough to make his throbbing head want to explode.

"Thought you were taking a break from rodeo for a while," Wade said.

"Changed my mind," Dirk replied.

"All right. I'll find someone to follow me over. Be there in a few…and, Dirk?"

"Yeah? What?"

"Call the folks. They really are worried sick."

"Right. Bye, Wade." Dirk clicked the phone off and stuck it back in his pocket, vowing to make the call home…after he'd come to some decisions.

Rejoining Grady and Janice, he slid into the booth opposite them, grunting absently to the waitress who came by with coffee. Still brooding over his conversation with Wade, he took up his cup and glanced at the television mounted over the lunch counter. The channel was set to CNN with a reporter giving an update on a recent bombing in Kabul, Afghanistan. A taxi packed with explosives had rammed a bus carrying thirty-three UN peacekeepers. The next story was on the Taliban bombing of an Afghani school for girls, one that had only recently been rebuilt.

"Animals. Fucking animals." Dirk shook his head with rage, cursing when his coffee sloshed over the brim of his cup, splashing his hands. "The Taliban deserves to be blown back to the Stone Age."

Grady gave a careless shrug. "Who cares about that wasteland anyway? We should just pull the hell out. They'll do themselves in eventually without any help from us."

Looking uncomfortable, Janice maintained silence. "So are you two back to traveling together now?" she asked as soon as the waitress returned with their food.

"Yes—"

"No—"

Janice frowned over the cup that was poised to her lips, looking from Dirk to Grady and back again. "Well? Which is it?"

"Told you last night that I'm looking to get in as many rides as I can to qualify for the finals," Grady replied, "while it seems Pretty Boy here don't know what the hell he wants."

Dirk had to admit that truer words had never been spoken.

College had gone by too damn fast. He might be four years older, but he sure as hell wasn't any wiser. He still hadn't figured out what he wanted to do with his life. Although ranching ran in his blood four generations deep, and he knew it would be what he turned to eventually, right now the idea of going home made him feel caged. Smothered. It was the same reaction he'd had when Rachel started dropping hints about an engagement. He just wasn't ready to settle down.

For the past few years, rodeo had seemed the perfect answer. Life on the road was rough and unpredictable as hell, but he'd enjoyed the freedom of it more than he'd minded the discomforts. When in the money, he and Grady had lived high on the hog, dining out on T-bones and sleeping in air-conditioned motels, but losing meant more than aches and bruises. It was a diet of saltine crackers and nights spent in the truck bed.

For four years now riding rough stock had taken the edge off, had relieved some of the restlessness that shadowed him, but now the twitchy feeling was back with a vengeance and he didn't know if rodeo was still the answer. There had to be something more, something to fill the void he felt deep in his gut. He just wished to hell he knew what it was.

He looked up to find Janice watching him. She quickly diverted her gaze back to her plate. Janice. That whole situation *really* had his head all screwed up. He never should have gone to her last night in the shape he was in. He felt a trace of guilt but had a hard time summoning any regret over it. On the one hand, he damn sure wasn't ready to jump feetfirst into a new relationship, but on the other, Grady's sniffing around her almost had him spitting nails.

Over breakfast, Grady's gaze tracked continually back and forth between them. It was obvious he suspected something. Dirk wasn't sure why he felt so compelled to hide what had happened between him and Janice. It just seemed wrong to reveal to the world what they'd shared in private. On top of that, the situation would get awkward as hell if the three of them were going down the road together.

As fidgety as she looked, he guessed Janice was thinking the same thing.

"You're awful quiet, Sweet Cheeks. Whatcha thinkin'?" Grady asked.

Janice glanced up at him, flushed-faced and looking guilty as sin. "Nothing much," she replied, plucking at her napkin. "Just dreading a whole summer spent on the road."

"I was wonderin' 'bout that," Dirk said. "How is it that you're running the stock alone now? Where's your ol' man?"

"He's been under the weather for months," Janice said. "He's never been sick in his whole life, but he's lost a lot of weight and has stomach complaints and back pain that won't go away. He saw a chiropractor for a while, but it didn't help any. When his eyes started turning kinda yellow, we convinced him to go to the family doc for a full checkup. That was last week. The doc didn't say much but ordered a bunch of tests that he's s'posed to have soon. I can't help fearing it's liver failure or something like that."

"I'm sorry to hear it," Dirk said. "What about your other hands? Isn't there anyone else to help you?"

"Not anymore. Ace walked out. Wanted more money than we could pay, even though he wasn't worth half what he was making to begin with. He was drunk most of the time and way too rough with the stock. I told Daddy I could do better, but he's a chauvinist to the bone. He didn't want to give me a shot until he didn't have any other choice. Truth be told, I've had to work twice as hard just to be thought half as good my whole life, but I don't see how I can do it all. If the doc confirms the worst, I'll be needed at home, but I can't be there *and* work the rodeos. We can't afford to lose the contracts, but if I can't find some help, things'll go to hell in a handbasket real fast. I can't even begin to tell you how much I've worried about this, how much it's been weighing on me."

Dirk was thoughtful. "I don't see why me and Grady couldn't lend you a hand for a while—long as you'd let us work around the rodeo schedule. What do ya think?"

Dirk looked to his traveling buddy, who slouched back in his seat.

"Don't see why not," Grady said. "We're traveling together anyhow and I've got nothing else lined up. 'Sides, I could use the extra cash—"

Dirk glowered at him. "Who said anything about money? Janice is a friend in need. We shouldn't take advantage of that."

"It's a reasonable request to get paid, Dirk," Janice protested. "I'd have to pay someone else anyway, so it might as well be you two."

"I won't take your money, Janice," Dirk insisted.

Janice looked shocked by the offer. "You really mean that?"

"Shit yeah," Dirk said. "At least until Cowboy Christmas. After that, if you're needed at home, we can haul the bulls for you."

"Thanks, Dirk."

He flashed a grin. "Don't sweat it, sweetheart. We've got your back." Her answering smile suggested a great burden had lifted from her shoulders. Oddly, he felt lighter too.

"Will you both excuse me?" she asked. "I need to make a quick trip to the ladies' room and then I've gotta get rolling. Need to get my bulls loaded up and hit the road."

Dirk and Grady looked after her in silence until Janice was well out of earshot.

"What the fuck was that all about?" Grady demanded. "You made me look like an asshole just now."

Dirk shrugged. "She needs help."

"And I need money to pay my entry fees. Some of us ain't as privileged as others," he added with rancor.

"If you're short, I'll spot you a couple hundred," Dirk offered. "You can pay me back when you win in Thermopolis...or whenever." He shrugged.

Grady's expression was still black. "That don't fix the poor impression she just got of me."

Dirk laughed. "Since when did you start caring what anyone thinks of you?"

"Since I started thinking about the future," Grady replied. "I figure I got five, maybe ten years of rodeo left in me—if I'm lucky—and then what? You got a ranch. I got shit. I need a retirement plan."

Dirk's gaze narrowed. "What are you getting at?"

Grady leaned back with a toothpick sticking out of his mouth. "Simple enough. Her ol' man's got a decent spread and a contracting business. He's real sick. If he kicks the bucket, someone's gotta run it. I don't see why it can't be me."

Dirk felt his fuse ignite. "What the hell are you saying, Grady? You think Janice is gonna be some kinda gravy train for you?"

"A man could do a helluva lot worse. She ain't hard on the eyes and she's a good hand to boot."

Dirk clenched and unclenched his fists under the table. "In case you haven't noticed, she ain't interested in you."

"Only 'cause I haven't properly applied myself. I can be Prince-Fucking-Charming when I apply myself."

"And you intend to do that?"

"Yeah. I do. Why do you think we're traveling together? Look, Pretty Boy, we've been friends for a long time now, so I'm feedin' it to you straight. I'm staking my claim. Right here. Right now. If you're smart, you'll go make up to your rich little rodeo princess and stay the hell away from Janice."

Chapter 6

IT WAS OPENING WEEK OF THE 106TH FRONTIER DAYS—
nine days of nonstop rodeo, come rain or shine. With
over a million dollars in prize money, there were over
a thousand competing cowboys and cowgirls and at
least half again as many bulls, steers, calves, and horses
to support the entertainments. This was the first year
Combes' Bucking Bulls had been chosen to provide
stock for the Rank & Ready Pro Bull Tour and Janice
felt the pressure deeply.

The past weeks on the road had gone by in a blur with
nonstop twelve- to sixteen-hour workdays since the collegiate finals. Her mornings had begun between two and
four a.m. with feeding, watering, and checking on the
stock. After that, she generally took a nap for a couple of
hours before gulping down coffee and maybe grabbing a
breakfast burrito from one of the vendor wagons.

During the later part of the mornings, she moved her
stock from the pens to their designated chutes and then
flanked the animals for their riders. It was then that the
cowboys usually came around to ask about the bulls
they'd drawn. Janice always tried to be available and
never withheld anything about a bull from anyone who
asked. A 175-pound rider backing a three-quarter-ton
bull needed every advantage he could get.

Once the bucking events began, she almost never left
the chutes. As Grady always liked to point out, the rough

stock events drew the biggest crowds. She never missed a ride, especially when one of her animals or Grady or Dirk was up.

After tending her own stock, she helped the chute boss or anyone else who needed it. It was damned hard work and downright exhausting. Janice didn't think she could have survived without Dirk and Grady's help. When not otherwise occupied, neither of them ever hesitated to bring her a quick meal or relieve her for a catnap. It was a routine they'd fallen into since Thermopolis and had continued through Sheridan and the Cody Stampede.

Although they'd both spent plenty of time with her behind the chutes, it seemed she was never alone with either of them for very long. Since they began working together she detected an underlying tension between the two cowboys that she'd never noticed before.

Janice still wondered what was going on in Dirk's head. He'd never made any mention of their night in Casper and she hadn't either. She almost would have believed it had never happened if it wasn't for the times she'd catch him giving Grady the evil eye for flirting with her. It was odd that Dirk hadn't shown any further interest but still seemed to resent Grady's doing so. His attitude was befuddling and frustrating at the same time. She'd known he needed space and hadn't pressured him, but maybe it was time to lay the cards on the table. If he wasn't interested, maybe it was time to quit pining after him and move on.

They'd pulled into Cheyenne with just time enough to give the bulls a chance to settle in before going back to work. Janice was exhausted and glad finally to have some downtime, even if just for one night.

It was Grady, not Dirk, who'd asked her out for drinks with some of the riders and contracting crews who were meeting for beers at the Outlaw Saloon, the most popular honky-tonk in Cheyenne. She'd agreed to go, but recalling the night of the party when things had gotten so out of hand, she'd insisted on driving herself. Grady didn't seem to like her stipulation, but she'd made it clear she wouldn't go otherwise.

She walked in to find the place packed with cowboys, cowgirls, and tourists. Although they all wore hats and boots, it was easy to distinguish the hands from the wannabes. The band wasn't bad but the volume made her ears ring. The dance floor was filled with couples two-stepping, elbow-to-elbow around the floor, an excuse many used to dance indecently close.

She lingered at the door watching and secretly yearning to be one of them out there, wrapped in Dirk's arms. Maybe he'd ask her to dance tonight?

Her gaze rested on a couple who were practically dry humping. They were making a lewd and lascivious display, but Janice couldn't tear her gaze away. She ached to feel the heat of his body again, to once more experience him moving inside her. She shut her eyes for just a moment, imagining she and Dirk on that same floor but without the crowd. There was a gnawing sensation deep in her belly every time she even looked at him, but sensing he needed his space, she'd waited, hoping he'd come around. But he hadn't. She chided herself for mooning like a lovesick calf. Sure he was physically present, but he was also emotionally distant. Reserved. Almost untouchable.

Feeling a presence beside her, Janice opened her

eyes to find Grady had sidled up. He must have been watching the door. "Wanna dance?" He jerked his head toward the floor.

"No thanks. I'm not really in the mood."

"Coulda fooled me. You seemed mighty interested a moment ago." A knowing smirk hovered over his mouth. "Or maybe it was something else happening out on that floor?" The remark sent heat flooding into her face.

"I only came for a drink." She spun toward the table where Dirk and a rowdy group of rough riders sat. Dirk nodded to her in greeting, but his end of the table was already full, so Janice had to sit on the opposite side. Grady straddled a chair beside her, ordering two beers and a bourbon.

She was only a few sips into her drink when Rachel Carson walked in the door. Her stomach dropped and then her gaze instinctively riveted to Dirk's face. The place was crowded, so they didn't see each other right away, but once he laid eyes on her, his hands gripped the table and his jaw visibly tightened.

She should have anticipated the inevitability of Rachel and Dirk running into each other in Cheyenne. It was the biggest rodeo event of the summer. As a contender for the Miss Rodeo America crown, Rachel would have countless PR events lined up over the next ten days, which gave Dirk ample opportunity to make up with her.

Janice covertly watched them, hoping it wouldn't go any further, but then Rachel saw him and smiled. It wasn't the smug kiss-my-ass kinda smile that Janice had hoped for, but more of an invitation. Although Dirk didn't make a move to go to her, his eyes didn't leave her face either. A moment later, the rodeo queen sashayed her way across the bar, her desire to mend fences perfectly clear. The sick feeling in Janice's gut reminded her of what she'd known all along—that she'd simply caught Dirk on the rebound.

"Didn't I tell you before that you were wasting your time on him?" Grady growled in her ear as if reading her mind.

"I never *said* I was interested in Dirk," Janice spat back, but the lie wasn't very convincing even to her own ears.

"You didn't have to *say* it," Grady replied. "You're easy as hell to read. Maybe I'm not your idea of Mr. Right, Sweet Cheeks, but I am right here and I can promise you a good time."

"I'm not looking for a *good time*," she snapped.

Grady's gaze met hers. "All work and no play, Janice... Maybe you should think about that." He shrugged, emptied his bourbon, and then left her to join Seth Lawson at the bar.

Janice's gaze trailed after him. Maybe he was right. Her life was such a dull and mundane routine and she still had weeks of it ahead of her before she returned home. And then what? She'd likely have more work waiting for her, not to mention the countless repairs on any number of things that always needed fixing on a ranch. She was barely twenty-one, but her life was making her feel so damned old...and lonely. It struck her even harder now that she knew what she was missing.

For the first time Janice was glad he'd kept his distance. With Rachel in Cheyenne, their reconciliation was all but a foregone conclusion. It was bad enough to watch the pair of estranged lovers play make up, but had she and Dirk become further involved it would have been nothing short of devastating. Too proud to make an ass of herself by hanging around like a lovesick fool, Janice gulped her drink, slapped down money for her tab, and hightailed it out of the Outlaw.

—∿∿—

Rachel had taken Dirk by surprise. He hadn't expected to run into her, although he probably should have, given the tight circles that formed the rodeo crowd. They'd both had plenty of time to cool down since the Casper Finals, and now that they were both in Cheyenne, here was his golden opportunity to make up to her. All he had to do was walk across the bar and buy her a drink or ask her to dance, but for some reason he couldn't rouse himself to his feet.

Janice had bolted almost the moment Rachel appeared. He'd just sat there watching like a bump on a log, making no move to stop her. In retrospect, he wished he had, but the situation was damned awkward and he hadn't known how to react. His feelings were still as clear as mud where Janice was concerned.

He told himself he was just being the friend that Janice needed, but his feelings for her were far from platonic. Being honest, he hadn't stopped thinking of their night together since leaving Casper, but those thoughts were mixed with guilt. He wanted her again. There was no doubt in his mind about that, but he didn't want to play the kind of games with her that Rachel had played with him, so he'd kept his distance hoping to get his head straight. He'd thought the time on the road would help him get his shit together, but after three weeks, he still wasn't any closer to making any decisions about his life…or about Janice.

He noticed Grady's continued interest in her didn't keep him from disappearing with a skanky brunette who'd had a few too many, shortly after Janice's departure. He and a wannabe bull rider named Seth Lawson had headed off in the direction of the restrooms when she'd offered them a threesome. Dirk just shook his head and ordered another drink.

For four years he and Grady traveled together and raised hell together, but Dirk didn't trust him any further than he could throw him, especially where Janice was concerned. He was a selfish, reckless, and ambitious opportunist who'd take whatever he could get and then move on when the mood struck him. Janice didn't deserve to be treated like that. No woman did—except maybe the ones who gave blow jobs in the men's room. He told himself that's why he'd played interference between Janice and Grady. He was just looking after her.

He didn't understand why she inspired his protective instincts, but he'd felt that way about her even before he and Rachel split. There was something about her that stirred him, but it was completely unlike what he'd felt for Rachel, leaving him damned confused. Tonight he hadn't gone to Rachel, or gone *after* Janice. Instead, he'd just sat like a dumb sack of shit. He was wishing he was just about anywhere else but Cheyenne, when he looked up to find Rachel standing there.

She looked great in her ass-hugging Wranglers and a snug Western shirt, her blond hair falling over her shoulders. Only a few weeks ago the sight of her would have made his mouth go dry, but now he felt somehow different. Sure he still liked looking at her—no red-blooded man could deny her appeal—but something had changed and he was damned if he could figure out what it was. He just didn't feel that instant stirring in his groin that she'd always evoked.

"Buy me a drink, cowboy?"

"Sure, Sunshine." He tipped his hat and turned up his palm in invitation, indicating the empty chair. "When did you get in?"

"Just this morning. It's been crazy these past weeks with all the traveling and campaigning." She sat across the table from him, leaning in close to be heard over the band. He got a whiff of her perfume. It was an expensive flowery scent that he'd once found provocative, but now he suddenly preferred the more subtle essence of vanilla.

She shrugged. "But you know how it is."

He signaled the waitress. "Yeah. It's crazy, all right."

"How 'bout you? How've you been? You look good…" She slanted a meaningful gaze through her lashes. "Damn good."

"I'm well enough," he answered.

The waitress appeared and took Rachel's drink order. After she left they studied each other in a protracted silence. Rachel traced patterns on a cocktail napkin, looking up only when the waitress delivered her cosmo. "Dirk," she ventured after a time, "we really need to talk. I think we both said some things we didn't mean back in Casper."

"Maybe one of us did, Sunshine," he said. "But I can't recall sayin' anything I've changed my mind about."

She frowned at him. "You aren't making this easy for me. Don't you think you could at least meet me halfway? I'm trying to apologize. All I want to do now is put this all behind us."

"And then what? You think we're gonna just pick up where we left off?"

"Well…yes. Why not?"

He sat back in his chair and pushed his hat up off his brow. "Because things have changed."

Her frown deepened. "Things? What kind of *things*?" Her green eyes flashed accusingly. "Are you seeing someone else?"

"Nope." It wasn't a lie. He and Janice weren't involved. "But I might ask you the same thing. You seemed to be getting pretty friendly with my brother."

"That? It was nothing." She waved her hand. "I was just hurt—"

"So you decided to use my own brother to strike out at me?" He slowly shook his head. "Don't seem right to come between us like that, Sunshine."

She had the decency to look abashed. "I already said I'm sorry."

"We don't want the same things, Rae," Dirk said after a time. "You're looking to settle down, and I'm not ready. I'd like to see a bit of the world first. Hell, I've never even seen the ocean."

"Then why don't we go together? Daddy's thinking about buying a condo in Hawaii."

He shook his head. "You just don't get it, sweetheart. I'm not about to live in your ol' man's pocket like that."

Another silence followed.

"Dance with me?" she suddenly asked. The band

had struck up a slow song, ironically, a cover of Rascal Flatts' "I'm Movin' On."

Dirk nodded, stood, and pulled out her chair, guiding her out to the floor with a hand on the small of her back. They found an empty spot and she stepped in close, twining her arms around his neck and pressing up against him with all her soft, feminine curves.

"See?" She smiled up at him. "Just like old times."

But it wasn't. Although he couldn't deny a stirring of sexual desire—he was still a man after all—the fierce lust he'd felt before was barely a flicker.

"You know, Dirk"—she stroked her fingers up and down his nape—"I've been thinking, maybe if we were really careful...and super discreet..." She shifted her position so she was almost riding his thigh, her message perfectly clear. She was trying to use his dick against him again.

"I don't think so, Sunshine." He anchored his hands on her hips and drew back a few inches, just enough to give his prick some breathing room.

Her gaze widened in surprise. "All right, have it your way for now, but just think about it, OK? I want to work this out between us. We're too good together to just give it up."

"It wasn't my idea to break up, Rae, but I'm thinking now it was all for the best."

Her blond brows pulled together. "You're just being stubborn and prideful, but I can be stubborn too when I want something—and I still want you, Dirk."

"We can't always have everything we want, Sunshine."

"Says who?" she quipped with a confident smile.

She was so damned sure of herself…of him…but he just didn't feel the same anymore. When the dance ended, Dirk led her back to her friends, tipped his hat, and wished her good night, leaving her staring in consternation as he headed for the door.

———

Lost in his thoughts and needing space to think, Dirk left the Outlaw without a thought to Grady until he was halfway back to the motel. He swore aloud and almost turned around but then figured Grady'd probably hitch a ride with Seth. They were all bunking at the same place anyhow, the Motel Six, the cheapest place in Cheyenne.

Dirk let himself into his room, bone-tired but still too wound up to sleep. He was restless and burning with sexual frustration—frustration that he probably could have relieved with Rachel. Her offer had been on the table, but he didn't want Rachel. Not anymore. His reaction to her, or lack thereof, still surprised the hell out of him. They'd been an item for over four years and he'd been proud to call her his, but now he wondered if it had ever been more than skin deep. Was he really that vain and shallow? He'd never thought of himself that way. The idea was mighty disconcerting.

He stepped into the shower, resolved to blow off some steam. Leaning against the tiled wall, he shut his eyes, but his mind didn't conjure visions of a pretty blond taking him in her mouth. Instead, it was a leggy redhead with freckles on her nose, gazing up at him with a shy smile. Although Janice had been inexperienced, he'd felt an intense satisfaction, a connection with her that went much deeper than mere flesh.

He remembered the smell of her, the taste of her. The incredible sensations of moving inside her, the way her walls squeezed him and the soft sounds of pleasure she made when she came. He pumped himself more vigorously, biting his lip and jerking his hips as he achieved a swift but ultimately unfulfilling climax. He rinsed off, feeling physically spent but still dissatisfied.

He consoled himself that tonight had been exactly the test he'd needed—he was over Rachel Carson. But where the hell did that leave him and Janice? He felt like nothing more than the proverbial cowboy who straddled the fence only to end up with a sore crotch—or in his case—a blistered palm.

He was only feigning sleep when Grady came crashing into the room at two a.m. about as quiet as a bull in a china shop. He stumbled into the john, where he spent ten minutes retching before falling headlong into bed with his boots still on. Within seconds, he was snoring like a freight train.

It wasn't long ago that Dirk would also have stayed out all night and come back in a similar condition. It was part of life on the road—the drinking and the whoring around. Though unlike Grady, Dirk had chosen to forgo the latter, one of the chief perks of bull riding. For four years, they'd wake in the morning hungover as hell and feeling fragile as glass, only to do it all over again. But he was done with it now. It was past time he got his shit together.

Rodeo had been a big part of his life, and Cheyenne was one of the biggest in the country, but Dirk felt like he was just going through the motions. His heart just wasn't in it anymore. Janice was the only reason he was still on the road. She was going through a tough time and deserved a guy who'd be there for her, someone she could lean on, someone to help shoulder her load, not to take advantage of her situation as Grady intended to do. Part of Dirk wanted to be that guy for her, but the other part of him just couldn't commit. Although he still didn't quite understand his own motives where she was concerned, he sure as shit didn't like Grady's. Traveling together seemed a reasonable half measure, but he sensed Grady's growing resentment and knew things were slowly coming to a head.

Tomorrow. Dirk promised himself he'd finally pull his head out of his ass and come to some decisions—about Janice, about rodeo and ranching—about what he was going to do with his life. Tomorrow. Come hell or high water. Dirk rolled over and glanced at the clock, suddenly stuck with a fateful feeling deep in his gut—tomorrow was suddenly today.

Chapter 7

BY FOUR A.M., DIRK'S MIND WAS STILL RACING. GIVING up on sleep altogether, he rose, dressed, and headed out to the rodeo grounds. With Grady dead to the world, he figured it was his best chance to catch Janice alone. Finding the water troughs already filled and the bulls eating their hay, he figured she'd probably gone back to her trailer for a couple more hours of shut-eye. Not wishing to wake her, he decided to get some breakfast and then come back. Tired of vendor wagon fare, he drove a few miles toward the outskirts of town to a truck stop where he bellied up to the counter.

He ordered black coffee and the three-egg special when two guys entered the diner sporting buzz cuts and Marine Corps khakis. "Mornin'." Dirk tipped his hat.

The two marines nodded in acknowledgment and then sat a few stools down. After a minute, the taller, leaner one of the two cocked his head at Dirk. "You in Cheyenne for the rodeo?"

"Yeah," Dirk replied.

"Thought I recognized you." The bigger guy grinned. "You're Dirk Knowlton, right?"

"Last I checked," Dirk replied. "But I'm sorry to say I can't place you."

"Reid. Reid Everett." The marine extended his hand. "It's been a few years, but I rode saddle broncs against you back in high school. You beat me out in the finals."

"Shit yeah! I remember you now. You're from Dubois, right? As I recall, your whole team left spur tracks in your cantles."

Reid shook his head with a laugh. "The victor always thinks he can rewrite the battle any way he likes."

"Damn straight." Dirk returned a shameless grin. "So you're in the marines now?"

"Yup." Reid nodded. "Home on leave. Garcia and me just finished boot camp."

"*Semper fi*, man," Garcia added with a toothy grin.

"We got ten days liberty," Reid said, "so me and my buddy decided to take a road trip."

"Did you just get into Cheyenne?"

"Yeah, but we've been travelin' a while. We stopped in Vegas, visited my family in Dubois and then my girl over in Riverton. We'll probably be hitting the road day after tomorrow. Gotta return to San Diego for infantry training, but I promised Rafael here some live rodeo action before we leave. He's from LA and probably doesn't know the front end of a bull from the back."

"Hey, give me some credit, *ése*," Garcia protested. "I can tell horns from *cojones*."

"If you want to see bulls, you're in for a treat," Dirk said. "Just a few miles up the road there's at least fifty of the rankest bovines you ever seen, just waiting for the chance to toss some dumb-ass cowboy like me fork end up."

"Oh yeah?" Garcia grinned. "This I gotta see."

"So you're ridin' bulls now?" Reid asked.

"Yeah. I started just to win the All-Around, but now I'm helping out a friend who's a bucking bull contractor.

Since I'm here with the bulls anyway, I might as well ride, right?"

"Makes sense…if you can keep from getting freight-trained by those big snot-slobbering bastards."

"Getting freight-trained is a given if you do it long enough." Dirk shrugged. "But I'm in the money more often than not…least I *was* until the past few weeks."

"You ever ride a bull, *ése*?" Garcia asked Reid.

"Hell no." Reid laughed. "It's bad enough to hang a pedal on a bronc. I can't say I've ever had a hankering to take a horn in the ass from a near ton of pissed-off bull."

"Still backing any broncs?" Dirk asked him.

"Negative. Not for a few years. I traded my spurs for an M-16."

"Know where you'll be deployed yet?" Dirk asked.

"Not yet, but with all the saber rattling in the Middle East, you can bet the ranch it'll be Iraq or Afghanistan." The marines ordered their breakfast and the three men continued their small talk.

"You staying in Cheyenne tonight?" Dirk asked.

"Nah. I figured we'd drive to Laramie. I've got some family there too."

"If you change your mind or have too many drinks and need a place to crash, me and my buddy are at the Motel Six. Here's my cell." Dirk borrowed a pen from the waitress and scrawled his number on a napkin. "Do you remember Grady Garrison?"

"Hell yeah. That crazy bastard hasn't got himself killed yet?"

Dirk laughed. "He was alive and breathin' as of last night, but today's a whole new day."

Reid laughed. "If a bull don't get him first, my money says some jealous cowboy eventually will."

Dirk was finished eating by the time the waitress brought Reid's and Garcia's food. He picked up their check as well as his own. When Reid made to protest, Dirk laid a hand on his shoulder. "Please. I got it. I want you to know I appreciate what you're doin'."

"Thanks, man," Reid replied. "Let me know if you ever get out to Southern California."

"Thanks. Maybe I'll do that one day. I've always had a hankering to see the Pacific Ocean." Dirk tipped his hat. "Stay safe, OK?"

"Ditto, *ése*," Garcia replied. "You're the one riding those badass bulls."

—∾∾—

Janice had looked forward to Cheyenne Frontier Days every July from as far back as she could recall. Frontier Park was the cowboy version of Disney World with its grand parades, Old West Museum, Indian Village, and giant carnival midway where she'd often eaten enough cotton candy and funnel cakes to make her puke. As a kid, it had been a magical place, but now that she was one of the myriad invisible people behind the scenes, the enchantment had pretty much worn off.

At eleven o'clock it was already hot as Hades, which only magnified the reek of manure. The stock pens swarmed with flies and bawling cattle, and the arena choked Janice's throat with dust. Looking out on the crowds, however, her chest expanded with a sense of pride to be part of it all. Rodeo was a pure American tradition that she hoped would never die out. Although the sport was struggling elsewhere, the stands in Cheyenne were packed to capacity and anticipation permeated the air with the announcer's booming proclamation that the grand entry was about to begin.

A moment later, the audience rose to their feet with wolf whistles and thunderous applause as the drill team entered the arena at a mad gallop that generated enough wind to send their banners flapping and snapping. Janice climbed on top of one of the panels for a better view. The team split into pairs, performed an intricate pattern, and joined up again in the center in a tight militaristic formation. What followed was a highly synchronized drill performed to a medley of patriotic music. The crowd's excitement and the sense of nationalism never failed to make her own pulse race.

A few minutes into the drill, Grady appeared beside her at the bull pens. She thought it odd that she'd seen no sign of Dirk. He usually dropped by with coffee, but for the first time in almost a month of traveling together, he hadn't materialized.

"Who'd you draw today?" she asked absently.

"Death Wish," Grady replied.

"Not one of mine. Know anything about him?"

"Yeah." He grinned big and bad. "He's my kinda bull. Twenty outs and no rides...yet. I've been aching all year to ride that nasty motherfucker."

"You really do think you're something, don't you?"

He hooked his thumbs in his belt loops. "The stats don't lie, Sweet Cheeks. I'm hot shit right now."

Janice shook her head with a snort. "What about Dirk? Who'd he draw?"

"Hell if I know. Ain't seen him. He was already gone when I woke up."

"Strange he hasn't come around." She wondered where he was but then remembered who had walked into the bar last night. Had he and Rachel left together? The idea that they might have made her heart sick. She still couldn't help asking. "Any idea where he is?"

"After who showed up last night?" Grady echoed her own thoughts. "I think we both know the answer to that. In case you're wondering, they hit the dance floor together after you left."

She was doubly glad she hadn't hung around. The thought of Dirk and Rachel melded together on the dance floor made her chest ache.

At the end of the drill routine, the rodeo queens entered in a dazzling spectacle. Janice couldn't help scanning the long line of glittering cowgirls for Miss Rodeo Montana. Although there were other blonds and palominos in the parade of beauties representing every rodeo organization in the union, Rachel Carson was impossible to miss.

The queens formed a circle around the periphery of the arena with the reigning Miss Rodeo America taking center stage with the American flag. The crowd rose once more for the national anthem. It always drew a lump into her throat, but today Janice's emotions were reeling for another reason.

Grady had doffed his hat and was holding it over his heart in true-blue cowboy fashion. When the music ended, he shoved it back on his head and then leaned against the panels. He reached into his shirt pocket. "I got a pair of tickets for Chris LeDoux tonight."

"That's great. I figure he might have sold out with this crowd."

"Wanna go?" he asked.

"You're inviting *me*?"

"Yeah." Grady grinned. "You might even call it a date."

She regarded him in genuine surprise. "Why me?"

For weeks she'd kept Grady at bay, laughing off his sexual innuendos and halfhearted attempts to coerce her into bed. She wondered why he still had his sights set on her when he had his pick of so many others. Maybe it was just the challenge? The fact that she kept saying no?

He kicked at the dirt. "Maybe I got a hankering for a change."

She laughed. "A change from what? Your steady diet of buckle bunny?" He was one of the best bull riders on the circuit and women flocked to the chutes after every one of his rides.

He grinned. "Don't worry, sweetheart. There's still plenty of me to go around. So, you wanna go or not? He's only doing a few engagements. You might never get another chance."

She leaned back to consider him, resting one booted heel on the bottom rung of the corral panel. The offer was mighty tempting. Chris LeDoux was one of the most beloved names in rodeo and she'd been raised on his music. She still hesitated. "Is there a hitch?" she asked. This was Grady after all.

He raised his brows and turned his palms in an innocent I-don't-know-what-you-mean gesture.

"Are there strings attached?" she prodded.

"No strings." One corner of his mouth turned up. "But I'd be more'n happy to use some rope if you're inclined."

"Ropes and spurs? Is that all part of your repertoire?"

His face split into his full coyote grin. "Only by special request."

She considered him for a long beat. "What time does it start?"

"Eight."

"No can do, Grady. I'm working the chutes, and won't even be done here by then." There was no shortage of work to occupy her. With seventy-some riders and just as many bulls, she'd be glued to the chutes for the long haul. She told herself it would get easier as the days passed due to rider attrition from injuries and no turn out, but tonight she sure could use a hand.

"Even if the rides are all finished," she said, "I still have to take care of the bulls and then clean up. I won't go out reeking of the stock pens."

"Then I'll come by and help you settle things for the night. That'll give you time to pretty up for me."

"Pretty up, eh?" She laughed. "Maybe your expectations are a bit high. But even if you do help me out, I still won't be done in time for the start of the show."

"Probably not, but there's always a warm-up before the headliner anyway. Worst-case scenario, we'll catch the second half. Truth be told, I'm as interested in the company as I am the music."

That remark took her aback. Janice gave him a bemused look. "That's probably the nicest thing you've ever said to me."

He shrugged with a flash of his cocky grin. "I can talk real sweet when I want to." His gaze roamed slowly over her. "Just give me half a chance and I'll sweet-talk those jeans right off you. I've a powerful hankering to feel those mile-long legs wrapped around me."

Janice rolled her eyes with an exasperated huff and then pushed off the pen. "I got work to do."

He'd said no strings, but she wasn't naive enough to think he'd do anything without an ulterior motive. She turned to walk away but then looked out at the arena where the queens were pairing up and filing out. For weeks she'd waited, hoping for some sign from Dirk, but now Rachel was back in the picture. Grady was right. It was past time to give up and move on.

She was fed up with waiting. Tired of only being thought of as one of the stock hands. Sick of being alone. Maybe Grady wasn't perfect, *pretty far from it actually*, but at least *he* was interested. He'd been good-humored about all of her prior rejections, mainly because he didn't need her company, but now maybe she needed his.

On a sudden impulse she spun back to him. "All right, Grady. I'll go with you."

His smile widened. "I'll come back around when my ride's done."

Janice watched him swagger off with mixed feelings. He wasn't her dream come true, but she really wanted to have some fun for a change. It's why she'd gone to the Outlaw the night before, to have a drink or two, maybe dance a little, and just unwind, but she hadn't even finished one drink. The last time before that had been the after-party in Casper—an even bigger disaster.

Thinking back to the party, she recalled how embarrassed she'd been at not have anything decent to wear.

Last night the rodeo queens had looked down their noses at her just like they'd done at the Plaza Hotel in Casper. She might not be in their league, but she wasn't about to set herself up for that kind of humiliation again. Although she despised shopping with a fiery passion, she wondered what it would feel like to look like a girl for a change.

She consulted the rodeo schedule. And then her watch. There were at least fifty bareback rides before the first section of bulls. If she left now, maybe she could find something to wear in one of the boutiques. Without giving herself a chance to rethink and back down, Janice checked the water buckets in her bull pens, grabbed her purse from her trailer, and headed over to the Frontier Village.

~~~

Janice was in the third shop, a high-end boutique, and growing more frustrated by the second. She stepped out of the dressing room to the three-way mirror in a brown broomstick skirt and blousy floral top. She turned one way and then the other, chewing her lip in indecision. She should have known the clothes would be expensive. She didn't mind paying if she could make some kind of a fashion statement, but couldn't help thinking she looked more like her mama on a church social day. She turned back to the dressing room ready to give up and just buy a new pair of Wranglers when a feminine voice stopped her.

"You're Janice, right?"

She spun around to find herself face-to-face with Rachel Carson.

"I thought that was you," Rachel continued. "Weren't you at the party in Casper?"

Janice was almost too stunned to respond. "I was there," she replied. "But not for long. I left once I knew the mischief Grady was up to."

"Grady Garrison?" Rachel's expression darkened. "Mischief?" she huffed. "That's putting it mild, don't you think? His raunchy karaoke routine ruined the party and then he started a brawl. He's lucky we didn't call the cops. You aren't seeing him, are you?"

"No. Not exactly," Janice replied. "But he did ask me to the concert tonight. It's why I'm here. I was just lookin' for something—"

"Please tell me you're not buying *that*," Rachel said. Janice flushed.

"I'm so sorry!" Rachel's hand came over her mouth with an embarrassed laugh. "That didn't come out right at all! I just mean the colors totally wash you out. You have such pretty hair and eyes. You should wear jewel tones. Blues and greens. It was part of my queen training you know, learning to make the most of color. Come here. Let me show you." She grabbed Janice firmly by the elbow and steered her to another rack. "These colors would be incredible on you." She pulled a sexy tie-dyed sundress off the rack and held it up. Her brows furrowed in a long appraising look. "Maybe this one would be better yet." She snatched a long colorful T-shirt off another rack. "You need to showcase those long legs."

Janice wondered what the shirt had to do with her legs. "Would I just wear it with my jeans?"

"No silly!" Rachel giggled. "With your boots! It's a dress."

"A dress?" Janice protested. "It would barely cover my ass."

"And I promise the cowboys wouldn't mind a lick! But if that bothers you, just wear some cotton leggings under it. Trust me. I know these things. I promise you won't recognize yourself when I'm done."

Janice grimaced. "That's what I'm afraid of."

Rachel ignored the remark and shoved several more garments into her arms before steering Janice back into the dressing booth. "Just give these a try, will you?" She glanced down at Janice's well-worn brown ropers. "Got some dress boots?"

"No. Just another pair of ropers."

"Nothing with a bit of heel or a splash of color?"

Janice shook her head. "Nope. Solid tan."

"You know they've got some really cool dress boots here. Let me go take a look for you while you're putting those on. What size do you wear?"

"Eight and a half. But I really can't af—"

Rachel held up a hand. "Just humor me, OK? This makeover thing is kind of a hobby of mine."

Janice fumed at the idea that she'd unwittingly become the rodeo queen's charity case but entered the dressing room anyway. She barely had the brown skirt pulled off before more clothes flew over the dressing room door—a gypsy-style peasant dress, a sexy slim-fitting halter dress, and a denim miniskirt with buckskin fringe with a matching denim bustier top.

An hour later, Janice had to reassess her entire esti-mation of Rachel Carson. She really wasn't the spoiled little bitch-girl Janice had always believed her to be. Rachel seemed genuine about her desire to help. They had never run in the same circles and had never even had a true conversation before today, but Janice knew the rodeo queen had plenty of other things she could have been doing besides helping a fashion-backward stock hand pick out a dress.

Now that Janice had seen another side of her rival, she grudgingly confessed that Rachel's appeal ran deeper than her flawless skin. She couldn't help liking her and understood why Dirk was so taken with her...*by* her. Although they'd split, there was no doubt in Janice's mind that he truly was *taken*—whether *he* realized it yet or not.

"You're working the rough stock, right?" Rachel asked.

"Yeah. I brought a few bulls." Janice wondered where this was going.

"Then you'll be seeing Dirk, right?"

"I'm sure I'll be seeing him eventually."

Rachel chewed her lip. "Do you think maybe you could give him a message for me?"

Janice almost laughed aloud at the irony of becoming Rachel's emissary.

"Could you tell him I'd like us to talk? We really didn't get much chance last night."

Janice bit her tongue. They were too busy "making up" to talk?

"I'm staying at the Cheyenne Marriott." Rachel pulled a card out of her purse and scrawled her room number on the back, then handed it to Janice. "I'd appreciate it if you'd give this to him. We have a lot to work out, but I'm sure you know how it is with these bullheaded cowboys." She winked.

"Yeah. I've been around a few in my time," Janice replied woodenly.

She'd been right about Dirk and Rachel getting back together. It was past time for a reality check. Cowboys like Dirk belonged to rodeo queens like Rachel. While stock hands like Janice... Although Grady's foul mouth and rough ways certainly didn't qualify him as Prince Charming, Janice's dirty jeans and callused fingers hardly gave her the makings of a fairy princess either. Grady's goal was to make it to the top in the bull-riding world and he probably had the talent to get there. Janice's own ambition—to join the big league of bull contractors and take her bulls to the finals—was compatible with that. It might not be a match made in heaven, but they were both focused, hardworking, and goal driven. Was she settling? Maybe, but she was pragmatic enough to accept reality.

Janice stuffed Rachel's card into her back pocket and left the boutique shortly after that. She carried two shopping bags, her heart hammering with a mix of excitement and guilt. Today's shopping spree had set her back.

Way back.

She'd never gone hog wild like that before. The Old Gringo boots alone were almost a month's pay. She'd have to live on saltine crackers to make up for it. She almost spun back into the store to return everything, but then took a calming breath. She'd saved a bundle by camping out in the stock trailer instead of staying at a motel. Would one selfish splurge in her whole life really hurt anything?

When she got back to her trailer she opened the bags and boxes with trembling hands. She fondled the supple leather boots that were almost identical to the ones she'd drooled over in Cody. The denim miniskirt would certainly show them off—along with her legs. She stared at the skirt and boots with a sudden feeling of discomfort, as if she was trying to impersonate someone else. Then she recalled the look on Dirk's face when Rachel had walked into the bar the night before.

Just once in her life, she'd like to have that jaw-dropping effect on a guy. She supposed tonight was her chance. She imagined the look of shock that would come over Grady when he opened the door. Maybe it was worth what she'd spent after all. His expression alone would be priceless—but part of Janice still couldn't help wishing it was on another cowboy's face.

Dirk took over two hours getting back to the rodeo grounds. He'd jawed so long with Reid and Garcia that he hadn't got back into town until they'd blocked off the streets. He'd forgotten all about the parade and had no choice but to sit and wait it out. Once he finally got back to the arena, the first events were in full swing. He'd hoped to catch Janice alone but probably wouldn't get a chance to talk with her until tonight—he hoped over a quiet dinner.

He still didn't know quite what he was gonna say. What did he really want from her? He wasn't sure of that either. There was a lot to figure out between them and opening that door suddenly seemed so hard. He'd kept his distance for so long that he wasn't even certain what kind of reception he'd get. For the first time he could recall, Dirk felt unsure of himself.

So he'd stalled.

He'd first hung out with the bronc riders, watching every ride—mostly young cowboys eating dirt. Then he hung around the timed event end of the arena for the barrel racing. Once the last rider finished and the final scores were announced, he finally headed over to the bull pens. Grady was already suited up in his chaps and safety vest, occupied with his preparations. He must be one of the first draws. Dirk was one of the last. He'd hit it lucky.

He had his chance. "Hey, Red." He tipped his hat.

"Hey yourself," Janice answered mechanically and continued her routine, throwing the rope over the bull's back and leaning down to hook it under his belly. "Haven't seen you today." She didn't look up at him even though he knew she could have flanked the bull blindfolded.

"I'm sorry I wasn't around to help you this morning. I came by early, but you'd already fed, so I went for some breakfast. I ran into an old rodeo buddy at the diner and then got stuck by all the parade roadblocks."

"You don't answer to me," Janice said, sounding irritated.

"No, but I owed you the courtesy of an explanation," Dirk replied. "Something wrong, Red?"

"No. Why would you say that?"

"I dunno." He shrugged. "You just seem out of sorts..."

"I'm just busy, Dirk. There's a lotta bulls to flank and a lotta riders to spot."

"Yeah, I can see that. I'll be glad to help until my ride. Do you think we can talk later? Can I maybe buy you dinner when you're done tonight?"

Janice stood, setting her hook against the chute, and then settling her hands on her hips.

"What's all this about, Dirk? You avoid me for weeks and then the minute Grady asks me out, you all of a sudden want to *talk*?"

"Grady asked you out? You didn't accept, did you?"

"Yeah. As a matter of fact I did. He bought tickets for Chris LeDoux."

Grady was watching them from the platform several chutes down. Even from this distance he could detect his buddy's scowl. He leaned in closer and dropped his voice real low. "Do you really think that's a good idea, Red?"

"What business is it of yours?" He could almost see her bristle. "You've got a lot of nerve, cowboy — especially after last night. Which reminds me...I was s'posed to give you something." She pulled a card out of her back pocket and shoved it toward him.

"What's this?" he asked.

"Rachel's hotel and room number. She's expecting you." Janice picked up her rope hook and moved on to the next bull.

He followed after her. "Please, Red."

Janice spun around. "If you wanted to talk to me so bad, you've had plenty of chances before now. Even last night — but I s'pose Rachel walking in must have been quite the distraction."

"This is exactly *why* we need to talk. There's some things I need to explain —"

"The look on your face last night was self-explanatory. There's nothing more that needs saying. Grady might be a horndog, but at least he doesn't play these head games."

He winced, feeling as if she'd slapped him. She had no idea who the real Grady was, or what he was really after, but if he tried to warn her off again it would just look like petty jealousy. *Shit!* Now what the hell could he do? He couldn't have dinked things up any better if he'd tried.

"Just give me a minute," he pleaded.

"I'm sorry, Dirk. I don't have time for this right now."

He had to talk to her, and swore he would, but she was in no frame of mind to listen. "Have it your way." He spun away, grinding his teeth.

Feeling all too raw and vulnerable, Janice watched Dirk stalk off. Did he think she was just going to wait around on him forever? He'd had weeks to talk to her but now, the very minute she'd decided to move on, he was all of a sudden interested? No way in hell was she going to let him manipulate her like that. In all truth, Grady couldn't hurt her if he tried, but if she gave Dirk half a chance, he'd surely break her heart.

Chapter 8

DIRK WALKED OFF, SHAKING HIS HEAD AS HE MOVED down to Grady's chute. He was coming up on Death Wish, one of the rankest and most dangerous bulls on the circuit with twenty-some outs and no rides. Grady was geared up and looking like the cat that ate the canary when Dirk stepped up to the chute.

"So, you used Chris LeDoux to get to her?" Dirk growled.

"Told you weeks ago I was staking my claim. Just had to figure out the right approach."

Grady climbed over the rail, placing his booted foot on the bull's back. Death Wish gave a loud snort, jamming himself against the panel, an act that would have crushed Grady's leg had he already been in position. He waited for the bull to settle down again before easing himself onto its back. Dirk pulled the bull rope taut and handed the tail to Grady.

"You're just using her, Grady, and I don't like it."

Their eyes met. "I don't give a shit what you like." Grady jerked his hand up and down, warming the rosin and then making his wrap. "She's mine now, Pretty Boy…" He looked up with a confident smirk. "Just like this bull right here." Seconds later, Grady pulled his hat down low, shifted his hips forward over the rope, and gave his nod to the chute man.

The gate flew open with Death Wish hurling himself

airborne and into a spin, coming down bucking and kicking wildly, while Grady sat the bull tight as a tick. The seconds sped by while Dirk watched his buddy spurring the bull, his body still balanced and moving in perfect synchrony with the animal's frenetic fits and sudden starts. Whatever his character flaws, there was no denying that Grady was a helluva bull rider.

At the sound of the buzzer, he looked up, released his rope, and threw his right leg over to dismount, landing on all fours and scrambling away from the bull. He'd made the whistle on the toughest bull for a record ninety-point ride. With that performance, he'd clearly go into the short round and qualify for the finals in Las Vegas.

It was during Grady's ride that Janice's phone jolted her. Pulling it out of her pocket, she found she'd missed three calls from home. She didn't understand how, until she recalled switching the setting to vibrate the night before at the Outlaw Saloon. She'd done it figuring she'd never hear the ring over the band and had forgotten to switch it back when she left. Her mind had been far too preoccupied.

With a strong sense of foreboding, she walked as far as she could away from the mayhem and then hit redial. A few rings later her mother picked up. "Hey, Mama, it's me. I saw you called. Is everything OK?"

A long pause followed. "Are you sitting down, baby girl?"

"No." Her heart raced. "Do I need to be?"

"It might be best," her mother replied.

Hugging the phone between her shoulder and ear,

Janice turned over a nearby feed bucket and sat down on it. "I am now. Tell me, Mama, what is it?"

Her mother audibly inhaled. "We heard back from the doc yesterday. Your daddy has cancer in his pancreas."

"What?" Janice gasped. "Oh my God! Are they sure?"

"Yes. They're sure. They did the CAT scan and all those other tests. They followed with a biopsy day before yesterday."

This could not be happening. He couldn't have cancer.

"Why didn't you call and tell me? I would have come home! I would have been there with you."

"There's nothing you could have done, baby, and I didn't want to worry you until we knew for sure."

"Where's Daddy now?"

"They admitted him to the VA up in Helena."

"I'll come now. Tonight."

"You can't, Janice. I know you want to, but I don't see that it's a choice at least until after the rodeo's done. We need the money, especially with all the medical bills."

"But I can't just stay here!"

"We need you to, baby girl. We need the contracts. You have to be strong for your daddy right now. He's countin' on you..." her mother added in a choking voice. "So am I."

"All right, Mama." Janice swallowed down the lump in her throat. "I'll stay until we're done, and then I'll come straight home. How's he doing? Can I talk to him?"

"He's on a lot of pain medication. Why don't you wait? I'm driving up to Helena tomorrow. I'll be staying a night or two with my cousin Claire who lives up there.

I'll call you from the hospital as soon as I get there. OK, sweetheart?"

"Yeah. OK, Mama," Janice replied woodenly.

"I love you, baby."

"Love you too, Mama."

"I'll call again tomorrow. I promise. Be strong."

"I will, Mama. I won't let you down."

"I know you won't."

Janice disconnected the call with a dull feeling of unreality. He *couldn't* be dying. He was only fifty-four. Her next thoughts were of her mother. What would they do? How would she and her mama go on without him? She just sat there stunned and staring down at the phone in her limp hand for what felt like hours. She looked up only when a scuffed-up pair of boots broke into her line of vision. Her gaze tracked upward over Grady's lean body to settle on his face.

His gaze met hers and then drifted to the phone, his habitual grin fading. "Bad news?"

"Yeah. You might say that." Janice bit down hard into her lip, drawing blood in her struggle against the sob that threatened to break out. "M-my ol' man... it's cancer," she whispered. "Pancreatic. He's gonna die, Grady."

She didn't know how it happened, but suddenly her face was buried in Grady's shirt. His arms came around her, holding her tight, stroking her back, and murmuring soothing words as she let loose the wave of fear and anguish she'd tried so hard to hold back.

"Don't worry 'bout a thing." His voice rumbled in her ear. "Whatever you need. I'm here for you, baby doll."

"Y-you mean that?" She hiccuped.

"Said it, didn't I? You goin' home now?"

"I can't. I have to stay in Cheyenne until the rodeo's done—or at least until I know if my bulls are needed for the short round. After that, I'm headed straight home."

"I'll go with you."

"What about the rest of the circuit?"

"Doesn't matter. I just scored ninety points, which means I'm only one ride away from qualifying for the finals. Even better, the payoff here will take me all the way to Vegas. As long as I finish in the money here, I don't have to ride again if I don't want to, which means I can take you home."

"Thank you, Grady." She gazed up at him through bleary eyes. "I thought I knew you, but sometimes you really surprise me, you know that?"

He tipped her chin and his mouth brushed softly over hers. "Yeah, Sweet Cheeks. I'm just chock-full of surprises."

Dirk's bull was being loaded four chutes down. The rider beside him was Seth Lawson, the same young cowboy who'd been with Grady at the Outlaw last night—the one who'd been Grady's shadow since they'd arrived in Cheyenne.

"Who'd you draw?" Dirk asked, but then instantly recognized the animal as one of Janice's bulls.

"Magnum Force," Seth replied. "Heard he spins like a son of a gun."

"Yeah, you heard right," Dirk replied.

"You rode him before?" Seth asked.

"Yeah," Dirk replied. "You might say that. I backed

him once and even made the whistle, but then got
hung up on my rope. Walked out of the arena with a
concussion, bruised ribs, sprained wrist, and dislo-
cated shoulder."

"Shit!" Seth replied with a nervous grin. "I'm up next.
Grady was s'posed to spot me, but he's disappeared."

So had Janice. She never missed a ride on her bulls,
but she was nowhere around.

Climbing the panel, Dirk scanned the bull pens and
the surrounding area. His gaze lit on a couple locked
in an embrace. It was Janice plastered to Grady. He
clenched his fists, his blood pounding a throbbing pulse
in his ears as Grady kissed her. He'd tried to play interference, but the snake had still gotten to her.

*She's mine now, Pretty Boy... Just like this bull
right here.*

How could he not have seen it coming? Janice's earlier brush-off made perfect sense now. The idea of the
two of them together, especially after Grady's behavior
only the night before, made him want to pound him into
the ground. *Fuck!* How had he let it happen?

Seth's voice broke into his thoughts. "That right
there's the biggest reason for ridin' bulls—the all-you-
can-eat pussy buffet." A big smirk stretched his mouth
as he jerked his head toward Grady and Janice. "Since
Grady's...er...occupied, will you spot me?"

"Sure," Dirk replied absently. Seth popped in his
mouth guard but shook away the helmet offer before
climbing over the rail. "You not gonna wear the helmet?
This SOB's damned unpredictable," Dirk warned.

"Grady doesn't wear one," Seth said, tugging his
Stetson lower on his forehead.

"He's been doing this a lot longer than you."

"I plan to keep my head out of the way."

Dirk shrugged. "It's your head."

He spotted Seth, bracing his arms on either side of the rider's body while Seth's buddy tightened the bull rope. Seth settled down onto the bull, glancing up at Dirk with a nervous grin before releasing the panel and giving his nod.

Seth's ride didn't last long. Within three seconds, he pitched face-first onto the bull's horns. He went instantly limp. The bull spun, hurling Seth from his back to land headfirst in the dirt—but his left spur was caught in the flank rope, trapping Seth beneath the bull for a deadly pummeling as the animal continued to buck, kick, and spin. The next seconds unfurled like a repeat of Dirk's own nightmare.

Without thought, he leaped over the fence to join the bull fighters, but the bull had already dragged Seth's unconscious body half the width of the arena before anyone could get in close enough to cut Seth loose. The announcer and barrel man distracted the crowd with jokes and antics while half a dozen men fought to free the unconscious rider. Once they'd cut the cowboy loose, the bull fighters coaxed the enraged animal back through the cattle chute and into the pen while the medical team sprang into action, surrounding Seth's inert, bloodied, and barely breathing body.

Dirk had seen plenty of bad wrecks before, but this one made his blood run cold. He stood helplessly looking on as the medical team swiftly transferred Seth onto a stretcher to carry him out to the waiting ambulance. As they passed, Seth's eyes flickered open to stare directly into Dirk's. Their gazes met for no more than a second but Dirk read the terror and helplessness before Seth's expression went utterly blank. A long and shuddering breath followed. Then he went perfectly still. The efforts at revival were frantic and fruitless. Seth was gone. He'd slipped away before their very eyes.

Everyone would later say the kid died doing what he loved, but he shouldn't have died at all. Seth Lawson should never have been on that bull. Dirk watched utterly numb as they carried him out. The smells, the sounds, and the look in Seth's eyes were forever etched in his brain. A long moment of silence followed Seth's exit, but then the announcer called the next rider. As always, the show must go on.

Minutes later, Dirk lowered himself onto his own bull, mechanically going through the motions, wrapping his fist in his rope and sidling his hips right up to his hand just as he had a hundred times before. Normally his heart would be pounding in anticipation and his blood fired to beat Grady, but everything had changed. He felt completely numb. The thrill was gone.

Fearing his head wasn't in the game—a damned dangerous thing while forking an eighteen-hundred-pound bull—it took all his concentration to tune out the distractions and blank his mind to all but the bull.

When the gate swung open, the animal came to life beneath him, hurling himself into the air and transforming into a furiously bucking cyclone. He clung like a burr to the wildly pitching animal for the longest eight seconds of his life. When the buzzer finally sounded, he released his hand and threw his leg over for a clean dismount, landing on both feet. His boots had barely hit the dirt before the bull spun around to face him, dropping his shoulders as if to charge, shaking his head and spewing snot. While Dirk's instincts told him to run for the panels, he just stood there, boots rooted in the dirt.

The bullfighters moved in shouting and waving their hats, but the silent showdown continued with bull and rider just staring one another down. Taken with a sudden crazy impulse, Dirk tipped his hat in salute. As if on cue, the animal gave a loud snort and turned away, trotting quietly back into the chutes. Dirk watched until the gate closed, then looked up to find Janice staring down at him, mouth agape. Their eyes met. He tipped his hat again and walked out of the arena.

Dirk found himself in the warm-up area behind the pens without even remembering how he got there. Hell, he hardly remembered the ride. It was as if he suddenly viewed himself through someone else's eyes. While the other riders laughed and jawed, he wordlessly stripped off his vest and chaps, throwing them into his rigging bag.

"What the fuck was that exit all about?" Grady demanded.

"I'm done," Dirk said.

"Whadaya mean done?"

Dirk released one spur from his boot, and then the other. "Done as in retired."

"Retired? Old men and pussies retire. You sayin' one kid gets killed by a bull and you go all chickenshit? You know the risks. He did too. Hell, the danger is more than half the reason we do it."

"It's why *you* do it," Dirk said. "I'm done now. I haven't lost my nerve, I've just gained some sense. You might call it an epiphany."

"An epiphany? What the fuck's an epiphany?"

"It's a 'shit, I finally get it' moment."

"Yeah and what do you get?"

"That it ain't rodeo. There's more I want to do with my life."

"And what's that?"

"Dunno yet. I'll figure the rest out on the way."

"On the way where? You goin' some place, Pretty Boy?"

"Yeah." Dirk stood. "I am. I got a hankering to see the ocean. I'm leaving tonight."

"Did you hit your head again? You're talking like you scrambled your fucking brain."

"Nope. I just need a change of scenery... Say good-bye to her for me."

Grady smirked. "So it's Janice? That's what this is really about? You're bowing out?"

Dirk threw the last of his gear in his bag. "Looks to me like she's already made her choice. Might not be the best one, but what's done is done. Just know that if you hurt her, I'll tear you a new asshole."

"Hurt her? Shit!" he scoffed. "I'll treat her like a fucking queen."

"For how long?" Dirk demanded.

"Till death do us part... I intend to marry her."

"Oh, yeah?" Dirk rose and slung his bag over his shoulder. "Then I just hope she has the good sense to refuse. You ain't husband material, Grady." He took a few steps and turned around. "I mean it, Grady. Treat her right."

"Or what?" Grady challenged.

"Or I swear to God, you'll answer to me."

———✦———

Janice showered quickly and then threw on her Dixie Chicks T-shirt before toweling her hair dry. She'd hung up the towel and was just about to rake a comb through her hair when a rap sounded on the door. Was it Dirk? His actions in the arena tonight had unsettled her. It was as if he'd dared the bull to gore him. The thought of it had made her knees buckle. All of her anger and resentment were washed away by a flood of fear. Try as she might to deny it, she still cared for Dirk.

"Janice? You ready?" Grady called through the door. "We gotta hustle to catch the second half."

She had no plans of going out after the news she'd received from home, but she hadn't told Grady. She answered the door, only realizing at Grady's stunned expression that she wore only the T-shirt. She hadn't even put underwear on.

"Wasn't what I expected." He grinned. "But I can sure dig the look."

"I'm sorry, Grady, but I'm not going anywhere tonight."

"Hey, I'm easy to please." He didn't wait for an invitation before stepping into the trailer. "I'm happy to stay in if that's your preference. I'm sure we can find plenty to entertain ourselves." His gray eyes raked over her meaningfully.

Janice felt a surge of irritation. "No. You don't under-stand. Too much has happened tonight. The phone call from home. Seth Lawson killed by one of my bulls. I can't even process it all—"

"You saying you wanna be alone?"

Did she? She had to think about that. No, she didn't want to be alone. "I guess not," she replied softly. "But I'm not good company right now."

Grady's hands came down on her shoulders. Janice fought the urge to shrug them off. He seemed too possessive all of a sudden. "Told you I'm here for you, Sweet Cheeks, and it looks like it's gonna be just the two of us from here on out."

"What do you mean?" she said. "What about Dirk?"

"He's gone."

"Gone? I don't understand."

"He packed up his shit and left as soon as his ride was done." He patted his shirt pocket. "Didn't even wait for his paycheck. Just got in his truck and split."

"Did he go home to the ranch?"

"Don't think so. He mumbled something about the ocean."

"The ocean?" Janice was truly baffled. "What ocean? There isn't any ocean in this part of the country."

"Hell if I know what he meant. Does it really matter?" Grady asked. "He's split and I'm here." He put his arms around her, drawing her closer. She fought the impulse to push away, but it felt so good just to be held by somebody—even if his weren't the arms she craved.

"No," Janice whispered woodenly. "I don't suppose it matters…not anymore."

"It's just you and me now, and I swear I'll take real good care of you."

"Take care of me? How?"

"I'm going to the finals in Vegas, Sweet Cheeks, and you're coming with me."

Janice stared at him speechless. "I don't understand. What would you need me for?"

"The wedding, baby doll," he replied with his cockiest grin. "After I win the World Championship, you're gonna marry me."

His words had stunned her into silence, and then his mouth had followed.

Passive and accepting, she'd just let it all happen.

Chapter 9

Las Vegas, Nevada

"WHEN ARE THEY GOING TO START, MAMA?" CODY climbed to his feet and began bouncing up and down on his seat.

"Soon, Cody. Real soon. Please sit down. The people behind you can't see."

"I can't see either. Where's my daddy?"

"He's not up yet, sweetheart. He'll be riding later."

"Why doesn't he get to go first?"

"Because all the cowboys have to draw a number. It's how they make it fair. They draw the bulls too, so we never know which cowboy is gonna ride which bull."

"Daddy said he'll win if he gets to ride that muver-fucker Gangbanger."

Janice cringed as three heads turned to gape. "Cody!"

His eyes widened, completely unaware of his transgression. "What'd I do, Mama?"

"Nothing, baby." She ruffled his red hair. "I'll take it up later with your daddy." It wasn't Cody's fault. He was just parroting Grady. He'd lusted after that bull for four years and tonight he'd finally get his wish.

Janice stared wistfully out across the dirt-filled arena to the bull pens, the place she'd once thought of as her second home, the world she'd left behind. Instead of standing in her old place behind the chutes, she now sat front and center at the Rank & Ready World Bull Riding Championships, surrounded by the wives and family members of the world's top-ranked cowboys—most of whom chattered in Portuguese. The Brazilians had dominated the sport for years. She hoped tonight that Grady would change all that.

She still loved bull riding and missed the sounds, the excitement, the feeling of connectedness with the riders. Hell, she even missed the smells. It still felt strange to be an outsider looking in—not that she could have done it anymore anyhow.

Her pregnancy had come as a shock. She and Grady hadn't even talked about kids and then suddenly they had one on the way. She'd had a real hard time of it too, almost miscarried twice. In the end, she'd had to leave the bull-riding tour and go back home to Montana. The last six weeks she'd spent almost entirely in bed.

Between her difficult pregnancy and her father's fight with cancer, they'd had to sell off almost everything—the horses, the cows, and even most of the ranch. Grady was constantly on the road, Janice couldn't help, and Mama couldn't run it by herself. They'd held on to Mag the longest, but even he had eventually gone to the highest bidder. Grady had counted on the ranch as his retirement legacy, but it was all gone and he resented the hell out of her for it. Grady was traveling almost all the time, which made it easier, but even when he was home, he paid little attention to either of them.

It wasn't the life she'd dreamed of, but she still had hopes to make it work. At least now Grady was winning more often than not. If he took the championship tonight, they'd have money enough to buy a place of their own, instead of living like gypsies in cheap motels.

"Janice? Is that you?" A light touch on her shoulder and an achingly familiar baritone voice broke into her thoughts. She spun around, feeling as if the breath had been crushed out of her chest at the sight of his face. For four years she'd tried to put Dirk Knowlton out of her mind, but try as she might, she could never forget him. His eyes were still the same startling icy blue, but they were also somehow different. Older. And shadowed. More sober. He'd matured.

"Dirk? Oh my God! I can't believe it's you! Wh-what are you doing here?"

"Just got back from the sand pits and I'm on leave. I was watching ESPN last week and saw Grady's qualifying ride so I decided to come out."

"But I thought you and Grady..."

"What's done is done." He shrugged. "It's been four years. Life's too short. Grudges and regrets both just get heavier the longer you carry them. So it's past time to get over it, right?"

He spoke rhetorically, but his gaze seemed too probing, as if it really was a question he expected her to answer. *Get over it or him?* She'd done neither. But he was right. What was done couldn't be undone.

"Mama! Who's that?"

Dirk's gaze darted to Cody and then back to Janice. "You have a kid?"

"Yes, Dirk. This is Cody." She turned to her son. "Cody, this is Mr. Dirk. He used to rodeo with your daddy."

"You don't do it anymore?" Cody asked.

"Nope." Dirk shook his head. "I quit four years ago. I'm a marine now."

Cody's face wrinkled. "What's a mawine?"

"It's kind of like a soldier and a sailor combined," Janice explained.

"Oh."

The announcer's voice interrupted the exchange, introducing the barrel man. Cody's attention riveted back to the arena. "Look, Mama! It's a clown."

Dirk tipped his hat. "I'll catch up with you afterwards? Maybe we can all have dinner?"

"Yes, Dirk," Janice replied. "I…we'd like that. Grady'll be really surprised."

—·∾∾·—

Dirk went to find his seat, shaking his head in disbelief. *She had a kid*.

He'd known Janice and Grady had married right after he joined up. His mother's letters had kept him informed about all the local gossip, but she'd never mentioned they'd had a son. The knowledge had lambasted him. He didn't know why. Maybe a piece of him hadn't wanted to let go of the past…let go of her. There was so much he'd wanted to say if he ever saw her again, but none of it mattered anymore. All that counted was that she was happy.

Dirk watched a dozen rides with a sense of total detachment until Grady's name came up. He'd drawn a bull named Gangbanger. The announcer called out the animal's stats—thirty outs no rides. Grady's kinda bull. He might be one of the top contenders tonight, but with this bull, there was no margin for error.

Dirk's muscles tensed involuntarily as he watched the action behind the chutes. He could almost feel the adrenaline rush that he'd thought long forgotten, or at least replaced with the state of total hyperawareness that preceded combat. He found himself on the edge of his seat by the time Grady gave the nod. A millisecond later, Gangbanger spun out of the gate like an F4 tornado. Grady was in near-perfect form the entire eight-second ride and his expression at the whistle said it all—it was the smug-as-hell smile of the new world champion.

After the last ride, Dirk made his way through the crowd to the bull pens. He found Grady already in full celebration mode. But rather than rejoicing in his victory with his wife and son, he was swigging from a foaming bottle of champagne while the buckle bunnies swarmed. Dirk searched the crowd for Janice and found her standing quietly in the background, holding Cody's hand, looking on with her lips pressed into a fake smile.

His gut churned at the realization that Grady never even looked in Janice's direction. He'd thought she was content until that moment, or maybe that's what his conscience had wanted to believe, but her eyes told a completely different story. He pressed his way through the revelers to her side.

"Mr. Dirk!" Cody squealed. "Did you see it? My daddy won! He's the champion of the whole wide world!"

"I did see it, Cody. It was a great ride."

"I'm gonna be a world champion too when I gwow up."

"I'm sure you will be." He ruffled the little boy's curls and stood back with Janice while Cody entertained himself by climbing the panel of an empty pen. He watched her watching the boy, with love and more than a little sadness reflected in her eyes. He'd give anything in that moment to take her in his arms and make it all better. But he didn't have that right. He'd given it to Grady. Now he'd never felt so helpless in his life. "You OK, Red?" he asked, trying to pose the question with just the right amount of concern and ease to open the door. He'd help her, if she'd let him. But that was a ridiculous thought. He couldn't help her, even if she would let him. And she wouldn't. Of that he was sure.

"Yes. It's just overwhelming. We hoped of course, but with bulls, you never know." She nodded to Grady and the autograph seekers. "Looks like he's going to be a while yet. I need to get Cody home to bed. I'm afraid we'll have to take a rain check on that dinner, but there's a big after-party at the PBR Rock Bar. You should go with him, Dirk."

"You aren't going?" he asked in surprise.

"No. I can't. Besides, I'm not much for parties, and this one is certain to get wilder than I like. I'm sure Grady's going to be out all night celebrating." She offered a weak smile. "You know how he is."

"Yeah. I know all right."

"Maybe you can look after him for me? I know he's gonna get wasted. I can't do anything about that, but I just want him to get home in one piece."

"Yeah, I can watch over him—as much as he'll let me, anyway."

"Thanks, Dirk." She paused. "Are you in town long? Will I—I mean—will we see you again?"

"Dunno. Don't really have any plans."

"Are you going home at all?"

"Nope. Not this time. It'd be too damned awkward."

"Awkward? What do you mean? Oh." Her mouth gaped. "I'm sorry…I'd heard about the wedding. I'm so stupid." She shut her eyes with an embarrassed head shake.

"It's nothing, Red. I wish Wade and Rachel well, but if I suddenly showed up…" He shrugged. "You know how it would be. It's a small town. They don't need any more fodder for gossip than they already have."

"So you're honestly OK with it? With Wade and Rachel?"

"They're consenting adults. Besides, her father never thought I was good enough anyway. He once said he'd rather see her with Wade. I just hope they're doing it for the right reasons."

"Yeah. The right reasons," she whispered. "Sometimes people make big mistakes. Huge life-altering mistakes. At the time they think they're doing the right thing, but they realize later that it was for all the wrong reasons."

He couldn't help himself. He had to hear it from her lips. "Are you unhappy, Red? Has he hurt you?"

"Does it really matter?" Janice gave a fatalistic shrug. "I made my bed. And Cody here is late for his."

"Has he hurt you?" he demanded, more insistent. "I want to know, Janice."

"He doesn't beat me, if that's what you're asking, but there are worse ways to hurt someone."

His mouth thinned. "Like how?"

She looked away. "I really don't want to discuss my marriage to Grady, especially not in front of Cody."

"I understand. Do you need a ride somewhere?"

She hesitated, her gazed locked with his for a long moment before breaking away. "No. I don't think that's a good idea. But thank you for the offer. I'll just take the truck back to the hotel if you can give Grady a lift later."

He nodded. "I'll see him back to you when it's all done."

Later that night he was glad he hadn't promised her it would be in one piece.

Chapter 10

"JANICE LEE COMBES! YOU AREN'T ACTUALLY GOING out dressed like *that*, are you?"

"It's Garrison, Mama. I don't know why you refuse to say it. It's only been my name for the past ten years."

"You know I never liked that boy. Now that he's gone, you should change it back."

"Don't be ridiculous," Janice hissed. "And please don't talk like that in front of Cody."

"Like what?" Cody asked.

"Nothing," Janice replied with a sigh. She was back home for good now, Grady was gone, and Cody was growing up just fine, in spite of her occasional clashes with his doting grandmother about his father.

"You didn't answer my question either," her mother persisted. "You aren't wearing *that* to work, are you?"

"She always dresses up in funny clothes for work, Grandma," Cody said.

"This is not your conversation, Cody. Now eat your peas."

Cody scowled at his plate. "I hate peas."

"But you like Gram's chocolate cake, right?"

"Yeah."

"No peas means no cake. I mean it." Janice directed the threatening look first to Cody and then to her mother. "You've got to stop spoiling him."

"It's my right as a grandma to spoil my only

grandbaby. You still didn't explain why you're dressed like that."

"Look, Mama, it's real simple. I'm working in a bar. Most of the patrons are men. Men like to look." Janice made a small adjustment to her cleavage but wasn't about to go change. She was already running late. Besides, a small show of flesh meant much bigger tips.

"Well, it ain't decent." Her mother huffed. "And I thought you were *looking* for ranch work."

"I was and I still am, but no one's hiring hands right now and we've got bills to pay. Look, Mama, I don't have time to talk about this right now. I'm gonna be late. Be a good boy for Grams, Cody, and I'll see you in the morning." She kissed the top of his head and grabbed her purse off the kitchen counter but then hesitated at the door, feeling a surge of guilt. Between the moving and her job search, she hadn't spent much time with her son. "Cody?"

"What, Mama?"

"I was thinking maybe we can do something special together this weekend? I know some great spots to go fishing. Would you like that?"

"Dunno." He shrugged. "Never been fishing. I got invited to a friend's house. Can I go?"

"Who's the friend?" she asked.

"His name's Caleb Croft. They have horses. I've never ridden a horse either."

Janice bit her lip, searching her memory. "I don't know any Crofts. Do you, Mama?"

"I do. They moved to town a few years back. Seem like nice enough folks. I think she's a teacher."

"Librarian," Cody corrected. "Caleb's mama works at the school."

"Oh?" Janice said. "Then I s'pose it'll be all right, but I'll still want to meet them first. Call and ask Caleb when I can bring you out there. I gotta run now, sweetie. Bye, Mama," Janice flung over her shoulder as she headed out the door.

Arriving at work twenty minutes later, Janice made a face in the mirror as she applied a shade of lipstick she never would have considered ten years ago. It seemed ironic, even laughable, how nothing in town had changed, while nothing about her would ever be the same.

In all truth, the last place Janice wanted to be was back in Twin Bridges, Montana, with her tail between her legs like some beaten-down dog. But that's exactly what she felt like—as desperate as a starving bitch with whelps to feed. Returning home was not what she'd planned, but as always, Janice did what Janice needed to do. Her family depended on it. They'd always depended on her and she'd never let them down. Not once.

The truth was the *only* person Janice had ever disappointed in her entire life was herself. Yes, she'd certainly let herself down—or better said—she'd let herself be beaten down. It should have made her happy to come back and make a new start, but she felt like a stranger in her hometown. She'd never been more terrified. Or more alone.

She reminded herself that all that mattered now was making a decent life for Cody, even if that meant aping a Hooters girl. Although they barely skated above the poverty line, at least they had a roof over their heads in a place where Cody could do all the things boys were meant to do—like ride horses and learn to hunt and fish. Hiking her breasts a little higher in her push-up bra, she left the ladies' room to clock in for her evening shift.

———◊———

It was a slow night, even for a Thursday, when Wade Knowlton walked into the bar. The sight of him took her aback. She'd heard he'd had some trouble with booze following what folks called "the Rachel tragedy." Janice had still been traveling the bull circuit when it had all happened, but she'd heard plenty of gossip about it. Their world was small—especially when the news concerned the Knowlton brothers. If only Rachel hadn't played them against each other, everything might have turned out differently. Given time and perspective, the whole situation was nothing short of heartbreaking.

Janice hoped Wade's appearance in the bar didn't mean he'd fallen back into old habits. God knew she was familiar enough with that vicious cycle. But contrary to her fears, Wade seemed perfectly at ease with the world, walking in with a grin and a pretty brunette that Janice didn't recognize.

He tipped his hat to the bartender, and then to several waitresses who lit up at the sight of him. Wade had that effect on lots of women. He was a damned good-looking man and a charmer to boot, but he'd never compared to Dirk in Janice's book.

Until now, she hadn't seen either of the Knowlton brothers. She wanted desperately to see Dirk again, but in the weeks since she'd been home, she hadn't yet worked up enough nerve to take the initiative. She was too uncertain of her reception. He'd been through so much and she feared her appearance would only resurrect bad memories. So she'd waited, banking her hopes that *he* would come to *her*, but so far those hopes hadn't paid off.

Janice's pulse sped up when Wade settled at a table in her section. Here was her chance at last, but she found her courage faltering. "Buck up, Janice. Who knows when you'll get another chance," she mumbled to herself.

Armed with a bright smile, she approached their table. "Hey, Wade. Been a long time."

He stared blankly for a few seconds, then recognition dawned. "Janice Combes? I'll be damned. I didn't know you were back in town."

His reaction didn't surprise her. She hardly recognized herself anymore—either inside or out. Janice Combes had left Montana as a tall and gangly girl but the brown eyes that gazed back at her in the mirror were darkly shadowed from years of sleepless nights. She felt so much older than her barely thirty years. She also felt suddenly self-conscious.

"I never thought I'd set foot back here either, but I had nowhere else to go with my kid and all." She always hated having to explain, but the subject inevitably came up along with all the awkward questions.

"I was sorry to hear about what happened to Grady." Wade shook his head with a sympathetic look. "What a gruesome way to go."

It *was* gruesome. The stuff of nightmares, but Janice didn't care to rehash all the sordid details. The papers and the *Cowboy Sports News* had already done that...

and then some. The worst part of it was when her son discovered videos of it on YouTube. Cody would probably carry the scars his entire life. It was part of the reason she hadn't come home sooner. She hadn't wanted him to have to deal with the questions or the looks of pity. So they'd stayed in Vegas.

Although the anonymity of the city had been her shield, it was no place to raise a kid—especially a boy without a father—so they'd eventually packed up and come home to Montana. Maybe three years wasn't long enough for the scandal to die altogether, but at least now it was all old news.

"He knew as well as anyone that it was bound to happen sooner or later. With the bulls, it's never a question of *if* you're gonna get hurt—it's just when and how bad. Least he didn't suffer much. He never regained consciousness." She shrugged, hoping Wade wouldn't ask any more about it, and that he'd interpret her terse response as stoicism rather than coldheartedness. After all this time, it was still hard to deal with, but at least she was free.

"I'm glad Dirk gave up rodeo, though the way it turned out for him, maybe joining the marines wasn't the best choice either," Wade said.

"I haven't seen him around. How's he doing?" Janice asked in what she hoped was an offhand manner.

Wade shrugged. "As well as can be expected, I guess, but he hardly leaves the ranch."

She wondered if he'd become some kind of recluse, but that seemed so out of character, she could hardly wrap her mind around it.

"You know about his injuries, don't you?"

"Yeah, I heard." When she'd first learned about it, her heart had bled for him.

"He's changed a lot from what he was before."

"I'd expect as much." Janice knew she should leave the couple alone now, but she was almost desperate for more news about Dirk. She bit the bullet and asked, "He seein' anyone?"

"Dirk?" Wade shook his head. "Not to my knowledge."

"Think he'd mind if I dropped by?"

"Don't know," Wade replied. "But I think he could use some old friends—as long as you aren't put off by his surly, badass behavior."

Janice almost laughed. "You're kidding, right? I'm not thin-skinned. Could never afford to be. You don't know what it's like to be a woman working the chutes with all those bulls and rough riders." She'd spent the better part of a decade in the rodeos and bull-riding circuits, even though it now seemed like another person's life. "For the record, I can give every bit as good as I get."

"Forgive me, Nikki," Wade addressed the brunette who had been eyeing Janice with open curiosity. "This is—"

"Janice," she supplied smoothly, extending her hand. "I grew up here and just recently moved back."

"Nikki Powell from Atlanta." The brunette briefly shook her hand.

"Welcome to Montana. First time?" Janice asked.

"Yes, and likely my last. Wade's helping me with some personal business. My father passed away."

"Oh," Janice replied, feeling awkward. "My condolences."

"We just came from the mortuary," Wade explained. "I thought she could use a drink."

Janice forced another smile. "Then you came to the right place. What'll you have?"

"The usual for me. The bartender knows." Wade looked to Nikki. "Sorry, I don't know your poison."

"I'll take a shot of Patrón."

"Salt and lime?" Janice asked.

"Of course," Nikki said. "What?" she answered Wade's querying look. "You thought I'd order some girlie umbrella drink?"

"Yeah, it was pretty much what I expected over straight tequila."

"This seemed like a tequila occasion," Nikki replied.

"You are full of surprises." Wade chuckled as Janice hustled away to fill their order.

"A shot of Patrón and the usual for Wade, whatever that is," Janice told Moe, the bartender.

She was surprised when he went in the back and returned with a bottle of nonalcoholic beer. "I keep a case for him," Moe said. "He's the only one around here who drinks this stuff."

Janice returned within minutes with a foamy mug for Wade and a shot glass sporting a paper umbrella that she set in front of Nikki with a wink for Wade.

"I suppose this is a joke?" Nikki said, plucking out the umbrella.

Wade laughed, a low, warm rumble that ceased the second Nikki licked the back of her hand to apply the salt. She took the shot, in a single choking swallow, made a face, and then bit into the lime.

At first Janice also chuckled, but then a wave of fierce

envy followed. They were hardly able to tear their eyes from each other. Was it so very long since she'd experienced that kind of attraction? It had been almost three years since she'd been with anyone. Yearning pierced her like a physical pain—not just for sex, but for intimacy.

She wondered if Wade would think to mention her to Dirk. Probably not. His mind was preoccupied with other things—pretty little brunette kinda things—and it looked like his interest was more than reciprocated. Judging by the way Wade later flung his money on the table and half carried her out the door, Nikki had certainly lit his fuse. By the looks of things, Wade was finally moving on. She was glad of it. At least one of them was getting their life back together. It gave her hope that maybe after three years of licking her wounds, she might be able to do the same.

Hours later when her shift ended, Janice was still thinking about Dirk. He continued to linger in her mind during the thirty minute drive home. Although she'd tried to move on, her heart had never belonged to anyone but Dirk Knowlton. She'd come back to Montana and so had he, but they were both damaged and broken. It was heartrending how many mistakes they'd both made, but the past couldn't be changed. The present was what counted. The here and now.

Dirk, by all accounts, was a shattered man. The question she intended to answer was whether his pieces could ever be put back together again.

Chapter 11

Flying K Ranch, Montana

"GODDAMNIT!" DIRK HOISTED THE SADDLE ONTO HIS horse's back with a curse. "And double damn Wade!"

His brother had ridden out late yesterday afternoon after strays and still hadn't come back. He had a half-dozen animals missing and Wade was too busy screwing around with his new girlfriend to care—as if there wasn't already enough bad blood between him and his brother already. Had Wade not taken the girl with him, Dirk might even have been worried, but now he'd bet the whole friggin' ranch they were holed up in the cabin doing what he could only fantasize about.

The only reason he'd sent Wade after the cattle was his own difficulty riding. He used the ATV most of the time for cattle work, but there were a number of strays on the mountain and some of the cow paths were too treacherous and narrow to chance it with the ATV. He rarely rode a horse unless he had to. He couldn't do it like he used to, so he didn't want to do it at all.

Unfortunately, there were still a few occasions where riding was unavoidable. It was the only reason he kept horses at all. It wasn't just the mounting and dismounting that made it difficult, but the chance of a hang-up was a constant danger. Riding with a prosthetic leg was a royal pain in the ass. He supposed his stubborn pride was an even bigger pain in the ass, but that's just how it was.

If the missing cattle wasn't already enough to fire him up, Allie Evans had just shown up with another offer on the ranch. He'd thought the issue of selling out was laid to rest a week ago, but here was Allie back again. She might have Wade in her pocket, but she was wasting her breath if she thought to change Dirk's mind. He had a legacy to protect and he swore he'd do so with his very last breath. It wasn't just a matter of guilt on his part, it was a matter of honor.

The Flying K was all he had left.

He'd screwed up his life so many times and in so many ways that all he wanted was the opportunity to start over. Just one stinking chance to see if he could finally get it right—whatever-the-hell "it" was.

He was damned tired of just scraping by and barely surviving. Hell no, he wanted the Flying K to thrive again as it once had, as he knew it still could. While his neighbors continued to complain about the low prices they were getting for their Angus and Herefords, Dirk had researched everything he could get his hands on about Japanese Wagyu and what it would take to raise a herd. His ideas meant taking chances and facing mockery, but he didn't give a rat's ass what others thought. Montana ranching methods were steeped in old tradition but it was time to break out of the box or perish.

He knew he could turn things around but a new breeding program didn't happen overnight. It took time. Not weeks or months but *years*. It was also risky, but he knew in his gut it would pay off in the long run—if only his damned brother would have a little faith. But instead of supporting Dirk's ideas, he'd teamed up with Ms. Allison Fuck-Me-Pumps Evans to sell the place out from under him. Allison's unexpected arrival had also forced him to deal with his handicap head-on, which pissed him off even more.

Copenhagen shifted uneasily. They were decades-old trail partners and the horse was sensitive to Dirk's every mood. While only a few years ago he could have effortlessly vaulted onto the back of the most skittish and ill-mannered horse, now he only picked the veterans out of the paddock, the old-timers with patience—like Red Man and Copenhagen.

"S'all right, boy." He soothed the animal and adjusted the saddle. Then, cursing his brother all the while, he swung himself up, positioning his prosthesis carefully in the custom-designed stirrup. He resented the hell out of having to drop everything to go up the mountain after Wade, but being honest, rage about Allie's appearance wasn't all that motivated him. He was equally eaten-up with envy. Wade had found himself a new woman and looked to be moving forward with his life, while everything Dirk was working for was slowly turning to shit.

—◆—

It was Sunday. Three full days since Wade and Nikki had walked into the Pioneer—and three long and sleepless nights that Janice had waited for her silent phone to ring. Although she hadn't given Wade her number, Dirk would surely know how to find her if he was inclined to. Maybe he wasn't inclined? She quickly canned that thought, instead favoring the possibility that Wade had simply forgotten to mention her.

For weeks she'd struggled to come up with any plausible excuse just to "happen by" the Knowlton place, but so far nothing had come to her—neither had Dirk. Although the idea terrified her to the core, she was growing more convinced that she'd have to just cowgirl up and take the bull by the horns. *Bull?* The thought stopped her in her tracks.

How ironic that bulls would be her link to him. Dirk was a rancher said to be branching out into a new breed of beef cattle. How hard would it be to go out there and strike up some talk about his bulls? Maybe even ask about a job? She was a bit of an expert in that arena, after all.

She sank her teeth into her lip and looked at her watch. If she drove out to the Flying K now, she could visit an hour or two with the Knowltons and still be back in time for supper. Even if she was a bit late, Mama would surely watch over Cody until her return.

She'd taken him to Caleb's house early this morning to ride horses. It'd been years since he'd been on one, but he was too young at the time even to remember it. They'd once kept a number of ranch horses for moving cattle, but the stock had been sold off long ago to pay medical bills and the bulk of the property had soon followed. Little good it had done. The cancer had not only eaten her father alive—it had taken his entire life savings. After the bills were paid only the old farmhouse and five acres remained of the original two-section homestead. Things had gone south real fast after that.

She'd realized too late that she was only an insurance policy to Grady. He'd married her in hopes of getting the ranch, but no one had counted on the bill collectors getting it instead. The ranch sale marked the beginning of the end of their marriage, or maybe better said, it was the nail in the coffin. At one time she was desperate to save her sinking marriage, even though she'd been bailing buckets out of it almost from the start. She'd wed Grady for all the wrong reasons but had hoped to make it work anyway. On that account she was also wrong.

Horribly. Horribly. Wrong.

She hadn't loved Grady. He hadn't loved her either. Nevertheless, she'd somehow managed to keep it together for Cody's sake. In the end, there was no saving it and no saving *him*. Now Grady was gone, but she couldn't shed any more tears. She'd wasted too many while he lived.

But the nightmare was finally over. She was safe from all the dirty secrets she'd struggled to keep hidden from the world. Now free of all that, she longed for a second chance to see what might have been. She'd lived too damned many years with what-ifs not to see this thing through once and for all. There was so damned much history and hurt to overcome, but she wasn't about to live out the rest of her life with added regrets.

That's right, Janice. Now or never. Just do it before you lose your nerve.

With her pulse racing, Janice shed her ratty sweats and pulled on her best ass-hugging Wranglers. Maybe she wasn't the lanky cowgirl she'd once been, but a lot of men preferred curves on a woman. Today, however, she was unable to decide whether she should emphasize or downplay. She didn't want to send the wrong message.

In the end, she settled for something in between, donning a fitted Western blouse in a turquoise shade that suited her well. She always tried to stick to blues and greens. She had Rachel Carson to thank for that. After dressing, Janice dug into the back of her closet for her only pair of dress boots—the worn pair of Old Gringos she'd spent eight hundred dollars on at Cheyenne Frontier Days a decade ago. She had Rachel to thank for that purchase too.

The boots represented the biggest act of self-indulgence in Janice's entire life, and one she'd never repeat. Although wearing them always invoked bitter-sweet memories, she'd never been able to bring herself to throw them away. Instead, she'd resoled them three times. Although they'd both seen some hard times, like the boots, Janice had held together all these years—even if sometimes by a thread.

Two hours later and halfway up the mountain, Dirk was still seeing red. Arriving at the spike camp and finding Wade's horses picketed outside had him ready to rip his brother a new one. Dirk tethered Copenhagen and approached the cabin, forcing himself to count slowly to ten but only making it as far as eight before he slammed his fist into the door. He didn't wait for an answer. The single knock was as much courtesy as his brother was going to get.

He shoved the door open with a thud, his blood pressure skyrocketing as he took in the scene—scattered clothing, two bodies huddled together in a single sleeping bag. It was exactly as he'd thought. He braced himself in the doorway with a glower while the startled couple disengaged and scrambled for their clothes. "Just fucking great, Wade. You told me you were going to bring down the strays. Instead, I come all the way up here to find you two knocking boots!"

Wade yanked on his jeans and tossed Nikki his shirt before stepping toward the door, blocking her from Dirk's view. "What the hell are you doing up here? I told you we'd bring them down, and we will."

"I'm playing the messenger boy for Allison Evans, that's what. Seems she has a new offer on the table and *needs* you, Wade. She won't go into it with anyone else."

"What's he talking about? Who's Allison Evans?" Nikki asked Wade.

"He hasn't a friggin' clue what he's blabbering about," Wade replied. "Allison is my partner's daughter. She's the ranch broker I've been working with. This is business, Nikki. Plain and simple."

"Plain and simple?" Dirk laughed outright. "Yeah, you just tell yourself that, little bro. Hell, it seems to me with such a fierce competition for that dick of yours, we should pin a blue ribbon on it."

"Shut the hell up, Dirk!" Wade snapped. "And get out!"

"You done fucking then?"

Wade's expression darkened. "I'm warning you, one more word and my fist is going to get mighty familiar with your face."

Dirk felt his body stiffen at the clear call to arms, but tamped down the explosion that was threatening to erupt. After considering how he would have reacted had the boot been on the other foot, he forced himself to back off. He then turned and stalked out.

He was already on his horse when Wade followed a few minutes later. At least he was saved the indignity of an audience as he struggled to mount up.

"What the fuck was that all about?" Wade demanded. "What possessed you to run your mouth off about Allie in front of her?"

Dirk shrugged. "Figured she'd be better off knowing now than getting ambushed back at the house. You should thank me. I saved you from having to deal with a big cat-scratching scene."

"You think you saved me?" Wade threw a saddle on his horse. "You're a class-A asshole, you know that, Dirk?"

"Maybe, but I'm also right. What do you think will happen when Fuck-Me-Pumps—"

"Quit calling her that—"

"—gets an eyeful of Peaches?"

"It's not like that. I've never promised Allie anything and never expected anything in return."

"Yeah, right," Dirk scoffed. "Not even her daddy's law practice?"

"You really think I'd use her like that?"

"What I think is that you're kidding yourself if you think Allie don't have designs on *you*. And my money says she's gonna make that pretty damn clear the moment you ride up with Peaches in tow."

"There's nothing serious between Allie and me. Our relationship has always been mostly business."

"Business with benefits? Hell, if that's the deal you have going, where do I sign up?"

"Jackass." Wade pulled himself onto his horse.

"Just calling your bullshit. She's not my type."

"Yeah, I recall your type all right—other men's wives."

Dirk's knuckles whitened around the reins. The reference to Rachel was a damn low blow. They'd avoided any talk of her for over three years. Wade's marriage had failed and she was gone. He knew the guilt ate at Wade, but it seemed easier for his brother to make accusations than to shoulder the blame for the death of his wife and unborn child. But Dirk had let it ride long enough. "It's time to pull your head out of your ass, brother. That's not how it was, and I think deep down you know it."

"She never wanted me. She wanted you," he accused.

"That doesn't mean anything happened. It ended between Rachel and me ten years ago."

"If that's true, why did she turn to you instead of me?"

"You refused to make time for her, so she played us against each other just like she always did. It was her juvenile effort to get your attention."

"Sure looked like more than that to me." Wade spun around and spurred his horse up the mountain.

Dirk mumbled another curse. He'd said his piece. There was nothing more he could do to convince a brother who wanted to believe the worst.

They rode the next hour in an edgy silence, looking for any sign of the stray cattle but finding only dried-up dung piles. They followed the dung trail farther up the mountain until Wade's horse unexpectedly shied. "What the hell's wrong with you, Skoal?"

The wake of turkey buzzards, closely followed by the putrid assault of decaying flesh, provided the answer. Wade made to dismount but Dirk stalled him with his rifle raised. "I despise the ugly mothers." Aiming into the cluster of birds, he fired to clear the view of the rotting carcass.

Shit! It was worse than he'd feared. The buzzards were picking the bones of not one, but three of the missing herd—a cow and twin calves. Dirk's chest tightened at the loss. It had taken three years of careful and highly selective breeding to establish the beginnings of a Wagyu herd—not to mention a huge financial risk that Wade wasn't about to let him forget.

Wade dismounted, crouching with a handkerchief over his nose to examine the half-eaten remains—the obvious work of wolves. A grizzly or mountain lion couldn't have taken down all three at once. Nor would they have torn away the haunches and eaten the viscera first.

Bad enough they were killing his stock, in this case they were killing his future too. Even if the insurance paid out on the dead cattle, it wouldn't come close to what he'd invested. He'd busted his ass for the past three years trying to keep the ranch going while everyone else around him was selling out. With the beef market going all to hell, he'd studied every angle in hope of doing better than they'd done in the past.

He couldn't afford to lose any more stock, but how the hell was he going to keep a pack of wolves away? He didn't have any help and sure as hell couldn't be a twenty-four-hour babysitter to a herd of cows. He seemed only to be running into obstacles at every damned turn!

"How many were you missing?" Wade asked.

"Seven," Dirk hissed through his teeth.

"Well, then I guess this accounts for almost half of 'em."

"Think the wolves got the lot of 'em?" Dirk asked.

"Not unless they took them last night," Wade replied.
"'Cause I swear I saw at least a half-dozen grazing up on
the ridge. Maybe more."

"Couldn't have been more. The rest are all accounted
for." Dirk gave Wade a dark look. "And we wouldn't
have lost *these* if you hadn't been so damned preoccupied with your prick."

"Bullshit! This kill is at least two days old. Besides
that, it would have been too dark to bring them down the
mountain last night anyway. I'm not about to risk my
life for a stupid cow."

"That's the difference between us. This cattle *is* my
life. I spent the past three years cultivating this breed,
and now I'm looking at over six grand in dead stock."
He slapped his hat on his thigh.

"How much can you reclaim from a wolf kill?"

"Hell, that's nothing but a crock to begin with. Unless
you can *prove* it was depredation by a wolf, they won't
pay a friggin' nickel." He dismounted. "C'mon. Wildlife
Service has to investigate, so we'd better cover these
carcasses and preserve what little we can of the crime
scene—not that I'm holding my breath. Even if they do
pay, it'll only be a fraction of what I had invested."

"Which begs the question—why do you still want to
hold on to this? You know there's no future in it. Private
ranching is as dead as these cattle."

"You're wrong. There is still an opportunity, but it
has to be the *right* cattle. In Vegas they're getting three
hundred bucks for a Kobe T-bone. There's opportunity for those who can think outside the box, Wade.
American Kobe is an emerging market."

It was purely by chance that Dirk had come upon that answer. The night Grady'd won the World Bull Riding championships they'd celebrated at Vic and Anthony's where Grady ordered the most expensive thing on the menu—a jaw-dropping three-hundred-dollar steak. Dirk had never even heard of Kobe beef before that night, but at thirty to fifty dollars an ounce, it didn't take a mathematical genius to figure out where money could still be made in cattle.

"There are all kinds of restaurants and gourmet food chains looking for suppliers," Dirk said. "It's going to take off in a big way. I just need to be able to meet the demand."

"You're crazy, Dirk, and I'm done! I'm not putting another penny into this operation. It's stupid to hang on. I finally had the ol' man seeing reason—until you laid waste to everything," Wade added bitterly. "Is that damned ego of yours worth giving him another coronary? He can't do this anymore. You're gonna kill him."

"Then we'll hire some help," Dirk argued. "There's plenty of hands looking for work."

"And why is that?" Wade scoffed. "You just proved my point. Name me one private ranch that isn't struggling just to survive."

"You've made yourself crystal clear, that you want to bail out. That's the difference between you and me. While you'd just walk away from four generations' worth of blood, sweat, and tears, I'm willing to fight to keep it."

"You're an ungrateful asshole, you know that? It's been *my* hard-earned money that's paid the taxes and grazing leases to keep this place going—money that would have been better spent on a condo in Arizona where our folks could retire."

"If that's how you feel, I'll buy you out. Whatever offer Fuck-Me-Pumps produces, I'll match a third of it—your share. All you've ever cared about is money, anyway. You've got no loyalty, Wade."

"Loyalty?" Wade snarled back. "You sure as hell are no judge on loyalty!"

"Back to that, are we?" Dirk's jaw tightened along with his fists. He refused to swallow any more of Wade's bullshit. "You got what you deserved, little brother."

Wade speared him with a murderous look. "Is *that* what you really think?"

"Does it matter what I think? It's what *she* thought and it's what killed her. *You* killed her, Wade."

"You goddamn son of a bi—" Wade reined in and pulled back a fist, but a ground-shaking sound of thunder halted him. "What the hell?"

"Holy shit!" Dirk echoed his cry as a band of madly galloping horses came barreling down the mountain toward them. In hot pursuit was a pack of half a dozen ravenous-looking gray wolves.

Dirk cocked his rifle, raised it, and took aim, but then held his fire at the last second. He could take down one or maybe two but then risked bringing the whole pack down on them if he missed, not to mention the litany of laws he'd be breaking if he shot any of them without a kill permit. As it turned out, the wolves were too preoccupied with their current prey to pay any attention to the two riders.

Dirk lowered his rifle with a head shake. "They've been having some wolf troubles down in Paradise Valley for a good while, and I'd heard there were a few who'd ventured farther north, but I hadn't seen any around these parts. Now a whole friggin' pack of 'em? How the hell am I going to protect my stock?"

"Guess you'd better bring in Wildlife Services," Wade said. "They'll probably just trap and collar them, but maybe you can convince them to relocate the pack."

"Yeah, that's real likely," Dirk snorted.

"What about those horses?" Wade asked.

"Hell if I know. I have enough on my hands without worrying about a herd of mustangs. Maybe if I'm lucky, they'll keep the wolves away from my cattle."

Chapter 12

Janice pulled into the drive of the Flying K just as a silver Lexus SUV pulled out. Recognizing the driver as Wade Knowlton, she waved, but he returned only a perfunctory nod. Based on the cloud of dust and flying gravel he'd left in his wake, he was in a big hurry. She hoped it didn't bode trouble.

She continued slowly up the half-mile-long drive to the Knowlton homestead. She'd been there dozens of times in the past when friends and neighbors all pitched in to help one another with sorting, roping, and branding. Not to mention castrating the calves. With an operation as large as the Knowlton's, it had taken a crew of twenty hands all day. It was hard and dirty work, but she'd enjoyed every minute of it. She loved the feel of a stiff rope in her hand and the challenge of roping cattle and missed it sorely.

Although the hours were long and the pay meager—even compared to waitressing—ranch work was what she'd hoped to find when she'd come back home. But she'd quickly discovered that jobs were scarce. Even though she was a more than capable hand, being female didn't help her chances when there were so many good cowboys out of work.

She parked her faithful red Dodge dually, the same truck she'd hauled stock with ten years ago, between the old white F-150 and a new Cadillac Escalade. She stepped down, shut the door, and then froze in her tracks. The Colorado plate and Majestic Ranch Brokers sign on the Cadillac door confirmed the worst. There was only one person who would be driving a car like that in Madison County—the same person who'd brokered the sale of her family's place.

Were the Knowltons selling out too? A giant knot lodged in her throat at the very thought. She couldn't imagine the Ruby Valley without them. They'd been in Twin Bridges for four generations, as far back as the gold rush that forged the town. But by the look of things, the Flying K suffered as much as everyone else. That was not to say it appeared neglected—just too quiet. Almost deserted. There was always *something* to do on a working ranch—horses to shoe, fences to mend, machinery to repair—yet Janice found no one around when she'd pulled up between the house and the main barn.

Realizing she'd come at a bad time, Janice debated knocking on the door and paying the briefest possible call, or just driving quietly away. She nixed that idea. If anyone had noticed her arrival, it would look really rude to drive off. She was still deliberating when an ear-splitting crash sounded from the barn, followed by the crack of splintering wood. Apparently the place wasn't deserted after all.

She heard it a second time and her pulse quickened. Was an animal loose? Had a horse got itself cast? She hustled toward the barn to check it out, sliding the metal door on its track and advancing inside. Her eyes were still adjusting to the darkness of the barn after the brightness of the afternoon sun, when a tall figure emerged from the tack room. He stepped toward her, or maybe it was more like a lurch and her heart almost stopped beating.

Even in the dim light with his hat tipped low, she knew it was Dirk. She'd come purposely to see him, but now face-to-face she felt like a deer in the headlights, poised for flight, but with feet rooted to the sawdust-covered ground.

"What the fuck do *you* want?" he growled, rubbing his fist.

His aggressive, almost unrecognizable tone told her everything she needed to know—coming out here was a mistake. A horrible, horrible mistake.

"I—I heard a noise," she stammered. "I thought an animal might be in trouble. I'm sorry I intruded. So sorry." With shaking hands and unsteady legs, Janice backed toward the door. Shoving it open, she strode briskly and blindly into the late afternoon sun, her only thought to get inside her truck before she broke down and started bawling.

"Janice?" Dirk's voice, low and gravely, called after her. "Holy shit! Is that you?"

She didn't turn around or even slow her pace, but he was on her in seconds. His powerful hands gripped her shoulders, whirling her around to face him. Their eyes met for the first time, his widening in shock. They were still icy blue and just as mesmerizing as she remembered. The effect they had on her hadn't changed either, but other things had. Though his hat was pulled low to throw his face in shadow, she could discern the scars that marred his handsome face—a long strip of angry red and pitted flesh that mismatched the surrounding skin—a graft. It made her heart ache for him.

"Red? Hell, I'm sorry for snarling at you like that. I thought you were someone else…"

"Who?" Janice choked out through her thick throat.

"Allie Evans." He released her arm and stepped back, shaking his head. "If I'd had any idea…I'm sorry, Red. I still can't believe it's you."

"Yeah, it's me, all right. I've been back for a couple of months now, me and Cody. We're out with Mama at the old homestead—or at least what's left of it."

"Just visiting?"

"Nope. I'm hoping to stay if I can find a way to make a living. So far none of the ranches are hiring, so I've been waitressing at the Pioneer."

"You? Waitressing?" He made a scoffing sound.

She scowled back at him. "What of it? I did it for three years in Las Vegas. It's an honest living."

"Not what I meant," he said. "It's just a damned waste of your talents."

"Oh." She smiled slowly. "Thank you."

"What brings you out here?" He seemed suddenly wary, almost suspicious. He kept his head cocked at an awkward angle, as if to hide the damaged part of his face.

"Curiosity. I heard you're raising some new breed of stock." Unable to look him in the eye and lie, she dug the toe of her boot into the dirt. "I wanted to see the bulls."

"You're curious about my bulls or maybe you heard the talk and wanted a look at me?" He ripped off his hat and slapped it against his thigh. "Go ahead and gawk your fill, sweetheart. There's not too many burned-up, one-legged cowboys 'round these parts. There's even fewer who wear their asses on their face."

Janice clenched her fists. She'd never wanted so badly to slap anyone in her life. How could he say such things to her? It hurt like hell. He'd lashed out, so she lashed back. "Then maybe that's fitting, Dirk, since you're *acting* like a complete ass to boot."

He winced. "What the hell's that supposed to mean?"

"You have no clue what it took just for me to drive out here. I've been trying to work up the nerve for weeks." She was trembling with hurt, rejection, and rage.

"Why? Thought you couldn't stomach the sight of me?"

"Just stop it!" She jutted her chin to look him squarely in the eye. "My reluctance had nothing to do with your injuries. I knew you were hurt and actually expected a lot worse."

"That so?" His brows met and his mouth compressed. "You've been back two months and you're just now coming around? Why'd you stay away so long?"

She swallowed hard, but it did no good. Her mouth was dry as sawdust. "I didn't know if you'd want to see me."

He clawed a hand through his short, sandy hair with a groan. "How could you have come to that fucked-up conclusion?"

"After the way you disappeared from Las Vegas—"

"Las Vegas?" He shook his head with a derisive laugh. "Yeah, a lot of ugly shit happened in Vegas and a lot more afterwards."

"What do you mean?"

"Grady didn't tell you?"

"Grady couldn't say much of anything for a while. He went out with you that night and came home with a broken jaw. What really happened, Dirk? And why'd you leave without even saying good-bye?"

He shrugged. "It's history best forgotten. 'Sides, what happens in Vegas is s'posed to stay there."

She chewed her lip. "Does it really, Dirk? I don't think so."

"Maybe not, but we gotta move on, don't we?"

"That's what I'm trying to do," she said, her gaze wavering. "It's why I came back. Cody needs a real home and I need a fresh start."

"So you're really planning to stay?"

"If I can make it, I will, but it hasn't been easy. Mama lives on social security and her health isn't good. She probably should sell what's left of the place." Janice gave a fatal shrug. "That's probably what it'll come down to in the end."

He pressed a hand to the small of her back. "C'mon, Red. We've got some serious catching up to do. Let's you and me go have a beer."

"OK," she replied. "But I can't stay long."

With a hand on her back, he steered her toward the bunkhouse behind the barn. Janice looked up at him in question.

"I'm not in the mood to deal with what's going on at the house right now," he explained. "There's time enough for that bullshit later. 'Sides, you and me need some private conversation." He opened the door and beckoned her inside. "It's not much, but it's home."

"Home? Wasn't this the bunkhouse?" Janice asked as she stepped inside. It was a typical log cabin with a clean-swept floor, scarred oak table, and leather-upholstered sofa and armchair angled next to the stone fireplace.

There were several of the requisite mounted hunting trophies marking it as a male domain, but not much else. The room seemed strangely devoid of personality. "Why are you here instead of in the main house?"

"It was empty and I needed space," he said. "I have a bed, shower, kitchen, and office." He nodded toward a corner desk and laptop. "Everything I need."

"So you've let all the hands go? Things are that tough?"

He shrugged. "It's no secret. It's tough for everyone right now. We only have a couple of part-timers left who come out as needed."

A number of ranching outfits had downsized in the past few years, and just as many had sold out, but she'd never expected the Knowltons to join those ranks. "Are you selling out too?" she asked. "I saw the broker's car."

Dirk's face darkened. "Wade's been pushing for it, but it'll be over my dead body. Seems it just may come to that too, 'fore all is said and done. How 'bout that beer?" He grabbed a couple of Coors from the fridge and popped the tops.

"Your hand's bleeding," she observed. She closed hers over it as he offered her the bottle. Their eyes met, the first contact of skin on skin seemed to startle them both. "Let me wrap it up for you."

"It's nothing." He jerked it out of her grasp. "I don't need a mother, Janice."

He handed her the bottle and then made a careless bandage from a paper towel he snatched from beside the sink. He waited until she sank into the sofa, before settling into an overstuffed chair to her right. She wondered if he'd done it to hide his scars from her.

"Wanna tell me now what really brought you out here?" he asked. "We both know it wasn't to talk about bulls."

Heat inflamed her face to be called out for her subterfuge. "I saw Wade the other night and asked about you," she confessed. "He said you could use an old friend—and frankly so could I. I've been away a long time now and I've lost touch with a lot of folks. Most of my connections were with the rodeos and I don't do that anymore, so I guess I'm just feeling kinda lonesome."

"And you wanna be *friends*?" He snorted.

"Yeah. Why's that so funny?"

"Because we've had this conversation before, Red. I told you a long time ago that men and women *can't* be friends. Sooner or later…" He let his words die off with a shrug.

"But time changes things, Dirk. People change."

He laughed outright this time. "Don't know why you think time makes any difference. I haven't *changed* genders and haven't changed my views either."

But he had *changed* in a lot of other ways. He'd become hard, wary, and cynical. She was comfortable with the old Dirk, but this version was different. He seemed edgy and volatile. She knew she'd changed a lot too, but in less obvious ways. His wounds were visible; hers were well hidden.

"For my part," he continued, "I'd only find the whole thing frustrating as hell if you started coming around, and I already have enough frustrations without adding to them. I hate to be so blunt, but I'd rather save us both the trouble and cut through the bull. If you came only looking for polite conversation, you've knocked on

the wrong door." His eyes drifted slowly over her with
the kind of look that made her insides stir. In reality,
his gaze hadn't left her since the moment he'd closed
the door.

She fully understood the implication, his interest in
things other than conversation was perfectly clear. Still
watching her, Dirk took a long swig from his beer. Janice
hadn't taken a single sip of hers. She shifted uneasily.
For the second time she felt the impulse to take flight.
Coward. You know why you came.

She'd been with two men in her entire life—Dirk and
Grady. She'd lost her virginity to the former and her
innocence to the latter.

Sex had been second only to bull riding with Grady.
And he was just as rough and aggressive—especially
when the adrenaline was still raging after a ride. And
he liked trash talk. The raunchier the better. It was tit-
illating at first but the novelty had quickly worn away.
Then there were other women. Lots of women. He was
discreet in the beginning but later… No matter how hard
she tried, Grady could never get enough and she could
never *be* enough.

The years with Grady had shaken her confidence to
the core. If it wasn't for that one night she'd spent with
Dirk, she might have been turned off from sex for good.
For ten years Janice had held that memory close to her
heart. They'd connected on a level she'd never experienced with Grady. It gave her hope that she could still
have a normal relationship, a normal life. She was desperate to reclaim that intimacy, but now that the moment
she'd fantasized about for so long had come, she was
suddenly terrified.

What if this was another mistake?

They were both so different now. Although their shared history still bound them, the old camaraderie was gone. There was a tension between them now. An edge. Even now he was studying her in that unnerving and wolfish way.

She concentrated on scraping the label from the bottle with her thumbnail. It was decision time. She could get up and walk out, or she could take whatever he was willing and able to give. She was so tired of feeling alone... of being alone.

Her heart hammered a rapid tattoo as she looked up and took the plunge. "What if I didn't come for polite conversation?"

"Then I'd say be damned careful what you wish for." His throat worked on a hard swallow. "You *don't* want to get involved with me, Red," he warned her. "I'm a fucking mess—inside and out. If you have any sense, you'll get up and walk out that door. Right. Now."

His words were harsh and self-deprecating, but Janice read the truth flickering in his blue eyes—he was every bit as scared as she was. What were they both so afraid of? It wasn't even their first time together.

No more regrets.

Her lips curved into a sad smile. "I don't have much sense. Used it all up, I guess. 'Sides, you might not be getting the best bargain either, cowboy."

He stared at her in incomprehension, his mind still reeling at her appearance. He still couldn't believe she'd walked into his life after all this time. He didn't understand her motivation either, but did he really care? He'd done his best to warn her, to chase her off even. He hadn't exaggerated. He was a fucking wreck, one that no sane woman would take on. But here she was, sane or not, and he wanted her with a desire that penetrated his marrow. The same need shone in her eyes, the kind of deep physical, gut-wrenching need that he shared, and the only kind he could fulfill.

He mumbled a stream of curses before hoisting himself to his feet. "Last chance, Janice. I can only fuck things up and make you miserable. It's all I've ever been good at."

Nevertheless, he offered his hand.

Her brown eyes met his unwavering. "I'm a big girl, Dirk. I think I can take it."

The softness in those eyes betrayed her tough words. That same softness and vulnerability cried out to him. After six years in the marines, there was nothing soft left in him. He wanted to bury himself in it…in her.

The words had barely left her mouth before he jerked her to her feet. The bottle flew out of her hands to explode in a foamy mess all over the oak plank floor. He didn't care. The only thing that mattered was his mouth devouring hers. Her hot, wet tongue tangling with his. The feel of her silky hair in his fisted fingers, the faint scent of vanilla, her body molding to his.

Mutual desire flared instantly. Urgently, obliterating indecision. Supplanting uncertainty with sensation. His mouth came down on her neck, sucking and biting while his hands tore at her blouse. One sound jerk had her pearl snaps sounding like Jiffy Pop. Then his heavily callused hands were on her breasts, fondling, squeezing. He wasn't gentle. But neither was she.

Panting. Groping. She fumbled with his shirt buttons and then gave up, wrapping her hand around the throbbing bulge in his jeans, fondling him through the thick denim with one hand while yanking frantically at his belt buckle with the other. In a frenzy of lust, he guided her body, backing her up to the sofa. "Boots. Off," he commanded.

Gripping his shoulders for balance, Janice toed off one boot and then the other. He peeled away her blouse. She unhooked her bra, letting it drop to the floor, his gaze following her every move with increasing hunger. Peeking through her lashes, she cupped and squeezed her breasts.

He groaned, then buried his face between them. She was working on his zipper when his mouth closed over her beaded nipple, drawing it into his mouth, alternating between soft bites and steady sucking until she threw her head back with a sob. He released her nipple to nuzzle his way to her other breast, scraping his teeth over her skin. Still kissing, biting, and sucking her breasts, he unzipped her jeans. His hands shook as he stripped them off, peeling them down over her hips.

She stood in just her panties. They were white and edged with lace—simple, but still sexy—much like Janice.

"Take them off," he said, his throat suddenly feeling full of gravel.

She ran her fingers provocatively along the waistband before sliding them off.

Their gazes met. His need was so bad his eyes

were crossing but he had to hear her say it. "You sure about this?"

"Yes, I'm sure."

"Good. Gimme just a minute."

He stalked toward the bathroom, flinging open the medicine cabinet and then rifling through every drawer, hoping like hell one of the stock hands had left a condom behind. Nothing. *Fuck. Fuck. Fuck.*

He went next to the bedroom, cursing another stream of invectives until he found a lone foil packet in the nightstand beside the bed. *Thank you, sweet Jesus.* But when he finally returned, Janice was curled up in the corner of the sofa, knees against her chest, chewing her thumbnail. *Shit.* He'd taken too long. She'd changed her mind.

"Having second thoughts?"

"No, but…" She bit her lip.

"But what?"

"It's just…I need…I need you to be patient with me, all right?"

Patient? He had a raging erection. His balls throbbed for release. His patience was a fine thread that was damned close to snapping. She was gonna kill him by slow torture.

"It's been a long time for me too," she blurted, "over four years."

"Four?" He digested that slowly. "Grady's only been gone for three."

"That's right. Things weren't good between us, Dirk. Not for a long time…there were a lot of…problems." She averted her gaze. "You can't understand how it was, and I don't want to talk about it."

"I tried to warn you about him, but you wouldn't listen. You *chose* Grady."

"Choice? What choice?" she cried. "My father was dying and I had a business and a ranch to run. I couldn't do it alone. Grady said he'd take care of me. I needed someone, and *he* was there." Her eyes spoke the rest. *You weren't.*

The unspoken words were like a knife to his gut. His conscience twisted that knife. No, she couldn't have done it alone. Hell, no one could have handled that much responsibility flying solo, let alone a twenty-one-year-old girl. He'd walked away, leaving her vulnerable. He'd let Grady have her without putting up a fight, and Grady had done exactly what Grady had always done. Married or not, he rode bulls, drank, and whored.

Dirk had lived with the guilt over it for ten years. A powerful surge of it hit him now. "I'm sorry I couldn't be there for you then, but I'm damn sure in no better shape now! What the fuck do you want from me?"

Her eyes widened. He could almost hear her jaw click shut. Then suddenly she was on her feet. Dirk watched motionless and wooden-faced as she snatched up her clothes and disappeared into the bathroom. She reemerged a few minutes later, fully dressed and stomping into her boots. "I don't *want* anything from you and certainly don't *need* any abuse. I thought you were worth it, but maybe you're not."

Her tearful words ripped through him, making his chest feel tight. The constriction increased the closer she got to the door, until he almost couldn't breathe, but he had no more words. What else could he say? It was all truth. And the truth hurt sometimes.

Nevertheless, he'd never felt so wrong as when he watched her walk out the door.

Chapter 13

A WEEK LATER, DIRK WALKED INTO THE PIONEER. IT was a slow night. Janice had finished wiping down tables and was polishing the glasses. She'd sworn to banish all thoughts of him, but it was much easier when he wasn't standing right in front of her—looking too damn good for her peace of mind.

He wore his town hat and boots with new jeans and a starched white twill dress shirt open at the collar. His scars weren't obvious from this distance and he reminded Janice far too much of the "old" Dirk. But it was time to let go of the past. Maybe the man she'd built up in her mind for so long never really existed... or maybe she'd never really known him at all. She'd expected too much.

He hadn't been there for her ten years ago when she'd needed him. Part of her had understood his reasons. He wasn't ready to settle down. How many twenty-two-year-olds were? But the other part of her resented him for leaving. She'd gone to him last week looking for comfort, for a shoulder to lean on, and he hadn't even offered her that shoulder. She'd beat herself up all week for making a fool of herself over him. She'd sworn when she came home to Montana that she'd move forward with her life. All she could do now was promise herself not to repeat her mistakes—and Dirk Knowlton now topped her list of biggest mistakes.

Although she tried not to acknowledge him, the bartender was in the back taking inventory with the owner. Otherwise, the place was almost empty. Not that it mattered. Dirk wasn't about to be ignored. He sat down on the stool directly in front of her.

"Evenin,' Red." He tipped his hat.

She wanted to ignore him, but he just sat there watching her, seeming to pay particular attention every time she reached up over the bar to take down or replace a glass, which put her breasts right at his eye level. His blatant interest made her feel nervous and clumsy.

"Do you have to stare?" she finally snapped.

He cocked a lopsided grin. "Can't blame a man for enjoying the landscape. You look good, Red... real good."

"What can I get you?" she asked tersely.

"Whatever's on tap."

She filled a mug and plopped it down in front of him.

He closed his hand over hers before she could snatch it away. His smile disappeared. "I came to talk to you."

"There's nothing to talk about." She jerked her hand away from his and reached over the bar for the next glass.

"Bullshit. There's a lot that needs sayin'."

"Like what?" she replied.

"First off, I never should have let you walk out like that."

She shrugged. "What's done is done. And this isn't the time or the place to hash through it. I'm working."

"Look, Red, I've been chewing on all this for days. I'm just asking you to hear me out."

"All right." He obviously wasn't leaving till he had

his say. She dropped her towel on the bar and settled her hands on her hips. "Go on. Speak your piece and be done."

"I was an asshole the other day."

"You got that right. What else you got?"

"I wanna make it up to you."

She frowned. "How?"

"I think we can help each other."

She held his gaze, her curiosity piqued despite her resolution to have nothing more to do with him. "What do you mean by that?"

"I'm planning to expand my operation as soon as I can get a few details ironed out."

"Expand? How can you do that when your brother's trying to sell out?"

His expression darkened. "I'll deal with Wade when the time comes. But it's not come yet. I'm not ready to give up. I think I'm onto something that'll turn us around. I just need more time…and some help."

"You want my help," she scoffed. "What makes you think I'm interested? You're the one who said men and women can't be friends, remember?"

"I'm sorry how I reacted the other day. And I was afraid you might not be amenable after what happened, but I'm talking strictly business now, Red. You said you came home looking for ranch work, and I need a competent hand."

He was offering her a job? Janice stared at him in incredulous silence and then answered with a snort. "Let me get this straight. You want me to work for you?"

"Yeah. It makes a lotta sense. I don't know why it didn't occur to me when you came out, but I wasn't exactly thinking straight. I'm sorry for acting like a dick-head. All I can offer by way of excuse is that I had the missing cattle and Allie to deal with, and then you turned up out of the blue. Shit, I didn't know up from down. Can we please just set all that aside and start over?"

"What do you have in mind?"

"It's only part-time right now with weaning and preg checks coming up, but it'll become full-time once the cows start dropping their calves. Since you're one of the best hands I know, I wanted to offer you the job."

She shook her head knowing this whole proposition reeked of trouble. "I don't know, Dirk. I don't think it's a good idea, you and me working together."

"Be pissed at me all you like, Janice. I deserve it, but don't blow off my offer so fast." His blue eyes held hers. "You need work and I need help I can count on. It's as simple as that. Just think about it, will you?"

He seemed so contrite that it would be easy to forgive him, but then again, he deserved to squirm at least a little after the way he'd acted. She propped her elbows on the bar and leaned toward him, giving him an up close and personal view of what he'd so openly admired. She felt a tug of self-satisfaction when he shifted in his seat.

She pursed her lips and then answered noncommit-tally, "Yeah, I'll think about it."

Dirk retrieved his wallet and slapped down a twenty and a business card. "Here's my cell number. Call me when you decide." His mouth kicked up in one corner. "I can't promise you great pay, but the hours are grueling."

He slid off the stool and walked out before she could give him change.

He hadn't even touched his beer.

—⁓—

Although Dirk avoided town as much as possible, he'd had no choice but to go in to see Janice. For the past week he'd tried to dismiss her from his mind and just focus on work, but she continued to infiltrate his thoughts. Part of him said to let it go, that it would be stupid as hell to get involved, but seeing her had unbalanced him. He'd thought about nothing but work for so damned long. She'd made him realize just how lonely and isolated he'd become. She was also a painful reminder of all his mistakes and regrets—of everything he didn't want to think about.

But he'd hurt her and he just couldn't live with that. He'd never be able to rest easy until he at least tried to make it right again. That wasn't to say he wanted any romantic entanglement. He didn't. He was way too far gone for that. He could never be what she needed, but that didn't mean he couldn't help her out. So he'd made the offer. The next move was hers.

He didn't have to wait long for an answer. His phone rang before he'd even pulled into his drive.

"Dirk here," he answered brusquely, not recognizing the number.

"It's Janice." She paused. "You didn't mention any specifics on hours or pay."

"You didn't ask."

"I'm asking now."

"I'm flexible, Red. Especially on the hours. I'll let you work around your schedule at the Pioneer—at least until things pick up. Right now I have an issue with missing stock. Got some cows and calves that didn't come down from winter gazing, and we've spotted wolves. I got to find them soon—or at least their carcasses."

"So you want me to hunt 'em down for you?"

"No. I'll do that myself, but I need someone to look after the rest of the herd while I account for the missing stock. There's calves to wean, preg checking on the cows and heifers, and then culling any that are still open. The ol' man can still do some of it, but he's got a heart condition and can't do everything he used to—just don't try to tell *him* that. He doesn't know yet, but Ma's hoping to convince him to spend this winter in Arizona. It's the only thing Wade and I agree on—that it's time for him to retire. The tricky part is gonna be convincing him that it's *his* idea."

"I can believe that!"

He was encouraged to hear her laugh. It seemed to break the barrier of ice that had built up between them. "So whadaya say, Red?"

"I'd like to give it a try." She paused. "If you're a bit cash-strapped, would it help if I just came out on my days off?"

"Hell yeah," he said. "When do you want to start?"

"I'm off for the next two days. I just have to be sure Mama won't mind watching Cody."

"You're a godsend, Red. I can't even tell you how important it is for me to track down my missing stock."

"I understand," she said. "Cattle were once my livelihood too. I'll be there by six."

"If you can make it by five thirty, I'll cook you pancakes."

"Pancakes? You cook?"

"Damn straight I do and not just breakfast. If I find

my missing cows, I'll grill you the best damn T-bone
you ever had in your life."

"That offer's hard to refuse."

"Then don't—" He was about to blurt "refuse" and
caught himself. Shit. It was too damned easy to forget.
He almost believed he could be normal with her.

"Don't what?" she asked.

"Don't be late," he replied tersely.

"I won't be. I'll see you first thing in the morning."

Dirk waited for the click that ended the call. He'd
told himself he was just helping her out. He really did
need a hand, but who was he really kidding? He couldn't
wait to see her again—no matter the terms.

With a nine-year-old son, Janice was accustomed to staying up late and getting up early, but it had been years since
she'd set her alarm for four a.m. It was a hellish hour.
She dragged herself out of bed with a groan, showered,
dressed, and braided her hair. She was glad she'd splurged
on the automatic coffeepot. She poured a cup in a tall
travel mug before heading out the door in her jeans and
boots, grabbing her old hat and the sherpa-lined Carhartt
jacket that always hung on a hook by the back door.

It was almost October and the morning air was brisk
enough to make her breath visible as she walked out to
her truck. She looked out at the surrounding mountains
and inhaled deeply, feeling lighthearted for the first time
in forever. Until this moment, she'd felt like she was just
going through the motions, trapped in someone else's
skin, but the prospect of going back to cattle work felt
like a real homecoming to her.

Ranch work was what she knew. It was what she'd been born into. It was damned hard. It was downright dirty, but it was what she loved. And it was the life she'd always wanted for her son. Grady had never shared that dream. Sure he'd wanted to raise bulls, but it was all for show, to be the star of the rodeo, not for the lifestyle. Real ranch work bored him. Dirk, on the other hand, was deeply committed to making things work at the Flying K.

He'd surprised her with the job offer, but she reminded herself that's all it was—a job. She refused to let her anxiety ruin everything. This was a business arrangement. There would be no personal involvement. He'd already made his feelings perfectly clear about that. He was simply her new boss.

So why had she agreed to meet him for breakfast? Why had he even asked her? Why was her pulse accelerating and her palms sweating on the steering wheel as she turned into the drive and through the gate of the Flying K? When he'd walked into the bar yesterday he'd been so different from how he was just last week. She remembered his teasing parting remark that had sounded so much like he used to be.

"C'mon, Janice," she groaned. "Pull yourself together. All you gotta do is go to work, collect your paycheck…and guard your stupid heart."

—∿∿—

Janice paused outside the door to the old bunkhouse, the knot in her stomach tightening at the memory of how badly the last time had gone. She shook those thoughts off, inhaled a deep breath, and raised her hand to knock, but the door opened before she made contact. Finding herself facing a solid wall of hard male, Janice took a step backward. Her gaze tracked upward into a pair of ice-blue eyes.

"G'morning," Dirk said. "Didn't mean to startle you, but I heard the truck. Diesels aren't exactly stealth vehicles."

"No, they aren't." She gave a nervous laugh. "And mine's in sore need of a new muffler. It's one of many things I've had to put off due to lack of cash, which is also why I'm here."

"I'm glad you didn't have second thoughts."

"No, but I don't have much choice. I really do need the money. Then again, the day hasn't begun yet. Maybe I'll hightail it outta here once I've had a good dose of manure and bawling cattle."

"I wouldn't blame you if you did." He laughed. "But I suspect this kinda thing runs in your blood."

Her mouth curved into a reluctant smile. "Yeah. Sadly, it does."

"C'mon, breakfast is ready." He stepped back and beckoned her inside. "Hope you're good and hungry."

Janice scraped her boots on the mat and followed him to the kitchenette. She sniffed the bacon-scented air and her stomach gave an embarrassing growl. "Smells wonderful. I can't recall the last time I ate anything in the morning besides Cap'n Crunch or Lucky Charms."

"Not exactly the breakfast of champions," Dirk remarked dryly.

He indicated a chair at the scarred oak table set for two. In the middle sat a plate of bacon and a large platter of blueberry pancakes. Janice sat down while Dirk piled a stack of four pancakes and as many strips of bacon onto both of their plates.

"Cody never touched anything that wasn't sugar-coated until Wheaties put Grady on the box," she said. "Then for the longest time he wouldn't eat any-thing else—breakfast, lunch, or dinner. I finally had to stop buying it. I feel a little guilty about that, but I was feeding an unhealthy obsession," she chattered on nervously.

Dirk seemed to fill the tiny kitchenette with his over-powering male presence.

"Coffee?" he asked.

She nodded. "Yes, please."

He filled her cup before sitting down with his own. "How old is Cody now?"

"He'll be ten in March."

"Is he really?"

"Yeah. I can't believe how fast he's growing up."

"How's he dealt with his father's death?"

Janice stared into her coffee mug. Recalling the look of stark incomprehension on her six-year-old's face when she'd tried to explain that his father would never be coming home again.

"Fairly well, actually," she answered at length. "Once he was over the initial shock, his acceptance surprised me. But they were never very close. I used to resent that Grady didn't take much interest in him, but maybe it was a blessing in disguise. On the flip side, I'm afraid I've overcompensated a bit."

"How's that?"

"I've kept him too close. He needs more freedom. He needs to be a boy."

"True enough." Dirk nodded. "All boys need to raise a little hell."

"You're right. And I think coming back to Montana has been really good for him. He's already made some friends and now he's learning to ride."

"He's riding? You still got horses?" Dirk asked with surprise.

She shook her head wistfully. "No, we don't. He's learning on a friend's horse, but I hope maybe one day we can get a couple of our own. We still have a small paddock and a hay shed. It would be nice to ride again."

"Dig in," he said, indicating her plate. "Syrup?"

Janice noticed four bottles of gourmet syrup and laughed. "Where's the Aunt Jemima?"

"Only the good stuff here. I might have something going soon with this same gourmet foods company. They want to expand into high-end meats. Here. Try this one."

Janice poured the blueberry syrup on her pancakes and took a bite. It was delicious. So were the pancakes. Dirk hadn't exaggerated his cooking skills.

"If you want to ride, why don't you bring Cody out here?" Dirk said after a time. "We've still got a couple dozen horses and Red Man's the best babysitter you'll ever find."

"You really mean that?" Janice's gaze met his over her coffee cup. "I don't even know what to say."

"They're all getting fat and lazy. Hell, they need to do *something* to earn their keep."

"Thanks," she said.

Dirk flushed. He seemed almost embarrassed by his offer. "Eat up," he grunted and then attacked his own plate, downing the pancakes in record time. He looked up in surprise when Janice pushed away her half-full plate. "You aren't gonna finish?"

"God no!" she exclaimed. "I'm about to burst."

"Waste not, want not." He stabbed his fork into the remains of her stack and wolfed them down as well. It suddenly seemed so natural, so comfortable to be sitting across the table from him like this. She'd never had that with Grady. He was too restless…too preoccupied…or too absent. Afraid to linger on domestic fantasies that could never come true, Janice stood and started clearing the table.

"Just leave it," he said. "Time's a wastin'."

"Cleaning up is the least I can do when you did the cooking," Janice protested.

"Fine. Just throw them in the sink."

But Janice was already filling it with hot, soapy water.

Dirk came up from behind, reaching around her to turn off the tap. "You don't take orders very well, do you?" he rumbled in her ear. "You need to know something straight up, Red. I don't brook disobedience to direct orders." His body was warm and hard behind hers, his breath sweetly scented. His tone, however, was anything but sweet.

She froze with her hands braced on the countertop. She swallowed hard. "I—I was just trying to help."

His other arm came around her, trapping her body between his and the sink, his hands gripping the counter top beside hers. His chest and hips pressed against her back, sending a flood of heat to her core. She shut her eyes and tipped her head back, breathing him in, filling her lungs to capacity with the scent of musky male. *Dear God, I want him. Right here. Right now.*

Did he feel it too? He must have but he continued, cool and controlled. "I know that, Red, but I'm in charge here," he said. "You can chalk it up to my time in the Marine Corps, but I'm gonna expect you to do *exactly* as I tell you."

"Or what?" she asked breathlessly and arched into him.

His breath hitched. His arms tightened. "You're playing with fire, Red. You better think real hard what you're doing, 'cause this time I'm not about to let you walk outta here."

He released the counter to skirt his hands slowly up her sides, cupping her breasts in his big strong hands, brushing his thumbs over her taut nipples.

She gasped.

"Last chance," he warned, nuzzling his face into her neck and inciting another ripple of pleasure deep in her belly. "If you wanna leave, you'd better do it right-fucking-now."

"No. I don't want to go," she whispered, making no move to escape.

He released her and took a half step backward before he anchored his hands on her hips and spun her around to face him. His pupils were dilated, his mouth compressed as he backed her up to the table.

"What about the cattle?" she whispered.

"Fuck the cattle." He tugged her shirttail out of her jeans. "They can damn well wait…I can't."

His mouth came down on hers, hard and possessive, his tongue sweeping the seam of her mouth demanding entrance. She parted on a moan and he plunged into her mouth, his tongue tangling with hers, every touch sending echoes of sensation straight to her sex.

Janice opened eagerly, greedily taking him deeper and grinding her hips against his.

He proved a fine multitasker, unbuttoning her shirt and unhooking her bra without even releasing her for a breather. Now he was working on her zipper. She wriggled out of her shirt and bra as he worked her jeans down. They were only as far as her knees when she found herself sitting on his kitchen table. He tugged her boots off. They hit the floor with a dull thud and then the jeans joined them. Grabbing a kitchen knife, his motions were clean and efficient as he slit the side seams to dispense with her panties. There was no doubt Dirk meant business this time.

"Lie back," he commanded low and husky.

Janice complied, only to be surprised by the sensation of something cold and wet on her chest and belly. She opened her eyes to find Dirk grinning down at her, and her upper body dripping blueberry syrup.

"Sorry, sweetheart. I couldn't resist the temptation." Hunching over her, he proceeded to lick her off with long slow lashes of his hot tongue, lingering to lick, suck, and bite her nipples

"Please," she begged, writhing in her need.

His mouth and tongue were all over her breasts and then her belly, his breath hot and moist against her skin as his mouth worked steadily southward. One hand ascended her leg to stroke between her thighs. She shuddered with raw pleasure.

He placed his hands on her ass, urging her to the edge,

then gripped the table and lowered himself to his knees. "You don't have to," she protested, realizing what he intended. Her pulse raced with panic even as her body remembered the pleasure. "I'm ready for you."

"I *want* to," he said. "Besides, if I don't get you off first, you might not get another chance. Once I'm gloved inside you, I'm gonna be blind and deaf and so caught up in my need to come that I'm not gonna give a goddamn about anything else… I told you it's been a long time, Red. A long fucking time."

He'd said almost the same thing the very first time they were together.

He draped her thighs over his shoulders and rubbed his face in her mons with a low groan that vibrated clean through her. Janice shut her eyes, throwing her head back with a whimper at the first hot swipe of his tongue. By the second slow, wet sweep, she ground her pubis against his mouth, agonizing in the sweet torture.

"Please. Don't stop."

Their moans mingled while he worked magic with his lips, teeth, and tongue, teasing, circling, and sucking, turning her mind to jelly. She glanced down at his face to find his eyes nearly black with lust and his lips curved up at the corners. He knew damn well what he was doing to her. His every touch invoked an increasingly needy response from her body. Her initial resistance forgotten, Janice lost herself in the pleasure of his mouth.

He nudged her thighs wider, gripping her hips tighter, and pulling her harder against his mouth working her with his skillful tongue as he plunged two fingers in and out, hard and fast in synchrony with the sweeps and swirls of his hot, velvet tongue. Her need for release was ramped to a fever pitch. She was quivering inside and out, her breath coming shorter, harder, as her climax coiled deep inside her belly.

"Give it up now, Red. Come for me. Now. I want *all* of it."

Her mind was so far gone, her brain so drugged by sensation, that she barely heard the words. As he closed his lips and sucked her clit, one thought exploded in her mind along with the sobbing climax that rocked her body. *Be careful what you wish for*.

Although his balls throbbed with need, Dirk wouldn't take back watching her climax for anything. In those last seconds, with her lips parted, her eyes shut, and her face flushed in ecstasy, he'd felt whole again for the first time in ages. In those precious seconds he was a man who could still please a woman. The knowledge made his chest ache almost as much as his dick.

He hauled himself to his feet with his mind conjuring visions of bending her over the table and plunging into her balls deep. Janice sat up and reached for his belt, but he'd already released the buckle and popped his jeans button. With shaking hands, he yanked his zipper down and released his erection. They were both panting with anticipation when he jerked her hips to the edge of the table and stepped between her parted thighs. He was primed and ready when he backed away, hissing a curse. "Shit! I almost forgot."

"You don't need it on my account," Janice blurted. "I can't get pregnant again."

"Thank you, Jesus. We're doing this bareback."

Parting her thighs, he took himself in hand, shutting his eyes on a groan at the sensation of his cock sliding through her wet folds. She raised her hips in invitation, crying out when he drove himself inside her, impaling his shaft to the hilt in a single deep, hard thrust. He stilled, his breathing ragged as he fought the urge to thrust again.

"You all right, Red?" He waited with sweat beading his brow.

"Dear God, yes. Don't stop."

Dirk murmured another prayer of thanks. It felt so fucking good to be inside her, filling her. He laid her all the way back, wrapping her legs tightly around his flanks. Her eyes were shut as if lost in pure pleasure. He partially withdrew, only to drive back into her again, setting a steady and relentless rhythm of thrust and retreat, riding her slow and hard until her body vibrated beneath him. His balls tightened, drew up. He gripped her hips tightly, pinning her body against the table as he pumped in and out of her. Harder. Faster. Her hips met him in counterpoint until her inner muscles contracted around him in orgasmic waves.

"Shit. So fucking good. Can't hang on," he groaned, driving into her again and again until a swell of sensation erupted. He squeezed his eyes shut on a groan, spending himself inside her in an explosive climax. Janice's body still quivered with aftershocks, and tears streamed down her cheeks.

"You OK, Red?" Dirk asked softly.

"Yes," she whispered. "More than OK."

Her expression brought a lump into his throat. He

withdrew, physically depleted and mentally confused after a release that no amount of jacking off ever could have satisfied.

He'd sworn not to let sexual frustration interfere with business, but all that went out the window almost the moment she'd walked into his kitchen. He'd thought he could hold himself in check, but he couldn't even be in the same room with her without wanting her.

Hell, she'd only come out for a job. He didn't even want to think about how many acts of sexual harassment he'd just committed. He didn't have a clue how to deal with himself—or with Janice. He jerked his jeans up and turned to the sink, feeling like the lowest kind of predator for taking advantage of her.

He wet a towel with hot water for Janice, but when he turned back, his breath seized in his throat. She was buck naked and propped up on her elbows, hair tangled, face flushed, torso smeared with blueberry syrup, and a slow, shy, sexy-as-hell grin on her face. The vision jolted him to the core.

She looked down at herself and shook her head with a chuckle. "You sure made a real mess of me—inside and out."

He was on her in two steps, marauding her mouth in a ferocious kiss that left them both reeling. He released her just as abruptly. "This towel ain't gonna cut it, Red. You need a shower."

"I couldn't agree more, but I'm feeling kinda sorry for those hungry cows."

"Another half hour won't kill them," he grunted.

"A half hour? I can shower in ten minutes."

"I don't think so. Blueberry stains. You're gonna need some help cleaning all that syrup off. It's dripped all over your back too."

"So you're offering to scrub my back?" Janice's smile grew, stretching to heart-stopping proportions.

"Hell, I made the mess. Least I can do is clean it up properly."

"You are such a hypocrite!" She laughed. "If I recall, all this began when I tried to clean up *your* mess."

"That's right, sweetheart. I manage my own messes. And believe me when I say I've had plenty of experience at it," he added dryly.

"Haven't you ever let anyone else take care of you?" she asked, suddenly serious.

"No. Never had to. I manage."

"But we all need help sometimes," she argued.

"And that's why you're here," he answered back. "I need help with the ranch...and now you need help getting that syrup washed off."

Before she could open her mouth to argue further, he swept her up into his arms and carried her toward the bathroom. She looked down at his chest with an expression of mock dismay. "Now there's syrup all over you too. Guess you'll have to join me? You wash my back and I'll wash yours?"

"You mean scratch," he corrected gruffly, using his elbow to nudge the bathroom door open.

"Doesn't fit the situation." She grinned back at him.

He set her down, jerked back the curtain, and turned on the shower. He waited for the water to heat up and then handed her a bar of soap. "Get in."

"You are too bossy by far, Dirk."

"I can get away with it because I *am* the boss. Now get in."

"Aren't you coming?"

"Already did." He grinned. "And now I'll wash you off."

"How do you expect to accomplish that without getting all wet?"

"I'll manage. Now get in the goddamn shower."

Janice crossed her arms over her chest with a scowl. "Only if you join me. It's only fair."

"Fair?" He shook his head in growing irritation. "Look, Red. There's a big fucking difference here. You're not missing body parts."

"Seems to me you still have all the ones that count."

Dirk didn't trust himself to answer that. Instead, he pushed her toward the shower and spun toward the door. "Come on out when you're done. We've got work to do."

───※───

Janice stared after him once more feeling hurt and bewildered. Until she'd suggested he undress, their exchange had been light and playful. Then he'd suddenly stormed out.

She didn't understand at all until she pulled back the curtain and saw the seat and metal bar on the wall—a handicapped equipped shower. It was only then that it sunk in that he wasn't really rejecting her. He was embarrassed. Dirk was so strong and able that it hadn't even occurred to her that he'd be so self-conscious about his injuries.

She tied up her braid, stepped under the hot water, and

briskly scrubbed herself. He'd made love to her almost fully clothed. She now understood that was intentional as well—he didn't trust her. The thought both saddened and angered her, but trust was a two-way street. Sure he'd been through a lot, but he didn't have an exclusive patent on pain and suffering. He had scars he was reluctant to reveal, so did she. Hers just weren't as visible.

Chapter 14

DIRK WAS WAITING FOR HER OUTSIDE, PACING AND wanting to kick himself. Once more he'd been a jack-ass, lashing out at her for no good reason. He should be happy as hell just to have gotten laid, but the situation was exactly as he'd feared. Being with Janice made him crave everything he couldn't have—a normal life.

He'd accepted long ago, four years to be precise, that he'd never have the kind of freedom or relationship that others took for granted—especially where sex was concerned. It wasn't just the prosthesis; his body was so scarred and mutilated that he'd never be able to reveal it to any woman in the light of day. Her pushing him to do so only reminded him of his inadequacies and frustrated the hell out of him.

Needing a distraction, Dirk headed out to the hay barn to load up the tractor to feed the cattle. He hated having to start feeding hay so early in the season, but it was a cost he would have to bear at least until he could find better winter grazing. The summer in this part of the valley had been dry, which made for lean grass, so he'd left the cattle up on the mountain pastures as long as he'd dared, but it was past time to bring them back down. The temperature up there had already dropped below freezing at night and the higher elevations were covered with snow. They could get more any day. He'd already gathered most of the herd, but he couldn't afford to lose the strays to wolves. He planned to go after them as soon as he got Janice settled. At least a light cover of snow would give him a better ability to track his missing stock.

Dirk found the door to the shop open and his father working on the tractor.

"'Bout time you showed yourself," Justin Knowlton grunted.

"It's barely seven," Dirk protested.

"And I've already been out here for a solid hour. Hand me that wrench, would you?"

"What's wrong with the damn thing now?" Dirk asked.

"Looks like a hydraulic leak. I'll probably have to go into town. We need a replacement hose. Why are you so late?"

"I was occupied with a new hand I hired."

"Oh yeah?" The old man stood up with a groan and then looked around the shop. "Where is he?"

"*He* is actually a *she*," Dirk replied. "Do you remember Janice Combes?"

"Yeah, I do. Didn't she marry that Garrison boy you used to rodeo with?"

"She did, but now she's come back home. She's been looking for ranch work, so I offered her a job."

"Did you now?" His father raised a pair of bushy brows. "Think she can handle it?"

"Yeah, I can handle it," Janice answered for herself. She entered the shop and extended her hand. "Nice to see you again, Mr. Knowlton."

Justin wiped his greasy hands on his coveralls before taking hers. "Been a long time, young lady."

"It has, but I've done just about everything when it comes to ranch work." She nodded to the tractor. "Even fixing machinery."

"Oh yeah?" He slanted his son a dubious look. "Think you can tell me what's wrong with this thing?"

"Probably," Janice said.

Dirk interjected, "We don't have time for you to grill her right now. I need that tractor running. You want me to go to town and get the part or are you gonna do it?"

"I'll go," his father replied. "S'pose I'll take the ol' lady with me. Come by the house later?" he asked Janice. "Donna will want to see you."

"Sure, I'll drop by for a few minutes before I leave."

He nodded to Dirk. "While I get that hose replaced, maybe you'll want to go ahead and take a look at the fence in the south section? The cows pushed part of it over."

"Already on it," Dirk answered. "Took a look at it yesterday. Gotta replace a few rotted posts. Guess I might as well tend to it now."

It took an effort to temper his impatience. His father had supposedly turned operations over to him three years ago. It rankled whenever the old man forgot who was in charge.

"Later then." His father gave a curt nod.

"Ready to get to work?" Dirk asked Janice.

"Not quite yet," she said, once his father was out of earshot. "This is new territory for me too, but it's my turn to apologize. I'm sorry, Dirk. I didn't understand."

"Understand what?"

"How you feel about your…loss."

"And now you think you do?" He scowled back at her and then started throwing fencing tools into the utility cart of the ATV. "I ain't buying that, sweetheart. No one can understand until they've walked in my boots—or maybe I should make that singular," he added bitterly. "I only wear a pair for appearances' sake."

She laid a hand on his arm. "Please. Don't be like this."

"Like what?" he snapped, jerking his arm away.

"I don't know…so…so…angry. Sometimes you seem like the old Dirk, and then at others you just turn like a rattlesnake. What happened to you over there?"

"What happened?" He glared back at her. "I'll tell you what fucking happened! I gave six years of my life and half my leg for nothing!"

"It wasn't for nothing," she protested. "Maybe I didn't believe in the war, but you were doing what you thought was right. I admire that and I respect you for it, but I still don't understand why you did it. Why, Dirk?"

His gaze met hers with a quelling look. "I don't want to talk about it."

"I'm sorry," she said. "I just wanted to understand—"

He hadn't talked about the war to anyone. Ever. Not since the long torturous sessions with the military shrink at Walter Reed. She was pushing him again, but he'd already been an asshole to her once today. Maybe once was enough.

He forced a deep breath in and then slowly exhaled it. "No more apologies," he cut her off. "Let's just move beyond all that, all right? There's a shitload of work to do around here. C'mon. I'll start by showing you around the place."

—∿∿—

Janice spent the day as Dirk's shadow, following his routine. Most of the morning he'd shown her where everything was, from tools to first aid, and then they'd ridden through the herd checking for sickness and injuries. It was all just mundane ranch work and nothing she couldn't have handled on her own, but she was secretly happy just to be with him.

After he'd shown her around and checked the herd, they'd returned to the shop to find the tractor repaired. Janice then offered to load up the hay and haul it out to the cattle. "I know how to operate the bale splitter," she insisted.

"All right," he agreed after a moment of hesitation. "If you can take care of feeding, I'll load up the fence posts."

She was proud that he'd trusted her to do the job and even more that she'd surprised him with her knowledge of farm equipment. After feeding, they'd taken the ATV out to repair the fence. Janice rode behind Dirk with her arms around his waist, and her face mere inches from his back. She loved the smell of him, all musky male with a hint of sweat and spice.

They'd spoken very little since the morning, mainly just exchanging questions and answers, but she was OK with that. She could sense that he still needed to decompress, that his distress from the morning still simmered close to the surface. In her experience, silence and mindless farm chores were the most therapeutic to a troubled soul.

They worked together with Dirk stretching the barb wire and Janice pounding the staples into each post. They'd finished the last strand of the last post when Dirk cut the wire with a grunt of satisfaction, straightened, and tossed the stretcher and wire cutters into the ATV basket. Janice's hammer joined the rest of the tools.

She stood as well with a low moan and a long stretch and then stepped away a pace to admire their handiwork. She massaged her lower back. It was killing her after hours of manual labor that she was no longer accustomed to. She didn't even *want* to think how much her abused body was going to ache the next morning.

"You stiff?" Dirk's voice broke two hours of near silence.

"Yeah"—she laughed—"but it's nothing a couple of Advil and a long hot bath won't fix."

"It's time for a break anyway," he said. "Let's go back to the house and I'll fix us something to eat."

She hopped behind him on the ATV but they didn't speak again the whole ride back to the bunkhouse, or while he fixed a simple meal of grilled cheese sandwiches. Just being in his kitchen again had her on edge. She sat at the same table where they'd joined so passionately only hours ago. She'd never be able to sit here again without thinking of him moving inside her. She wanted to feel him again. With his back to her, she was free to watch him unobserved. Her gaze tracked over him, inciting a quiver of desire. Even injured as he was, Dirk was still one big, strong, and very desirable man.

Dirk worked with a fascinating economy of movement, his actions in the kitchen just as brisk and efficient as he'd been setting fence posts. In minutes he placed a plate in front of her and then pulled a couple of beers from the fridge, popped the tops, and handed her one.

"Go ahead," he urged.

Janice took a big gooey bite of her sandwich and rolled her eyes in rapture. It was absolutely delicious. Definitely not Wonder Bread and Kraft American. "What kind of cheese is this, anyway? It's fabulous."

"Gouda with fresh basil on sourdough." He took a long swig from his bottle but didn't touch his sandwich. "You ever miss him?"

"Who?" His question had taken her completely off guard.

"Grady. You said Cody adjusted quickly to his death, but what about you?" His gaze searched hers. "Can't be easy losing someone you've shared years of your life with."

Janice didn't want to sound cold, but she also couldn't lie. "You asked if I missed him. Maybe I miss the man he *used* to be, but not who he became. Things changed…*he* changed. There's a lot of stuff you don't know, Dirk. Stuff I don't want to talk about."

"Maybe I know more than you think. He and I traveled together a long time. I know how he was, especially with women. I know how he treated them. Did he hurt you?"

She looked away. "Please. It's an ugly story that I don't want to talk about. I just want to move beyond it." She took another bite but it might have become sawdust between slices of cardboard. She'd been starving moments ago, but now her appetite was replaced by a giant knot in her stomach at the thought of reliving the nightmare. She pushed her plate away and watched him watching her. "Look, Dirk, I didn't press you when you didn't want to talk about the marines."

"That's different," he said.

"How? I've been through a hell of my own."

"Then tell me. We're damned well gonna talk about this, Red. I have some Pendleton or Jack Daniel's if you need fortification, but you're not leaving here until you tell me everything that happened. There's stuff I need to know. Did you love him?"

Janice sighed. There was no point in fighting him. He'd either pull it from her piece by agonizing piece, or she could just bite the bullet and get it over with once and for all.

"No, Dirk. I didn't love him."

"Then why did you do it? Why'd you take up with Grady?"

"I told you why! My father was sick. I needed help and he was there." She'd been desperate and felt like she had no one else to turn to. She'd even thought she might grow to love Grady in time, but she hadn't really known him at all.

"You told me that part, but it doesn't explain why you married him." He was watching her too closely. He suspected there was more to the story and there was.

She looked away, her voice dropping to a whisper. "Shortly after he and I got involved, I found out I was pregnant. My father was sick. My mother couldn't help me. What else was I to do? Grady said he'd take care of me. It wasn't so bad at first, but you and I both know what an addictive personality Grady had. He was hooked on the adrenaline rush of bull riding. His drinking got heavier. Then there were other women."

She was too embarrassed to mention the porn. That was her private humiliation. He'd even made her watch it with him. Rather than being a turn-on, it had made her feel dirty. Once he was gone, she'd conducted a thorough search-and-destroy mission.

He shook his head. "Shit, Janice. I had no idea. No," he corrected himself. "That's a lie. I just hoped it would be different, but men like him don't usually change."

"Grady was always arrogant and full of himself, but his success only brought out the worst in him. He was incapable of love…of fidelity…but it was meth that pushed him over the edge."

"Meth?" Dirk almost choked on his beer.

"Yeah. I think he'd been using a while before I ever knew. He probably got turned onto it by one of the buckle bunnies he'd been screwing around with. A lot of people use it to enhance sex. It's supposed to heighten arousal and delay orgasm, sometimes for hours. I'd never been around drugs, so I didn't recognize what was happening until it was too late. I only noticed the changes—the mood swings, sudden rages, insomnia. I had already refused to have sex with him anymore, but by then he couldn't get it up at all. They call it crystal dick. Of course that only incited more rage. It was a horrible cycle."

"Shit, Janice. Why didn't you just up and leave him?"

"I was going to. I knew he was out of control. I was even saving up money to come back home, but when it came down to it, I couldn't just walk out on him if there was any chance I could help him through it… God knows I tried."

"You can't help someone who doesn't want to help himself."

"I know that now."

His expression grew grimmer. "What happened?"

"He finally agreed to rehab, but it only lasted a few weeks. He left the program early for fear the bull-riding association would find out where he was. It wasn't long before it started all over again. I knew it would kill him if he didn't get off it... I was right." Her eyes burned and her throat knotted but she refused to shed any more tears.

"All the reports said his death was a bull-riding accident," Dirk said.

"It was," Janice replied, "but the accident probably wouldn't have happened if he wasn't high. Meth would have killed him anyway—even if the bull hadn't. No one else knows about all this, Dirk. There was an inquiry by the bull-riding association, but the idea of a drug-related scandal scared the shit out of them, so I was able to keep it all quiet. I thank God for Cody's sake. My greatest fear was that he'd grow up under that shadow—that stigma.

"By then I felt so beaten down. Cody was pretty much my reason for being...and the hope of making a better life for him is the only thing that's kept me together. Now I'm just trying to put it all behind us."

He was quiet for a long time. "I knew things weren't right when I came out to Vegas for the World Championships, but I thought it was just the whoring. Why the hell didn't you tell me the rest?"

"Part of me wanted to, but when did I ever have a chance? You left without a word."

Another heavy silence weighted the air.

"Why did you leave like that, Dirk? What happened between you and Grady?"

"You did."

"Me?" she exclaimed. "What's that supposed to mean?"

"I didn't like what I saw in Vegas, so I kept a promise."

"You aren't making any sense. What do you mean?"

He gave a resigned sigh. "I told Grady the night I left Cheyenne that he'd answer to me if he ever mistreated you, so I beat the shit out of him, just like I swore I would. I left thinking I'd set him back on the straight and narrow... Apparently I was wrong."

"*You* broke his jaw? He said he was assaulted by a drunk in a bar."

"It was in the parking lot outside the bar and neither of us was drunk...well, not completely drunk."

Janice gazed at him incredulous. "I don't understand you at all. If you cared anything about me, why did you leave in the first place?"

He swallowed hard. "I had my reasons. Look, Red, it's one thing to talk about what really happened but what-ifs are a waste of gray matter. It's all water under the bridge now. There's no point in rehashing it."

Her gaze searched his. "So where does this leave us now?"

"Us?" he repeated with a humorless laugh. "There can't be any 'us.' I'm afraid that train's done left the station."

"What was this morning?"

"This morning was great. It was fucking incredible," he added with emphasis. "But it doesn't change anything. Great sex doesn't mean happily ever after, Red."

"Is that all this was about to you? Great sex?"

He shrugged. "What did you expect? I told you how it is. If that's not enough for you, you want more than I can give you."

Her eyes blazed. "Why you selfish bastard! You *could* if you wanted to. You just *won't*!"

"Look at me! I told you already, I'm a fucking mess and my life is turning to shit. I can never *be* what you need."

"What I need? What makes you the authority on what I need? Did you ever think that maybe I might be what *you* need?"

His defensive walls came up. "I don't want or *need* your fucking pity!" He knew his reply stung her, but he was scared shitless and was just doing what he'd done before—pushing her away. This time, however, she pushed him right back. Literally.

"Just. Stop." Eyes blazing, she poked him in the chest. Hard. "You know that's not what I meant! I'm not gonna let you do it again. You can't have it both ways. We need to resolve this—one way or another. I can't work for you like this. Either you want me or you don't." She stared him down, hands on hips.

"Please, Red." He raked his hair. "You already know I want you. That's not the issue—"

"Then what *is* your damned issue? You're gonna have to make up your mind, Dirk, because I'm not playing games. I'm not gonna wait around until you decide you're ready, because I'm ten years *past* ready."

"I've already told you. I *can't* do a relationship."

"And I can't *do* meaningless sex. If you want me you get the whole package. Nothing less. We've both messed up our lives, but it's not too late, don't you see that?"

"I don't see it that way. This whole thing was a big mistake, one that can't happen again. Continuing would be nothing but senseless torture—for both of us." It was pointless. The last thing he wanted was for her to walk out on him, but what she was asking…demanding…was just too friggin' hard. She deserved far more than animal copulation, but that's all he had to offer. Anything more was impossible.

"Last chance, Dirk. If I walk outta here, I'm not coming back." She looked to the door.

"You have to know I don't want that," he answered softly. For four years, he'd wrestled with bitterness and self-pity, isolating himself even from his immediate family. Now Janice had entered his life and offered him his heart's desire—the chance to reclaim some of the normalcy he'd lost. But the thought that he'd only fuck it up all over again scared the shit out of him.

"Do I? Frankly, I have no clue what you want," she answered. "Maybe you can tell me?"

"What I want?" He scrubbed a hand down his face. "Right now it might as well be the fucking moon."

—∿∿—

Janice left the bunkhouse palming her burning eyes and feeling completely drained. She'd been riding an emotional roller coaster almost from the moment she'd laid eyes on Dirk, and she had a sinking feeling the ride was far from over. Was he worth it?

He'd certainly shaken her faith, but deep down she still believed he was. She'd pushed him really hard, but he needed for someone to do exactly that. His walls were so thick, it would take nothing short of a battering ram to knock them down. One step at a time, she reminded herself.

Lost in her thoughts, she was beside her truck with keys in hand before she remembered her promise to Dirk's father to drop by before leaving. Although emotionally and physically spent, she'd never be able to look Justin or Donna Knowlton in the face if she reneged.

"Janice Combes!" Donna Knowlton wore a look of pleased surprise when she answered Janice's knock. "You sure don't look anything like the gangly little redheaded tomboy anymore. I don't think I would even have recognized you if Justin hadn't told me you were coming by." She stepped back to invite Janice inside. "Come on in, sugar."

Janice wiped her boots and stepped inside. Her gaze surveyed the huge living room with its massive stone fireplace and floor-to-ceiling windows offering a breathtaking view of the Tobacco Root Mountains. She'd always loved the Knowlton place. It was exactly the kind of rustic but elegant home she'd always fantasized about.

"Would you like some coffee?" Donna asked.

"No thank you, ma'am. I really can't stay long. I was hoping to be back by the time Cody gets home from school."

"Cody's your son?"

"Yes, ma'am. He's nine now and keeps me pretty busy."

"Don't I know it." Donna laughed. "Dirk and Wade gave me most of these gray hairs before I even turned thirty!"

"You wear it well, Mrs. Knowlton." Janice always thought Donna Knowlton's silver hair was particularly attractive and set off her vivid blue eyes.

"Thank you, sugar," Donna replied with just a hint of Texas twang. "But please call me Donna. 'Mrs. Knowlton' makes me feel so *old*. Come and sit a short spell. It's not often I get a chance for any girl talk."

Janice perched uneasily on the edge of an overstuffed leather couch.

"How's your mama?" Donna asked. "I haven't seen her in a good while."

"I'm afraid she's developed a few health issues the last couple of years. She's not able to get out much. That's part of the reason I came home. She helps look after Cody, and I help look after her."

"And who looks after *you*?" Donna asked softly.

Janice looked away, discomposed by the question. "Well, I guess I do, ma'am."

"You're a young and attractive woman, Janice. You should have someone to take care of you. Justin told me you came looking for work. I was surprised by Dirk's offer, but I couldn't be happier. If any man ever needed a good woman…"

The heat of a flush invaded Janice's face. "I'm sorry, Mrs. Knowlton, but it's really not like that. I'm just here for a job—"

"Sugar, I sure hope not," Donna protested. "Dirk's too much like his daddy. Neither wears his heart on his sleeve, but I know my son well enough to see he has feelings for you."

"What makes you say that?" Janice asked.

"For starters, he's spent more time here at the house in the past week than he has in the past three years. It began the day after you were out here."

A moment later her gaze flickered past Janice's shoulder. "Well, speak of the devil and he always appears." Donna beamed a bright smile when Justin Knowlton entered. Dirk followed.

Justin tipped his hat to Janice. "Good to see you came by, young lady."

"Mama." Dirk doffed his own hat to kiss his mother's cheek. He then nodded to Janice. "I'm glad I caught you before you left."

Donna gave her a knowing look.

"Your mother and I have just been catchin' up a bit," Janice blurted, uneasy at Dirk's entrance. "I've enjoyed the chat, Mrs....I mean Donna...but I've really got to go now." She took to her feet.

"So soon?" Donna cried in dismay. "Please tell me you'll come back for Sunday dinner. I'll be making brisket. Bring your mama and your son with you."

Janice looked to Dirk with uncertainty. The last thing she wanted to do was impose on his family when he'd made it clear he needed some time.

"Come out at noon." Dirk spoke up before she could decline. "That'll give Cody and Red Man a couple hours to get acquainted."

"Are you sure about that?" she asked. "You don't have to do this, you know."

"I know that," he said. "I want to."

"All right then." Janice smiled and addressed his parents. "I'll look forward to seeing you both again on Sunday."

"C'mon, Red, I'll walk you out." Dirk pressed a hand to the small of her back. "There's a couple things I shoulda told you earlier." His tone was bland and matter-of-fact, but his expression was anything but. He didn't speak again until they stood beside her truck. A minute of strained silence ticked by.

Janice reached for the door.

"Wait," he said, his hand coming over hers. "There's something more I gotta say. I was afraid I might not get another chance."

She turned to face him, leaning back against the door, arms crossed over her chest. "Whatever it is had better be damned good."

"What you asked me in the bunkhouse…I want my old life back. But I know I can't have it. I know there's no going back."

"No," she whispered. "There's no going back. Too many things have changed. *We've* changed."

He rubbed the back of his neck and exhaled. "I don't know how to go about this. I don't know what you want from me, or *how* to give it to you. I'm fucking clueless, Red, don't you see? You have no idea what you'd be getting into." He was trying to warn her off again but at the same time a flicker of hope seemed to light in his eyes.

"Maybe I know better than you think," she challenged. She knew that if they got further involved, their entire relationship would have to be rebuilt on a completely different foundation from what they'd had before. But she was prepared for that.

"This has happened so damned fast. You gotta give me a little time to learn the game. I don't even know the rules."

"I don't know all the rules either."

He reached out for her hand and pulled her in close. "I don't want you to go. Do you think we can maybe just try playing this thing by ear?" He looked so uncertain, so vulnerable.

She instantly relaxed against him. "Yeah," she replied. "I think we could maybe try that."

He brushed his lips brusquely over hers. "You deserve a lot better than me, Red. I can't promise you I'll be worth it, but I'll damn sure try."

Chapter 15

It was almost an hour before sunrise when Janice drove into the Flying K. She hopped out of her truck, tightening her collar against the frigid morning air. Dirk was already outside waiting with two saddled horses. Her heart sped up when he greeted her with a nod and a half smile.

"Morning, Red. I'm glad to see you," he said softly. "I can't even tell you how glad."

"I guess I'm a true sucker for punishment," she replied. "You goin' after the missing stock now?"

He nodded. "I shoulda gone yesterday, but I got a bit sidetracked." His gaze met hers, a heated reminder of how they'd spent the earlier part of the day.

"So I guess you're not making pancakes first?" she taunted with a slow, crooked smile.

"Hell, no. It'll be coffee in a travel mug and a wad of beef jerky in the saddlebags. Don't know if I'll ever be able to make pancakes again. I'm already afraid of getting a hard-on if I even look at a bottle of syrup."

"Need any help?" She nodded to the horses.

"Nope, got it covered."

"Can I ride with you? It might not be easy if you end up having to carry down an orphaned calf or something like that."

"Already thought of that. The bay here's yours. Are you dressed warm enough to ride?"

"Yeah. I'm good." She eyed the twelve-gauge shotgun holstered with the saddle. "Grizzlies?"

"Not expecting any, but it pays to be prepared for them." He tossed her a twenty-two-caliber carbine. "Know how to use it?"

"Of course," Janice replied. "But what for? You already have the shotgun."

"Seems we got ourselves a wolf problem on the mountain," Dirk replied. "Wade and I encountered a pack last time I went up there." He added grimly, "I'm hoping we locate live cattle, but I'm taking some rope and tarp just in case we find more carcasses instead." He patted the pack behind his cantle.

"If the wolves got them, won't the Livestock Loss Board cover it?" she asked.

"Yes and no," Dirk replied. "There's a bunch of hoops to jump through in order to file a claim and then they're only going to compensate for average value when I've got three times that invested in each head. That's not even taking into account the years and expense of breeding them. They're damn sure worth more to me alive."

"Then I hope we find them," Janice said.

"The weather report predicted a light dusting last night in the higher elevations. If so, it'll make tracking a whole lot easier. Course Toby and Tallulah are coming along. Best cattle dogs you'll ever find."

The two lolling canines rose smartly to attention at the mention of their names. She reached out her hand to let them sniff. Toby nudged it. Janice scratched his head. "Toby and Tallulah?" She eyed the mottled pair curiously. "They don't look like any herd dog I've seen before. What breed are they?"

"Catahoula Leopard dogs," Dirk replied. "Not just herd dogs, but bred to track and hunt too. If there's still any live cattle up there, they'll find 'em and flush 'em out."

It was still dark when they guzzled down some coffee and set out. Janice rode behind, her gaze locked in admiration on Dirk's back. Sitting tall and straight, he still cut a helluva figure in the saddle, whether he realized it or not. It seemed the more time she spent with him, the less she noticed his injuries. They'd come a long way in a short time. She only hoped she might one day help him to forget them too.

They rode a couple of miles with the two dogs trotting eagerly alongside, before hitting the main trail leading up to the mountain pastures. The sun was now cresting, painting colors across the eastern horizon.

Janice drew up her horse. "It's so beautiful. I can't tell you how much I missed the sunrises and sunsets when I was in Las Vegas."

Dirk pulled up beside her. "We can take a short breather here if you like."

"Thanks. I'd like that. Although many people wax poetic about the desert, it just seems so desolate compared to this."

"I've seen some amazing skies in the open desert," he said. "Endless with so many stars at night that it boggles the mind." His voice drifted off.

Their horses stood side by side, panting vapor into the frosty air as Dirk and Janice watched in awe-filled appreciation as the sun rose, streaking its gold and pink hues across the big Montana sky.

"Do you think about it much?" she asked. "Your time over there?"

"I try not to," he said. "But it invades my thoughts every single day, whether I like it or not."

"Why did you join the marines?"

"Told you I don't want to talk about it."

"I didn't want to talk about my past either."

Dirk stiffened in the saddle. "You want me to unload all my shit on you? Is that what you want?"

His dark expression and gruff response told her she was pushing his comfort zone again, but she wasn't going to back off so easily. "Don't you think it's only fair when you made me unload mine?"

⸻

He said nothing for the longest time but the clouds of vapor came harder, faster as he fought the impulse to spur his horse and leave the questions behind. But he couldn't outrun the memories even if he tried. They were always with him. Part of him. Even now, it was still a daily struggle to keep thoughts of that time and place at bay.

"I'd been floundering for months," he began. "Didn't know what the hell was wrong with me. I was so restless, like I wanted to crawl out of my own skin. But watching the life drain out of Seth Lawson flipped some kind of switch. I had to get away. Clear my head, so I got in my truck and drove. Didn't even know where I was going, just had a powerful yen to see the ocean. I headed west on I-80 and didn't stop until I hit San Francisco. I remember parking the truck at Ocean Beach, pulling off my boots, and wading out into the surf. Jeans and all. Jesus, it was cold! I hadn't expected that.

"I stayed a couple of days and then headed south

down the Pacific Coast Highway and ended up in San Diego. An old rodeo buddy of mine was stationed there at Camp Pendleton. I called him up and then suddenly it was perfectly clear. I enlisted the next day in the U.S. Marine Corps. *Oorah. Semper fi.*

"At first I was zealous for the war, certain we were right. That the cause was just. Yeah, that's exactly what I told myself. We took down the Evil Empire and cleaned up the whole fucking mess in Iraq. Mission accomplished. Or so we thought." He shook his head with a bitter laugh.

"When I re-upped, I thought it was the same war, just a different mission. But it wasn't the same war. We were stalking that murdering sonofabitch Bin Laden in a place where you couldn't ever know who was the enemy. The day I lost my leg was just a normal day patrolling a quiet mountain village. We were walking among men, even women and children, who nodded, smiled, and salaamed even as they were planting IEDs to blow us to kingdom come.

"We didn't see it coming. Maybe we should have. It had been too quiet for too long. Without warning, all hell broke loose. Explosions everywhere. Men screaming. Bodies disintegrating before our eyes. Do you have any clue what an IED can do? Helmets and body armor are useless. They don't kill. IEDs vaporize. I had to have pieces of my best buddy surgically plucked outta me. That's the fucking devastation of an IED."

Janice whispered, "I can't even begin to imagine it."

"No. You. Can't," he replied through clenched teeth. "No one can who hasn't seen it." He shut his eyes finding it hard to breathe. He never allowed himself to think about it because it always sucked him down into the dark place—a hell filled with smoke and fire, sweat, and blood, excrement…and death.

The old feeling of panic started closing in, the terror that still jarred him awake in a cold sweat. Janice's soft voice pulled him back. "But you *lived*, Dirk. At least you got to come home."

"Yeah. I lived. Small consolation when I lost six men and then had to deal with a fucking court martial to defend our actions."

"Dear God. I didn't know. What happened?"

"Acquitted and came home. End. Of. Story."

"But—"

"I've told you about as much as I can stomach. I don't want to talk about this shit anymore…or ever again for that matter. Ready?"

Dirk didn't wait for her reply but urged his horse forward and up the steep and rocky incline. They rode another hour in a tense silence before discovering the first tracks in the snow. On examination, they proved to be equine rather than bovine.

"Horses?" Janice asked. "Who would have ridden horses up here?"

"They weren't riding. These tracks are from a band of renegade mustangs that Wade and I saw."

"Mustangs? Where the heck did they come from? I thought the only herd left in all of Montana was over in the Pryor Mountains."

"Not anymore," Dirk said. "'Bout twenty miles north there's an outfit that took on a bunch of them from the BLM."

"Really? I hadn't heard anything about it. Which outfit was that?"

"The Circle S, old man Sutton's place," Dirk replied. "It seems his widow has pulled out of cattle and now plans to turn the whole spread into a wild horse sanctuary or some shit like that. Of course she doesn't know what the hell she's getting into, but the BLM don't care. They're just desperate to get as many horses off their hands as possible."

"Isn't that the truth." Janice shook her head. "There's a real problem in Nevada right now with the ongoing drought. It was on the news all the time. There's over twenty thousand wild horses living in that desert and not enough water to sustain them. They were planning some emergency roundups when I left. Hopefully some of those horses will find homes."

"Lottsa luck there," he scoffed. "What kinda fool's gonna mess with a Mustang when even dead-broke ranch horses are a dime a dozen?"

"So what's the Suttons' plan?" Janice asked.

"Dunno and ain't too keen to find out, but I s'pose I'll have to go by there soon enough. I need them to move those horses outta here before calving season. I'm not about to lose any more stock because a herd of Mustangs ran the calves to death."

"But, Dirk, how the heck are they going to catch them?"

Dirk shrugged. "That's their problem. There's a lot of good cowboys looking for work. They'll figure something out."

Toby froze, ears perked and nose raised. Tallulah began sniffing the ground.

Dirk pulled up his horse. "Got something, boy?"

Toby gave a single bark and bounded off to the right through a large patch of sagebrush with Tallulah hot on his heels.

"They found a scent all right. If it's the cattle, they'll herd and hold 'em for us." Dirk spurred his horse with Janice following. A moment later, he reined up again to listen, head cocked to the side. "Sounds like a bawling calf to me."

Janice listened intently, trying to isolate other sounds from that of the two panting horses but heard nothing until the dogs sounded a cry.

"Yup. They got 'em, all right. Thank you, Jesus!" Dirk declared with a smile and spun his horse around in the direction of the baying dogs.

Three hours later, Janice dismounted to open the wire gate, the dogs standing sentinel as Dirk drove the two cows and solitary calf into the pasture.

He sighed and dismounted from his horse. "Recovered three. Not a total loss, I s'pose. I just hope the damned wolves stay on the mountain. For now, I guess the dogs'll have to put in some over-time babysitting the herd. Least until I find some safe winter grazing."

"What about installing fladry lines?" Janice asked. "I've heard they help keep wolves away."

"It's cost prohibitive and it's only a short-term solu-tion," Dirk said. "The wolves eventually get used to them flapping and then pay no more heed. I'm not too worried about it right now though. Don't anticipate any real trouble until next spring when I move the herd back up the mountain. I may have to bite the bullet at that point and hire someone to babysit."

"Got anyone in mind?" she asked.

He shook his head. "No, but I've got enough on my plate right now without fretting about that. Speaking of plates... I'm just about starved."

"Me too," Janice confessed. "I'm not a big fan of jerky."

He shook his head. "I warned you ahead of time what was on the menu."

"You did, but I also recall you promising to grill me the best T-bone I ever ate if you got your strays back."

"I did at that," he said. "You free tonight?"

"Tonight?" She hadn't really expected him to take her taunt seriously. "I could be," she replied. "But I'd want to run home and check on Cody and Mama first and of course take a shower and change."

"Tell you what, Red. I'm so damned happy, I feel like celebrating. Since you plan on getting all cleaned up anyway, how 'bout I take you out instead of cooking? I got a place in mind if you don't object to a bit of a drive. Might not be *quite* as good as my home-grilled T-bone, but it's pretty damned close."

"Oh yeah?" Janice smiled. "It sounds great, but if I'm gonna be out for very long, I'd need to get Cody settled for the night." She looked at her watch. It was almost four o'clock. "It could be two or three hours before I could be ready."

"Then I'll make us a late reservation."

"It would have to be after seven." She tried to keep the disappointment out of her voice. "You probably don't want to wait that long for supper."

"Don't be so sure about that, sweetheart," he replied. "I'll pick you up at seven thirty. I may be a slow starter, but I'm learning that some things are worth waiting for."

———∿∿———

Arriving home twenty minutes later, Janice came in the back door and hung her hat and coat on the pegs. Her mother was already starting supper and Cody was at the kitchen table doing his homework.

"Hey, Mom!" Cody looked up. "Think you can help me with my spelling words?"

"Sure thing." Janice smiled and ruffled his red hair before sitting down beside him.

"How was your day?" her mother asked Janice.

"Interesting. Cody would have loved it. Dirk and I rode up the mountain and brought down some missing cattle. His dogs, Toby and Tallulah, found them for us."

"Really? What kind of dogs are they?" Cody asked.

"Catahoula Leopard dogs."

"They're part leopard?" Cody asked.

"No, silly. But they do have spots."

"Can I have a dog?" Cody asked.

"Make an A on your spelling test, and maybe we'll talk about it."

"But I hate spelling!" he replied sullenly. "Spelling sucks!"

"Cody. You watch your mouth."

He hung his head. "Sorry, Mom. I'm just no good at it."

"Then you need to work at it more. You can't get good at anything without practice, Cody. Just like riding horses."

"I sure like horses better than spelling…or math… or reading."

"All right, I get it." Janice laughed. "I didn't like school much either at your age but had to keep my grades up in order to compete on the rodeo team."

"Can I do that too when I get bigger?"

"Sure you can," Janice said. "Which leads to some news you're gonna be real happy about."

"What's that?" Cody asked.

"The Knowltons invited us all out to the ranch on Sunday. Dirk said to come out early 'cause he has a horse for you to ride."

Cody's eyes lit up like a Christmas tree. "For real?"

"Yeah. He's a big sorrel named Red Man. Now, let's get to work on your spelling."

Janice could hardly remember the last time she'd put on a dress, or eaten out at any place that required reservations. Even though there wasn't a place in the whole state of Montana where jeans weren't welcome, Dirk's parting words inspired a desire to "wow" him. Although she was once a clueless cowhand, her years of waitressing in Vegas had taught her the value of a feminine appearance.

She rifled through her closet for a little black dress she'd bought after Grady had qualified for his first world championship. There was a sponsored big pre-event party for the bull draws and she'd wanted to do him proud, but he wasn't the only male who'd taken notice when she'd worn it. Although the dress was several years old, the sheath style still worked, and—more importantly—it still fit, albeit a tad tighter through the hips and boobs. Her matching pumps were also a bit outdated, but she doubted anyone in rural Montana would notice.

She pinned up her simple French braid into a chignon and then applied a touch of makeup, knowing this was a version of her that Dirk had never seen before. Would he like it? At the sound of his truck pulling in the drive, she stepped in front of the mirror her heart pounding with sudden self-doubts, but she had no time to change her mind. She exited her room and descended the stairs, feeling far too much like a nervous schoolgirl on prom night.

She was on the landing when he entered. He wore a crisply pressed dress shirt in a shade of blue that set off his icy colored eyes and a pair of snug-fitting jeans with knife-edge creases. He looked up the staircase in a sudden double-take that made Janice freeze in her tracks. Her pulse raced as his gaze swept slowly over her. His mouth curved into a slow wolfish grin that heated her from the inside out.

She descended the rest of the stairs on shaky legs. Dirk met her at the bottom step. His arm came around her waist and his lips brushed her cheek. "My, my, Red," he murmured in a tone that promised very wicked things. "You take my breath away."

His words made Janice acutely self-conscious, but she still managed a flippant reply. "You don't clean up so bad yourself, cowboy."

"Where's Cody and your mama?" he asked.

"Mama's arthritis is acting up real bad and Cody's upstairs playing video games," Janice said. "I'd call him down here but you're already gonna get more than your fill of him on Sunday. He's beside himself with excitement."

"I'm looking forward to it too," Dirk said.

His reply surprised her. "You are?"

"Sure. I'd like to get to know him better. I haven't been around a lot of kids, but I like 'em well enough."

"Well, be prepared. Cody'll talk your ear off. He's not the least bit shy and has a mind of his own. He hasn't quite learned when to back down on an argument and is always getting called out by the teachers for it."

"He might suffer for it now," Dirk said, "but it'll play to his advantage later in life." He glanced at his watch. "We'd better be going. Our reservation's for eight thirty and it's an hour's drive."

―――∿∿∿―――

Janice began peppering him with questions almost as soon as he pulled onto the highway. "Where are we going?"

"You'll see when we get there," he replied.

When he turned north on 287, she remarked, "There's nothing in Whitehall, and Bozeman's a good ninety minutes away."

"Yup," he agreed.

"We going to Belgrade?" she asked.

"Nope." Dirk shook his head.

"Manhattan maybe? I've heard Land of Magic's really good."

"It is at that," he concurred with a nod.

"So that's where you're taking me?"

"Wrong again."

"C'mon, Dirk! Quit tormenting me and spill it."

"No way. Anticipation is half the pleasure. Besides, I'm having way too much fun torturing you."

Janice huffed.

He chuckled and flashed a teasing grin. "Guess you don't read many mystery novels, do you, Red?"

"No. Haven't read much of anything since high school, but why would you say that?"

"'Cause you can't stand suspense. Bet you talk during movies too, don'tcha?"

"Maybe," she replied.

"I'll have to remember that." He gave her a teasing leg squeeze. Then his hand rested there. She laid hers on top of it.

"Bet I can make you talk." She slid her skirt up a few inches.

His mouth firmed. "I don't think so, sweetheart." He shook his head, determined not to give an inch, but she gave him several more—inches of bare thigh that is.

"You *sure* you don't want to tell me where we're going?"

She guided his hand a little higher. She wasn't wearing panty hose. Her skin was silky smooth. He got a whiff of vanilla mixed with just a hint of feminine arousal. He inhaled deeper and shifted in his seat. His gaze briefly strayed from the road to meet hers. "I don't think you want to continue this, Red. Not if you're hungry, anyway."

"I'm hungry all right." She licked her lips and slid his hand a little bit higher. "Matter of fact, I'm about starved, but I always like to think about what's on the menu ahead of time. Don't you?"

He didn't have to. His mind had been stuck in that one gear almost from the moment she'd shown up.

He snatched back his hand and pulled off the road,

cutting the ignition and yanking her across the bench seat. He groaned in surrender as his mouth claimed hers for a searing kiss.

She opened to him with a soft moan and their kiss deepened, their tongues dueling, every slick stroke sending surges of sensation rippling through him. She guided his hand deeper between her thighs. He jolted in surprise when his fingertips came into direct contact with her wet sheath. "No panties, Red?"

She flashed him a half smile. "Call me optimistic. I'd hoped to get lucky tonight." She squeezed her thighs on another soft moan when he sank his fingers inside her. He released her to adjust the seat, sliding it all the way back, but there still wasn't room to get her on his lap.

"Fucking steering wheel's in the way," he growled. "Put yours back. All the way."

Her gaze widened. "Right now? In the truck? What about our dinner reservation?"

"Guess we're gonna be late. I warned you where this was headed."

"But somebody could see us!" Janice cried with a look of panic.

"You started it, Red. You're gonna have to finish it."

"I don't think so, cowboy," she replied. "You're gonna have to deliver on that steak dinner first."

He mumbled a stream of curses. "I never counted you a cock tease, Red."

"I'm not a tease," she protested. "You just said yourself not a minute ago that anticipation is half the pleasure."

"Anticipation? I've lived like a fucking monk for the past four years. If you think I'm gonna drive the rest of the way with a stiff dick, think again."

"I'm sorry 'bout that, but you're gonna have to feed me first."

He started the truck up with another mumbled curse.

"How far away are we?" she asked a minute later.

"Still thirty ball-aching minutes," he ground back.

"You know," she began with a sly smile, "if this really is such an unbearable trial for you, maybe I can alleviate your discomfort." She unsnapped her seat belt and slid closer, her hands working deftly on his belt, then popping his fly button. "Of course, I'm pretty sure this is all kinds of illegal."

"What the hell are you—" He sucked in a breath as she eased his zipper down and slipped her hand inside his jeans, wrapping her fingers around his swollen dick.

"Keep driving, Dirk."

He was rock-hard and finding it harder to keep his eyes on the road as she slowly jacked him up and down, squeezing and stroking.

"Better?" she asked.

"Damn, Janice," he hissed. "You're gonna kill me."

"Oh, I doubt that."

Next thing he knew, her head was in his lap. Her mouth and hot, velvety tongue were moving up and down his shaft, rasping along his length, circling his head and lapping at the slit, turning his mind into jelly. The lines on the road blurred when she closed her lips around him, sucking him into the hot wet cavern of her mouth.

Holy shit! He released one hand from the wheel and curled the other around her nape. She drew harder with her lips, working him deeper into her throat. Her lips and throat muscles contracting, milking him. He was drowning in sensation, in mindless pleasure. He was losing it fast. Maybe he was already lost. Either way, it felt so fucking good to give himself up to her.

His balls contracted. His hands squeezed the wheel. He was panting with the effort to hold back. He pulled off the road again as the urge to come swelled inside him.

"You gotta stop now, Red...right fucking now... unless you plan to finish me off."

"Oh, I'll finish you all right." She sucked him even deeper, swallowing harder.

His eyes fluttered shut as his orgasm came crashing over him, his cock pulsing in a long series of body-wracking eruptions that left him physically spent.

A moment later, he opened his eyes to gaze down at her through a helpless haze. Her soft brown eyes met his and her mouth curved into that slow, shy smile that always crushed his lungs and left him heaving for breath.

To Janice's dismay, Dirk was quiet the rest of the drive, almost too quiet. Although she'd managed in only a couple of weeks to penetrate his first lines of defense, the question remained whether he'd ever let her all the way in.

They pulled off I-90 at the Trident and Three Forks exit and then headed toward town. "Three Forks?" Janice asked. "What's in Three Forks?"

"You'll see," he answered her cryptically.

A few minutes later he pulled up in front of an elegant white clapboard building. "The old Sacajawea?" she declared in surprise. "I thought it closed years ago."

"It did. But then a new owner bought it and completely restored the place while you were away," Dirk explained. "It's now on the register of historical hotels, and the food is top-notch. Good as anything you had out in Vegas."

He handed her down from the truck and then led her through an elegant foyer to the entrance to Pompey's Grill. Greeting Dirk by name, the maître d' guided them to a cozy booth near the massive stone hearth where a welcoming fire blazed. The hotel restaurant was dark-paneled, candlelit, and intimate, the perfect setting for a romantic dinner.

The maître d' smiled. "Your server will be with you momentarily with a wine list."

"I'm not much for wine myself," Dirk remarked to Janice, "but they have a respectable selection if you'd care for a bottle."

"Not for me, thanks." Janice gave an embarrassed smile. "I admit I'm more of a beer girl."

Their waiter arrived almost instantaneously to present the wine menu and take their drink orders.

"A Blue Moon for the lady and I'll take a Bud," Dirk said.

"Very good. Would you care to hear tonight's dinner specials?" the waiter asked.

"Sure." Janice nodded.

"For starters, we have a crab harumaki, which is a Japanese-style spring roll with red crab, fresh cilantro, napa cabbage, shiitake mushrooms, and fresh ginger, served with a spicy ponzu. Our entrée this evening would be the USDA Prime dry-aged American Kobe tenderloin, locally supplied from the Flying K Ranch."

He presented the full menus. "I'll be back in just a moment with your drinks."

"The beef is from the Flying K?" Janice cocked her head in surprise.

"Yup." Dirk nodded with pride. "Been doing a bit of test marketing in some local places. I hear it's become one of their most popular entrées."

"That's fantastic!" Janice exclaimed.

He beamed back at her. "I admit I'm encouraged. I'm working on something even bigger now. I have some serious interest from a gourmet foods company, but I can't hope to bid for the contract until I can show that I can meet the demand. That means growing the herd, which will require more investment in breeding stock."

"That's the expansion you were talking about."

"Yes." He nodded. "They are only interested in organic, grass-fed beef, which means I also need more grazing pastures. Wade and I have gone head-to-head over this for the past couple of years." Dirk's brows met in a scowl. "He's too damned shortsighted to see the new opportunity."

"Then you can't give up."

"I don't intend to."

The waiter returned with their drinks. "Do you have any questions?"

"Mind if I order for both of us?" he asked Janice.

"Not at all. Please do."

Dirk never even opened the menu. "The crab hamaruki to share, two wedge salads, and two of the Wagyu tenderloins."

"Excellent," the server replied and disappeared.

The service was exceptional and the entire meal superb, especially the beef. In truth, it was the best she'd ever tasted, which only confirmed in Janice's mind that Dirk really was onto something. On top of that, Dirk appeared more relaxed than Janice had ever seen him. They lingered over dinner, laughing and talking until they were the only patrons remaining in the restaurant.

"Would you care for coffee or dessert?" the waiter asked.

"Nothing more for me," Janice groaned, near bursting. "But it was all fabulous."

Dirk's blue gaze met hers. "I agree. It's been the best night I can recall in a very long time."

It was almost eleven o'clock when they finally left the restaurant. Dirk walked her to the passenger side of his truck and paused before opening her door. "It's just occurred to me that I've gone about all of this completely ass backwards."

"What do you mean?" she asked.

"I just realized this is our very first date."

Janice stared at him for a moment and then cracked a smile. "You're right. It is at that."

"Mind if I kiss you?"

"You're *asking*?" She laughed outright.

He grew suddenly serious. He cupped her face with both hands. "A man should never take a woman for granted." His lips met hers, gliding over them with a toe-curling and breath-stealing tenderness. He released her slowly and then stepped back to open the truck door.

"I s'pose that goes both ways," Janice said as he handed her in. "But after *that* meal, I promise you I'm a sure thing."

He held her gaze for a long moment. "That so?"

"Yeah." She licked her lips, tension coiling deep in her belly. "I told you I left the house tonight with a certain optimism."

"Then I'd hate to disappoint you, Red." The words were barely out of his mouth before he spun back toward the inn. "Wait here," he tossed over his shoulder.

Dirk returned a few minutes later, room key in hand. "Last one," he explained. "There's a big wedding party."

She stared at the key. "You got us a room?"

"I want us to do this right for a change. I don't want a quick and dirty fuck in the truck like a coupla horny teenagers. You deserve better than that."

Janice swallowed hard, the significance of his act and his words nearly overwhelming her. It seemed a monumental step from him.

"I admit I'm nervous as hell right now," he confessed, as if reading her mind. "I haven't had a woman in a bed since before… Shit! I've never felt *this* anxious before."

Although he was accustomed to taking charge, she could see he was facing a major crisis of confidence. She twined her arms around his neck. "There's no reason," she said. "All I want…all I need…is you inside me."

He withdrew a few inches, searching her face. "I want that too, Red. So you wanna go inside now?"

"Yeah. I do," she replied.

Moments later, Janice slinked through the lobby, acutely self-conscious about her lack of luggage and knowing she'd feel far more embarrassed when they left after a couple of hours. She hoped they'd be able to sneak out without anyone noticing. As if reading her thoughts, Dirk walked on the inside as they passed by the check-in desk, wrapping his arm protectively around her. He punched the button to call the old-fashioned elevator and pulled her inside the moment the doors opened.

Once they closed again, he hit a button for the second floor and then pinned her to the wall, his thigh wedged between hers. His mouth descended on her neck, licking, sucking, gently biting. Desire bloomed until she thought she'd melt into a puddle on the floor. Her legs were almost ready to give way when the elevator dinged and the doors opened.

<center>~~~</center>

The scent of vanilla had enveloped him the minute the elevator closed. She smelled so damn good that it made him light-headed. She tasted even better. When the bell dinged, he peeled her arms gently but firmly from around his neck, forcing himself to break the kiss before he lost himself in it...in her...completely. He guided her down the hall with his hand poised just above her ass, unlocking the door, his heart pounding erratically with a mix of fear and anticipation. It wasn't their first time together, but this was different. By taking her to bed, he'd be letting his guard down. Completely. And it scared the shit out of him.

The room was dark, but he intentionally bypassed the light switch. He could barely stand to look at himself in the mirror. The thought of seeing revulsion reflected in her eyes terrified him.

Without breaking the kiss, they backed unevenly across the floor toward the bed. Her hands matched the eagerness of her mouth, unbuttoning his shirt and peeling it back to explore his torso. He experienced another instant of panic when she reached for the bedside lamp.

"No." He stayed her hand. "One step at a time, Red. If this is gonna happen, you'll need to grant me a few small concessions."

As if reading his fears, Janice rose up on her toes and cupped her hands around his face. "This is about trust, Dirk. You told me you want to make this work between us. If that's going to happen, you need to trust me."

Holding him, she brushed her lips over his, then worked her way over the scar that marred his face. He stiffened beneath her touch, but tamped down the urge to wrench away.

"Please, Dirk," she whispered, her brown eyes pleading. "Just let go. Let me prove to you that your injuries don't matter to me. Show me we can do this…that we can have this." She feathered more light kisses over the mangled flesh before pressing her warm, lush body against him and sealing her mouth to his.

He kissed her back, his mouth melding with hers, exploring, tasting, growing hungrier when her tongue darted out seeking his, spiking his desire another notch. Edgy as he was, she still had him hard as a post in no time.

She stripped off his shirt, but he knew it was too dark for her to see very much. Even with their eyes adjusted, the dim light wouldn't reveal the worst of it. She tugged his jeans and boxers off his hips, but stopped shy of pushing them all the way down. He sprang free into her warm and eager hands. She caressed his length as she trailed hot and humid kisses down his torso. Lust had him swaying drunkenly on his feet by the time she was face level with his swollen dick. He had to clasp her shoulder for balance.

His lids fluttered shut on a low moan as she drew him into her mouth. She took him deep, gently rolling his balls between her fingers. They tightened beneath her touch. He rocked his hips. She gripped his flexing buttocks and he was gone, his mind blurred to all but sensation. He realized with annoyance that once more he'd let her take control. It wasn't what he wanted, not how he'd planned for this to play out, but it still took a supreme force of will to withdraw from her mouth.

As she'd sucked, stroked, and caressed, his pleasure became hers. She was quickly caught up in his salty taste, his musky scent, and the guttural sounds emerging from his throat. He had to be close to coming. His eyes were shut, the muscles in his neck straining, his chest rising and falling erratically when he abruptly withdrew.

"What's wrong?" She looked up at him with surprise.

"Nothing," he growled. "I appreciate the gesture, but it's not what I want."

"I thought it would help you relax."

He brought her back to her feet. "Not this time, Red. This has gotta happen on my terms."

She'd gone down with the single thought of making him forget his fears, but if he needed to exert control, she wasn't about to balk. He'd never be able to handle any kind of relationship until he reclaimed his sense of manhood. And that would never happen until he regained his confidence in bed. She was determined to do whatever it took to help him.

"And what are those?" she asked.

He pulled her close, rocking his pelvis into hers and squeezing the globes of her ass. His big hard erection pressed into her belly. He kissed her deeper, licking up her neck and then around the shell of her ear. He sank his teeth into her lobe. "Take off the dress and I'll show you," his voice rumbled low and deep. "Leave the shoes on."

"I need help with my dress," Janice said.

He spun her around and unzipped it. The black sheath slid down her shoulders, over her hips, and hit the floor. She wore nothing underneath. He grunted in approval. "You have one beautiful ass, Red."

He stepped into her from behind, nuzzling along the juncture of her neck and shoulder with his lightly bristled jaw. His breath was hot and moist on her skin. She shivered. Her breasts were heavy, her nipples painfully erect. His every touch had her aching with want. Cupping and molding her breasts in his hands, he continued kissing, licking, and biting her neck and shoulders while teasing her nipples with his thumbs. Cranking her need tighter. Higher.

His chest hair tickled her back as he nestled his hard cock between her ass cheeks. He felt so damned good— all big, hot, and aroused male. Her sex throbbed like a beating heart, her inner walls convulsing with the excruciating need to be filled.

"Please," she whispered, grinding her backside into him.

"On the bed," he said, ripping back the covers. "I want you on your hands and knees."

His commanding tone sent ripples down her spine.

She kicked off her heels and climbed on top of the bed, kneeling with legs apart. Her body thrumming with the anticipation of penetration, only to be surprised by his mouth instead. Her skin stung with sharp nips of his teeth on her butt cheeks, soothed by hot wet kisses and long raspy licks.

He explored her deeper with his tongue while his hands slid over her hips, stroking and circling the dimples of her lower back and then farther south, fondling her ass and then sweeping up and down the cleft. His finessing fingers excited every nerve ending, pushing her closer and closer to the brink of climax.

"Now, Dirk. Please." She whimpered over her shoulder. "I want you inside me."

His tongue probed her deeper. He circled a finger over her puckered entrance.

She froze, clenching her butt cheeks with another whimper—this time in fear. "Please don't."

Dirk drew back. "What's wrong? You don't like that?"

"No. I don't. Grady…he was rough."

He pulled her into a sitting position. "Let's get one thing straight. I ain't Grady. And I'd never force anything on you that you don't like. I'd never hurt you, Janice."

"I know," she whispered. "If I thought you were anything like him I wouldn't be here."

"Trust is a two-way street, sweetheart."

"I know. I'm sorry."

"There's no need to be." He soothed her with a kiss and a caress. "Are you all right now? Do you still want this?"

"Yes," she said. "I'm OK, and I do." In truth, she ached like hell to have him buried deep inside her.

"Then just relax and let me take care of you."

"No, Dirk. I want to feel you inside me. Now."

"Now?"

"Yes. Now." She kissed him hungrily, her desire coming quickly back to life with every flick and stroke of his questing tongue. She lay back on the bed, pulling him down with her. He released her just for a moment. His hands came down between them. She heard the stiff rustle of denim, and then he plunged into her, impaling her fully in a surge of pure pleasure that rocked her to the core.

She shut her eyes, reveling in the sheer sensation of Dirk filling her emptiness, relieving the ache. They remained joined and locked, stock-still, until he began a slow and deliberate thrust and drag that wiped her mind clean of all thought beyond the feeling of him moving inside her.

"So good," he murmured hotly, licking and sucking her neck. "So damned good."

She urged him deeper, digging her heels into his flanks and straining into his ebb and flow of motions. He increased his pace, pounding into her until the air echoed with their mingled moans, synchronized with the erotic slap of flesh on flesh, until her senses were swimming in a mind-erasing rush of sensation.

"Give it up," he growled, driving into her in a ravaging rhythm of thrust and retreat that sent her barreling toward the edge. She clawed the sheet on an endless moan as her climax sluiced through her, her inner walls contracting and convulsing in searing waves.

He followed with a primal roar as he emptied into her in a hot and pulsating rush. It was everything she'd wanted. Everything she'd wished it could be. She only hoped he felt the same.

———∿∿∿———

Dirk was sitting on the edge of the bed lost in his thoughts and staring at his boots when Janice emerged from the bathroom. She left the light on and the door open, he guessed intentionally. She scooped up her dress from the floor with a look of uncertainty. "What now?" she asked softly, a tiny frown wrinkling her brow.

He didn't immediately answer, mainly because his brain still wasn't fully functioning yet. He'd been so lost in the moment...in her...that he hadn't given any thought to the aftermath. Her brown gaze continued to search his. Her question had caught him off guard. Staying together the whole night seemed a huge step... but then again...maybe it was time to get off the fence.

"Bed looks real comfortable." He bounced lightly a couple of times. "Feels comfortable too. Seems a shame to waste it."

Her brows scrunched together. "You saying you want to stay?"

"The room's ours for the night," he replied, "but the choice is yours, Red."

She chewed her lip. "I would like to stay, but I'd need to be home before Cody gets up for school."

"OK with me, as long as you don't mind getting up at a hellacious hour to drive back."

She smiled. "I don't mind as long as you're planning to join me in that bed."

"I don't intend to sleep in the chair."

"But you're still dressed," she observed.

"Yeah," he said. "I'm well aware of that."

"You gonna undress?"

The idea had him feeling twitchy. "I'd rather not."

"Time to cowboy up, Dirk. I'm not giving you a choice."

"Why are you pushing it?" he asked.

"I told you your injuries don't bother me, but I know you don't believe me. I need you to know that I can handle it. This is about trust, Dirk. Now lie down." She pushed him backward onto the bed.

He was uncomfortable as hell with the idea but still too dazed and spent to make much protest when Janice knelt and pried off his left boot. She then grabbed the heel of the right.

"No," he said. "The right one stays on with the prosthesis."

"Then how do I do this?" she asked.

"I take the jeans down first and then off with the leg."

"Oh. Then you'll need to lift your hips," she commanded, already tugging at his jeans.

Dirk sighed and then lay back, hands behind his head, staring up at the ceiling, grim-faced, letting her draw them down over his thighs to just above the knee—or where his knee used to be. He didn't want to see her expression when she got a good look at his stump. He shut his eyes, forcing himself to relax, but held his breath, acutely attuned to every movement and every sound. It was a major struggle to lie there, to just give himself up to her.

"How do I remove this?" Her hands stroked down

his thigh to the top of the silicone sleeve that attached his prosthesis.

He reached down to roll the sleeve off his thigh, but she laid her hands over his.

"Please. Let me do it. Just tell me how it works."

"The leg's held on by suction. Roll down the silicone sleeve and it'll detach."

She did as he instructed, and the device came free. A moment later, his jeans were off and then his boxers followed. He released the air from his lungs on a long hiss, but was almost afraid to open his eyes. His chest was tight and his heartbeat pounded in his ears. Other than what little was still covered by his unbuttoned shirt, his entire scarred and mutilated body was now bared to her view. He'd never felt more exposed…or more vulnerable.

He sat up abruptly, tore off the shirt, and threw it at her. "Satisfied?" he growled. His gaze darted to her face, but rather than the disgust he'd expected and had prepared himself for, she was grinning back at him.

"Hardly," she replied. "But I'm hoping you'll take care of that as soon as you've had enough time to recover. Maybe I can help you with that?" She cocked a brow.

Her suggestive look had his spent dick stirring instantly back to life.

"No need," he replied. "C'mere." He beckoned her closer, drew her down to him, and kissed her passionately. He cupped her ass in both hands. "Straddle me."

She dropped the dress and climbed onto the bed. His erection reared up rock-hard between them as her knees sank into the mattress on either side of his hips. She pitched forward, raising up to mount him, but he stopped her. Although he wanted inside her something fierce, he held her back. "Not yet," he said.

"What's wrong?" Her brown eyes widened in surprise.

"Nothing's wrong. I want you to touch yourself. I want to watch you get off."

"Why?" Her brow wrinkled.

He knew he was pushing her comfort zone, but she'd already blasted clean through his.

"Because it excites the hell out of me, Red…because I asked you to. Does that make you uncomfortable?" He knew Grady had put her through a lot of shit. It made him wonder where her limits were. How far *she* trusted him.

It was a moment before she answered. "No, Dirk, it doesn't as long as this is just between you and me. No cameras. No videos."

"No, Red. I'm not into that kinda shit," he reassured her, breathing easier as the uncertainty passed from her eyes. "This is only about us. It's all just between you and me."

Janice sensed that he was intentionally testing her, trying to make her feel as exposed and vulnerable as he felt, but she wasn't about to retreat. She'd told him before that it was gonna be all or nothing. If he wanted a show, she'd give him one.

She leaned forward to kiss him, using her breasts and hips to tease him as she dragged her body slowly up his. Her mouth sought his hungrily, but she didn't prolong the kiss, instead withdrawing from it the moment he would have pulled her deeper in. Wordlessly, she brushed her fingers over his damp lips.

His blue gaze darkened in instant understanding. He caught her hand, drawing her fingers into his mouth one at a time, licking and sucking and then slowly releasing. He watched with a spine-tingling intensity as Janice cupped her breast with one hand, toying with her nipple as her other hand crept down her belly toward her nest of short curls.

"Oh yeah, just like that, sweetheart," he murmured hoarsely. His pupils flared when she dipped into the wet folds of her cleft.

Feeling increasingly shy and embarrassed, she shut her eyes but continued to stroke and tease herself until her body quivered with the first tiny orgasmic tremors. Throbbing to feel him inside her, filling her, she rubbed her mons up and down his shaft.

He gripped her hips almost painfully tight. His hip bucked beneath her, but he still held back. "Don't stop."

She squeezed her lids tighter, imagining him pumping into her. Her climax hit like a tsunami. She let loose a low moan, rocking her hips rhythmically as it washed over her in breathless waves. She opened her eyes to find him staring up at her with a ravenous look.

"Holy shit." His voice was low and gravelly. "Do you have any idea how hot that was? How hot *you* are?" He pulled her down for a long, deep kiss that sent a series of aftershocks resonating through her.

"Please, Dirk. I need *you*," she whispered urgently. She wrapped her hand around him, guiding him toward her aching core, dragging his shaft through her wetness. Holding him primed at her entrance, she slid her hips slowly forward and back, then circling and teasing until he emitted a long groan that made his body quake beneath her. But just when she thought he'd finally lose it, he usurped control from her.

The next thing she knew, she was trapped beneath him, his arms caging her head and his mouth devouring hers. They gasped in unison when he entered her in a single, breath-catching thrust.

She wrapped her legs tightly around his flanks, urging him deeper. "Please don't stop. Don't ever stop."

—∾∾—

Hours later, Dirk found himself once more staring at the ceiling. He couldn't remember the last time he felt so content...or so confused. In just a few short days, she'd turned him upside down and inside out.

Her head rested on his shoulder and his left arm had gone completely numb, but he didn't want to chance waking her. He glanced down to find her gazing up at him with a sleepy smile. "What are you thinking?"

"I'm trying not to," he said. "Thinking seems a highly overrated activity compared to others."

"Yeah, you might be right about that." She chuckled and then rolled on top of him, plying soft kisses to his face. She then worked her way lower, trailing her fingers and mouth over the various scars on his body.

He winced under her touch.

"You don't like that?" she asked.

"It's still uncomfortable for me," he admitted.

"I'm sorry, Dirk, but I'm afraid you're just gonna have to get used to my hands on your body."

Janice had a habit of pushing him too hard and too

fast, but she also held nothing back. For the past four years he'd believed he could never have a normal life again. Now he wondered if that was true. He'd also told himself he'd never find a woman who'd accept him without reservation, but by the looks of things, it seemed he might have been wrong about that too.

Morning came way too fast for Janice. The only saving grace was that they checked out early enough that she was spared the walk of shame she'd dreaded the night before. They drove home in a thought-filled silence broken only when they stopped for coffee at a drive-through. Had Dirk not held her hand on his thigh for almost the entire drive, she might have worried about his lack of conversation, but they both needed the quiet time to digest, and to adjust. Their night together had changed everything, had put their relationship on new ground. Now they both had to regain their footing.

The sun was only starting to crest the horizon when Dirk pulled up in front of the house. She was glad to see the lights were still off. Hopefully, she'd have time to sneak upstairs and change before her mother or Cody caught sight of her. Janice reached for the door, but Dirk pulled her back. "Guess this one's for good morning instead of good night." His lips met hers in a slow and tender kiss. He released her with a smile. "Will I see you later?"

"I'm working at the Pioneer the next two days, but I'll be out on Sunday with Cody…that is, if the offer is still open."

His brows drew together. "Why wouldn't it be?"

She replied with a nervous shrug. "Didn't know if you might need some time alone…after everything."

His frown deepened. "You saying that for my benefit or yours, Red?"

"I don't have any regrets if that's what you're asking."

"Yeah. It is what I was asking."

"None, Dirk, but I don't know where this puts us."

"I don't either," he replied. "One step at a time, remember?"

"Yeah." She gave a nervous laugh. "But last night seems like a Neil Armstrong kind of step."

"It was at that." He grinned. "Noon Sunday then?"

"Yeah. I'll be there." Their eyes met briefly and then Janice let herself out.

Chapter 16

By Sunday, Dirk was almost aching to see Janice. It'd only been two days since they'd spent the night together, not that they'd done much sleeping. Now by comparison, his own bed seemed cold and way too empty. He was growing in the certainty that he wanted her with him every night—but Janice came complete with a kid.

He hadn't even considered *that* aspect of a potential relationship...until now. Was he really prepared to take on a ready-made family? A month ago, he would have said no friggin' way, but now? A lot of things had changed in the short time since Janice walked into his life.

He was leading Red Man out of the corral toward the hitching post when her old red Dodge pulled into the yard. Almost before she'd cut the ignition, a redheaded kid in a cowboy hat bound out of the truck.

"Cody Garrison!" Janice jumped out behind him. "You get yourself back here!"

"He's all right," Dirk said, unable to suppress a chuckle at the kid's exuberance.

"I'm afraid he's been like this for hours," Janice apologized. "He's near bursting with excitement and pestered me almost incessantly about coming out here since the minute he woke up this morning."

"Hey, Cody." Dirk stepped toward the boy and extended his hand. "'Member me?"

"Not exactly…well, maybe…I think I saw your picture with my daddy." Cody stepped back and scrunched his face. "But you look real different from the pictures I seen. What happened to your face?"

"Cody!" Janice gasped. "Oh my God, Dirk, I'm so sorry!"

Dirk shrugged it off. "Kids tend to speak their minds. There's nothing wrong in that. It was an explosion that burnt my face," he answered Cody. "Same one that took my leg."

Cody's eyes grew impossibly wide. "What do you mean? You got a fake leg?"

"Yup," Dirk said and lifted his jeans just over his boot top.

"Cool!" Cody exclaimed. "Does it come off?"

"Cody," Janice cried again, her face and neck coloring.

"Yeah, I take it on and off," Dirk answered. "It's got microprocessors and batteries that need to recharge every night—kinda like Iron Man's suit."

"Can I see it when you take it off?"

"I s'pose sometime," Dirk replied noncommittally.

"My daddy was a bull rider," Cody announced, puffing his chest proudly.

"Your daddy was a *world champion* bull rider," Dirk corrected.

"Were you a bull rider, too?"

"I was once," Dirk said.

"I want to ride bulls."

"Do you now?"

"Yeah. Can you teach me?" Cody asked.

Dirk looked to Janice who shook her head. "I never

knew he had the least interest in it. He's never said anything about it to me until now. Never."

"Maybe he was waiting for the right time and place
to speak up about it. I s'pose I could teach you," Dirk
answered Cody, "but let's start with the horse for now.
You'll find they're a lot more cooperative than bulls.
C'mon. Red Man's been waiting on you. Janice, why
don't you go in and visit with my mother? Cody and I
will join you when dinner's ready."

"But—" Janice protested.

"No buts," Dirk said. "This is guy time. No females
allowed."

"Yeah." Cody beamed and repeated, "Guy time.
Sorry, Mom."

Janice still hesitated.

"Go," Dirk commanded. "Cody and I need to get
acquainted. 'Sides, he's gonna take instruction a lot
better if you're not here. Give us an hour or so, then
come back out to watch him ride."

"All right," she huffed.

Dirk watched her trudge off toward the house.

His curiosity about the prosthetic apparently satisfied,
Cody asked him, "Can I meet your Leopard dogs too?"

"Sure, when we're done with Red Man here. Your
mom says you've been riding with a friend?"

"Yup. A horse named Slug. He's old and don't go
very fast."

"Red Man's getting up in age too, but he's still got
enough piss and vinegar to go when you ask him to."

"How old is he?" Cody asked.

"He was born when I was about your age, so I guess
that makes him about twenty-three now. I had one

that looked just like him before that, a sorrel named
Buckshot. C'mon. We're done jawing. Let's go into
the barn and I'll show you how to get this horse saddled up."

—∿∿—

Janice couldn't help feeling a little hurt when Dirk sum-
marily dismissed her, but she knew he had a point. Cody
would have been far too distracted had she hung around.
Still, she couldn't help being anxious because Dirk hadn't
been around many kids. He'd surprised her with the
patient way he'd handled Cody's questions though. She
reassured herself that they'd seemed to hit it off just fine.

"Hey, Janice." Donna Knowlton greeted her with a
smile. "Come on in. I just made a pot of coffee."

Janice followed Donna to the kitchen where she sat
at the breakfast bar while Donna poured out two cups.
"Where's your son and your mama?" Donna asked.

"Cody's outside getting acquainted with Dirk and
Red Man. Mama's still feeling under the weather."

"I'm sorry to hear that." Donna's brows met with a
look of concern. "Is she OK?"

"I honestly don't know." Janice shook her head and
stirred her coffee. "She says it's just her arthritis, but
we're gonna talk when I get back. I think keeping the
place up is way too much for her. Besides that, the old
house needs repairs we can't afford. I know she'd considered moving up to Helena before Cody and I came
home. She has a widowed cousin who has a nice place
in one of those high-end retirement communities. She
invited Mama to move in, but I think she's stayed here
for Cody and me. Now I feel guilty about it. I thought

things would work out for all of us once I got here, but it's been a lot harder than I expected."

"Times are tough for a lotta folks," Donna replied sympathetically. "We were considering selling our place as well, but it looks like Dirk might finally be able to turn things around *if* I can only keep Wade and Justin out of his way."

"So you believe in Dirk's new breeding program?"

"I do, but Wade wants nothing to do with ranching anymore, and my husband's too set in his ways to give Dirk the free rein he needs to make a go of it. With any luck, Justin and I will be wintering in Arizona this year, which will give Dirk a free hand to do things exactly as he sees fit without Justin's well-meaning interference. He'll need help though. He can't run the place by himself." She gave Janice a thoughtful look. "How's it working out between the two of you?"

Janice diverted her gaze into her cup. Her relationship with Dirk wasn't exactly a secret from his family, but she wasn't ready to talk about it, especially with his mother. "I don't know. Has *he* said anything about it?"

"No." Donna laughed. "He wouldn't, but I have eyes in my head. You've been good for him, Janice. I can't tell you how different he's been. I even caught him whistling once. If that isn't proof of a Knowlton man in love, I don't know what is. Justin only whistles after… well…" She gave a slow sly smile. "Let's just say, only when he's particularly…content." Donna winked.

Janice flushed from her neck to her hairline. "I'm just taking this one day at a time."

"Smart girl." Donna nodded.

Janice drained her coffee cup and glanced out the

window. "I'm a bit anxious about how it's going with Dirk and Cody."

"Then why don't we go out and see?" Donna suggested. "I need to call Justin in to clean up for dinner anyway. He always loses track of time when he's tinkering in the workshop."

"But I promised Dirk I'd stay away for an hour," Janice said. "He thinks Cody won't listen as well if I'm there. He's probably right."

"Well that doesn't mean we can't watch them unobserved for a few minutes," Donna said. "Come and sit on the back porch with me. We might not be able to hear everything, but we can see the corrals just fine from there."

"If you're sure we won't get caught."

"I'm sure. I kept tabs on my boys for years unnoticed. They didn't get away with half the things they thought they would."

Cody was already on the horse, sitting solid as a rock and trotting circles around Dirk who looked on with an expression of approval. The sight of them together filled Janice with emotions she couldn't even name.

At Dirk's nod, Cody nudged the horse into an easy lope.

"Will you look at that!" Janice declared, but Donna didn't answer. She glanced at the other woman to find her leaning heavily on the porch rail. Her face had visibly paled.

"Are you OK, Donna?" Janice asked.

"No, Janice. I don't think I am," Donna murmured in reply. "Please excuse me. I need to go inside for a moment."

"Should I get Dirk? Or Mr. Knowlton?" Janice asked in growing alarm.

"No. I'll be fine. I—I just need a minute."

Janice had never seen Donna Knowlton so discomposed. As soon as Donna left her, Janice descended the porch steps, heading toward the corral in rapid, ground-eating strides.

"Mama, I loped the horse," Cody exclaimed. "Mr. Dirk says I'll earn my spurs in no time."

"That's wonderful, Cody! I'm so proud of you," Janice declared, then slanted an anxious gaze to Dirk. "I'm worried about your mother. She seems to have taken ill all of a sudden. She got real pale and quiet. Does she have any heart problems or anything like that?"

"Not that I'm aware of. Shit! Where is she?" Dirk demanded.

"In the house. I think maybe you should go and check on her. I'll take care of Cody and Red Man."

Dirk looked like he wanted to vault over the panels but then thought twice. "Go get my father, would you?" He was out the gate and jogging toward the house before she could even reply.

"Mama! Where the hell are you?" Dirk opened the door with a bellow.

She was slowly descending the stairs, her hand tightly gripping the banister and her face unusually pale. He bounded up the stairs as fast as his C-Leg would allow. "Are you OK?"

"I am now. I've just had a bit of a shock is all."

"What do you mean? What kind of shock?"

"I need to sit down, Dirk…and so do you."

He led her to the sofa and lowered himself beside her. "Damn it all, Mama. Tell me what's wrong."

"Take a look at this." She produced a Polaroid photo. It was Dirk as a kid in hat and boots smiling at the camera from atop his favorite horse, Buckshot.

"It's me and Buckshot. What of it?"

"Can't you *see* it?" she demanded.

"See what?"

"My God! The resemblance can't be denied. That boy out there is the spitting image of you!"

"Impossible. You're seeing things, Mama." His chest constricted even as he spoke the denial.

"How old is Cody?" she demanded.

"He'll be ten soon. In March I think," Dirk choked out his answer while counting months backward. *Holy fuck. It couldn't be!*

"Were you and Janice ever… Did you and she…"

He could barely hear her anymore over the roar in his ears. He shoved the photo into his pocket, pushed off the sofa, and banged out the door. He was halfway across the yard when he met his father and Janice hurrying toward the house.

"She's fine," he answered his father's look of alarm.

"Thank you, Jesus!" Justin exhaled.

Dirk dug his keys out of his pocket and headed toward his truck. He didn't even trust himself to *look* at Janice.

She trailed after him. "Where are you going?"

"Not now, Red." He kept walking.

"Please!" She latched onto his arm. "You've got to tell me what's wrong?"

He shook her off, snatched the Polaroid out of his shirt pocket, and shoved it in her face.

"I don't understand." Janice frowned at the picture, her forehead wrinkling. "It looks just like my son, but how could you have a picture of Cody?"

"That ain't Cody."

"Then who…" She looked up at him with brown eyes growing fearfully wide. "Oh my God. It can't be…"

"You got some major explaining to do, Red, but I can't trust myself to hear it right now."

"Let go, Dirk," she whispered. "You're hurting me."

He released the arm he hadn't realized he'd taken hold of. "That so?" he hissed. "Well, I can barely fucking breathe."

Dirk headed straight to the Stockman, the only watering hole in Twin Bridges, settling into a corner and ordering a bottle of Pendleton. He'd knocked back several shots of the whiskey and was already halfway to shit-faced when his brother walked in. "What the hell are you doing here?" Dirk sneered over his glass.

Wade straddled a chair with a shrug. "They say misery likes company, and since you're one miserable sonofabitch, here I am."

"Thought you went back to Bozeman," Dirk remarked after a time.

A pretty waitress in a low-cut top came to take Wade's drink order. "Nothing for me, thanks." He waved her away and then pushed back his hat. "I did for a few days, but I've got a court date in Virginia City tomorrow, so when Mama called to say she was making a brisket, I drove down a day early. As it turns out, most of Sunday dinner went to those ugly dogs of yours. Seems no one but them had much appetite."

Dirk threw back another shot. "You see Janice?"

"Briefly," Wade replied. "She left almost the minute I got there. Can't say I blame her. She was pretty distraught."

"*She* was distraught?" Dirk gave a derisive snort. "I just found out she had my kid and never even told me! How could she lie about something like that…to me… to Grady. I still can't fucking believe this!" Dirk shook his head.

"Do you know for sure he's yours?" Wade asked. "You and I both know that Mama's got a powerful yen for grandkids."

"That may be, but she ain't delusional, Wade. You seen the picture?" He made to refill the glass but then changed his mind and swigged straight from the bottle.

"Yeah, I saw it."

"I have half a mind to demand a DNA test."

"You need to think carefully about that, bro," Wade warned. "I can understand your desire to know for certain, but think what it could do to the kid. Do you *really* want to go there? Besides, Janice has every right to refuse."

"What the hell am I supposed to do then?"

"I don't know, but seems there's a helluva lot of unanswered questions—questions only she can answer. There's probably nothing worse than living with the knowledge that you made bad decisions over misunderstandings—I speak from experience. You accused me of jumping to conclusions about you and Rachel. I made that mistake and have lived to regret it. Deeply. Maybe you're doing the same thing to Janice."

"I can't talk to her, Wade. It'll get real ugly real fast if I even try."

"I know the photo's pretty damning, but it's not enough to try and sentence her without even giving her a chance to explain. Don't you think she deserves to speak her piece?"

"Yeah, like all the chances you gave me and Rachel?" Dirk scoffed.

Wade groaned. "I was an asshole, all right? Rachel might be alive today if only I'd listened instead of making accusations."

Dirk set the bottle down and sharply eyed his brother. "What are you saying?"

"That I know you and she *didn't* betray me. Deep down I've always known it. I wanted to believe it to assuage my own guilty conscience. I was wrong. I'm sorry."

"Took you damn long enough to see it," Dirk grunted.

"Look, I can't change what's happened between us in the past, but I want to help you through all this shit. Don't make the kind of mistakes I made."

"What's the point?" Dirk demanded. "Whether she lied or not, I don't see how we can ever get past this. How could I ever trust her?

"There you go again. At least hear her side of the story before you pass judgment."

"Will you take off the fucking lawyer hat already?" Dirk snapped.

"I'm not speaking as a lawyer, Dirk. I'm trying to be a brother, just like you were for me when I nearly drank myself into a coma. By the way, you don't need this any more than I did." Wade snatched the bottle from Dirk's hands. He held it at a distance, shaking his head with a wistful look. Dirk could see the desire for a drink in his brother's eyes and grudgingly admired Wade's self-restraint. He'd never expected Wade would give up booze completely, especially given how long and hard he'd hit the bottle after Rachel's accident.

"I can't even tell you how much I'd like to join you in that bottle," Wade said, "but I'm done with self-destruction." He shoved it across the table and out of reach.

"I'm guessing things ain't so peachy with Peaches?" Dirk remarked.

"Her name's *Nikki*, dammit! And, yeah. I fucked it all up royally by issuing ultimatums when I should have given her some time and space. I was a dickhead. Nikki is the best thing that's happened to me in nearly four years, and from what I've heard, you could say pretty much the same about Janice."

"Then you don't know shit," Dirk retorted. "There's no fucking comparison!"

"Then you better get your damn head straight and think real hard about what's really on the line here. You've spent the past four years busting your ass…for what? I was there once too. Didn't care about anything but proving myself to the world. I thought I was making a better future for my family but what did that really get me? I lost it all, Dirk. Wife and baby. Now you're doing the same thing. So I gotta ask, what are you killing yourself for?"

"For the ranch, dammit! You might not give a shit about the place, but I still do."

Wade raised a hand with a black look. "Wait just a damn minute. It's time we got this straight between us. It *isn't* that I don't care. I just don't see *how* any private ranch is gonna survive into the future, let alone thrive, when we've got fat-ass government bureaucrats legislating the life out of farmers and ranchers across the country."

"Then why don't you put your money where your big fat mouth is and *do* something about that?" Dirk challenged. "You've got the friggin' law degree. Why not put it to work for some real good?"

Wade sat back. "As it turns out, I've been thinking about just that. A lot of thinking actually."

"That so?"

"Yeah," Wade said. "I might take a job up at the capital. I'm thinking I might try to work my way into the state legislature."

"Then that's all the more reason for me to keep on at the ranch," Dirk said. "I've got a plan to get us back in the black. It's on the brink of coming together. I only need more time."

"I still have my doubts, but let's just say it does happen as you planned. What then? You really think you're gonna be satisfied with your thankless ranching life? The cattle ain't gonna keep you warm at night."

"Look, I already had it all figured out—before she walked in and wreaked havoc with my life."

"That so?" Wade cocked a brow. "So now you're just gonna let her walk back out again? You're deluding yourself if you think everything is just gonna settle back the way it was before. You need her and you know it."

"Screw that. And screw you too."

"You saying you don't care about her?"

"Fuck off, Wade!"

Wade smirked. "I'll take that as an affirmative."

"All right. If you have to stick your goddamn nose into my business. Yeah. I do care about Janice. I always have, and that already scared the ever-lovin' shit out of me even *before* all this!"

"If you were wanting to take her on with a kid before this happened, what's the real problem here? You should count it a damned blessing if the boy is really yours. Seems to me you've all the more reason to work this out."

"Now you're making me feel like a self-centered asshole."

"If the boot fits…" Wade slouched back and cocked his hat with a grin. "You might actually be the biggest asshole I know, but you're still my brother and I care about you. What's more, whether you deserve her or not, Janice seems to care too."

Wade was right. He'd been an asshole. But now he realized he had nothing to lose and everything to gain.

Chapter 17

JANICE'S HEART LEAPED INTO HER THROAT AT THE sight of Dirk shadowing the doorway, but she refused to let him see how much she hurt. "How'd you get in here?" She opened a drawer and emptied the contents onto the bed beside the suitcase.

"Your mother let me in," Dirk said. "What are you doing?" He had to navigate around the boxes and Bubble Wrap that littered the bedroom floor to get to her.

"What does it look like?" She glanced up at him. "I'm packing." She slammed the drawer shut, barely missing her own fingers.

"We need to talk."

"*Now* you want to talk? What about two days ago?" She snatched up a pillow and hit him with it. It wasn't nearly enough, so she followed with an attempted punch to his gut, but he grabbed her wrist before she could land it.

"Maybe I was a dickhead two days ago."

"Yeah, you were." She laughed bitterly. "But maybe that hasn't changed. Now is not a convenient time, Dirk."

"What I came for can't wait any longer." He stepped beside her and shut the suitcase, forcing her to acknowledge his questions. "Is he really mine? Is Cody my son?"

Janice drew a deep breath against a sudden wave of

nausea. In truth, the revelation had come as much of a shock to her as it had to him. "You've got to know I never would have dropped a bomb like that on you. Not in a million years." She averted her gaze and reached for another box. He laid his hand over hers.

"Answer the question, Red."

Her gaze flickered upward, from the hand that covered hers and then back to his face. His expression was grim, his gaze searching. Janice sank her teeth into her bottom lip. "I don't know for certain, but I think maybe—"

"How can you not *know*?" Dirk cried.

"Because it was only that one time between you and me. And even then, we used protection. After that, I was only with Grady and we didn't use anything, least not after he said he wanted to marry me."

"You never questioned? Never wondered?"

"Did *you*?" she threw back at him. "You saw Cody when he was about five. Did it ever occur to *you* that he could be yours?"

"No. Why would I?"

She cocked her head. "So you think I have ESP or something?"

"Shit I don't know. Aren't women supposed to just sense these things?"

She shook her head on a sigh. "Maybe a tiny part of me always wondered if he could be yours, but I pushed it down, not wanting to think about it too hard. Life with Grady was complicated enough. It wasn't until your mother said something that I even noticed the resemblance between you and Cody. I'd never seen it before, but then the photo hit me like a bolt from the blue. Other than my coloring, he does look just like you. But this doesn't make any difference, Dirk."

"The hell it doesn't! You're not going anywhere with my son."

"He's *my* son," she replied in steely tones. "There's no *proof* of anything beyond that."

"Damn it all. That was not what I came here to say." Dirk snatched off his hat and threw it down with a curse. "This is not how this was supposed to go down. Shit! I'm only here five minutes and I've already fucked the whole thing up." He grasped her chin and tilted it upward until she was looking straight into his eyes. "Janice, please listen to me. You asked me a while back why I left you in Cheyenne. Why I joined the marines? I need to tell you the whole truth of it."

She turned slowly, hands on hips. "I'm listening," she replied, feeling wary but keeping her tone and expression neutral.

"I knew ten years ago that you were the one for me. But by the time I finally decided to tell you that it was done between Rachel and me, when I finally pulled my head out of my ass, it was too late. I'd waited too damned long."

"What did you expect from me?" Janice cried. "You took my virginity and then barely spoke to me for weeks—"

"*Took?* Seems to me it was an even exchange, sweetheart."

"Maybe that's true, but how could I know you gave a damn about me by the way you acted?"

"I told you it was a big mistake. I never should have let you walk out of the Outlaw that night. I should have gone after you then. I should have made you listen. I should have protected you from Grady."

She was hanging on every word she'd waited ten long years to hear. She could barely swallow, let alone speak. "If you cared at all," she whispered, "why didn't you speak up before?"

He grasped her by the shoulders in an almost painful grip. "You listening good?"

Janice nodded.

"Because I was having trouble dealing with it. Because I was a chickenshit. A coward. Plain and simple. I knew that if we got together, I'd never leave Montana—I'd never leave you—and that scared the hell out of me. I just didn't feel ready. By the time I worked through it you were with Grady." He raked a hand through his hair. "I've screwed up so many times in my life that I've long lost count. I don't want this to be another one. I'm not gonna lie. I still don't feel ready, but I guess I never will be until I just cowboy up and deal with it. I want us to work this out."

"You think that's what Cody and I want? For you to *deal with us*? No thank you!" She spun away, fighting the tightness in her chest and the tears burning behind her eyes.

"Goddamnit. You're twisting my meaning. That's *not* what I meant."

"Then what *do* you mean? I'm trying real hard to understand—"

———— ∿ ————

He was nearly boiling over with frustration. He'd come to apologize to her, to try and make things right, but he just seemed to mangle his words at every turn.

"Fuck it! This is what I meant." He yanked her into his arms, closing his mouth over hers, kissing her, on and on, long and fierce, refusing to let her go, refusing even to let her breathe. Dirk poured himself into the kiss that he hoped would overcome his ineptitude, the kiss that he hoped spoke for his heart. He released her slowly, knowing he'd laid it all on the table. There was nothing more he could say or do.

She stared back at him in silence and slowly shook her head.

It was done. Another royal fuckup. The lump in Dirk's throat choked out any other remark he might have made. He picked up his hat and turned to leave.

She cocked a brow. "Where are you going?"

Dirk shrugged. "I've got nothing more to say."

Her gaze met his. She licked her kiss-swollen lips. "Wait a minute, cowboy. I'm not really sure I understood all that." She slid her hands up his chest, linking her fingers around his neck. His pulse sped up with rising hope. She drew his head down to hers and kissed him until his head reeled. "Is this what you meant?"

"Yeah, Red." He grinned when she drew back. "I think that's about the gist of it."

He sat on the bed and hauled her onto his lap, wrapping his arms around her, holding her tight. "So, are you saying you'll give us some time to figure this out?"

"Said I would before, didn't I?" she replied stubbornly. "I'm not one to change my mind when I want something."

"You sure you still want me?" he asked.

"Yeah, I am. I'm kinda obstinate that way. You think we can make this work?"

He dipped his forehead to touch hers. "I dunno, Red, but I sure wanna try."

"I need you too, Dirk, and Cody needs a good man in his life."

"And you think that's me?" He shook his head with a scoffing sound.

"Yeah. I know it is."

"I don't want to let either of you down."

"You won't," Janice reassured. "What are we going to tell Cody?"

"I think there's no reason to say anything right now. I want to get to know the boy. I want us to be a real family, Red, but I want to build a genuine relationship with him first. I don't want to force myself on him. If he accepts me in his own time and on his own terms, there won't be any cause for resentment later. Can you understand that?"

"Yes, I do. Are you saying you don't want a DNA test?"

Dirk considered the question. "No. Maybe one day, if Cody wants it, but it doesn't matter to me anymore."

Janice's eyes misted. "You really mean that?"

"Said it, didn't I?"

Dirk shoved the suitcase to the floor, wanting nothing more than to lay her down on the bed and kiss her senseless. He pushed the remaining clothing aside, grimacing at the pile of white cotton granny panties and cross-your-heart bras. He held up a pair with a scowl.

"Please tell me these aren't yours."

"No." Janice laughed. "They're Mama's. I'm packing her things for her. She's decided to move up to her cousin's place in Helena."

"So you *weren't* packing to go back to Vegas?"

"No," she said. "Told you I'm stubborn. I was hoping if I stuck around long enough, you'd eventually see the light."

"I've seen it all right, sweetheart. The whole damn sun is blazing in this room right now."

Chapter 18

Janice backed the stock trailer slowly up to the gate where Dirk, Wade, and Cody stood ready to unload the last shipment of heifers. They'd hauled three stock trailers full of cattle they'd brought in from a big Wagyu outfit in Idaho.

"I still don't know how you maneuver this great big thing," remarked Wade's fiancée Nikki.

"Years of practice," Janice said. "I was driving a tractor before age ten, and a truck and trailer by fifteen."

"Do you think you could teach me?" Nikki asked. "I might be a silent partner, but I really do want to learn about ranching."

Janice was surprised at how eagerly the Georgia native had embraced the ranching life, especially given that only a few months ago Wade had wanted to sell out. Nikki's investment in Flying K Wagyu had changed everything. It seemed that Dirk's dream of turning the ranch around would finally come to fruition. Nikki's twelve hundred acres in the Ruby Valley would provide mild winters and plentiful grass for Dirk's cattle, and the free lease had allowed him to expand his herd with two more bulls and fifty cows and heifers. Most importantly, Nikki's involvement had helped to end the long estrangement between the Knowlton brothers.

"Sure," Janice replied. "I'm happy to teach you

anything you want to know. We can practice driving in the pasture once the snow melts."

She put the truck into park and shut off the ignition and then hopped down into the mud. The trailer shook as the men dropped the ramp to unload the cattle. The next few minutes passed in organized chaos as the lowing cows trotted off the trailer to join the rest of the herd.

Janice observed Dirk and her son with a smile. Cody had always been energetic, but he seemed to positively bloom whenever in Dirk's company. Although she'd tried her best to fill the roles of both mother and father to Cody, it wasn't until observing him and Dirk together that she'd realized how sadly insufficient she had been.

The boy had become Dirk's shadow over the past couple of months. Dirk had shown infinite patience in teaching Cody how to ride, gather cows, and handle a rope. Although she'd been a little hurt that Cody had asked to ride with Dirk when they'd made their road trip to Idaho, she realized the time together would only strengthen their growing bond.

He now stood by the gate with prod in hand, intently watching and mimicking Dirk's every move. "Hey, Mama!" he greeted her with a mile-wide grin. "Mr. Dirk has something real important to ask you."

Dirk scowled. "This isn't exactly the right time, Cody."

"Oh yeah?" Janice looked from Cody to Dirk. "And why's that?"

Dirk replied, "Because it's not the kind of thing you discuss in the middle of a cow pasture."

"Really? Then where do you suggest we discuss this thing?"

"How about over dinner tomorrow night?"

"Sure," Janice replied. "I've got a lasagna made up that I was planning to pop in the oven. What time do you want to come over?"

Cody and Dirk exchanged a conspiratorial look. "Wade said he and Nikki would watch Cody so we can go out."

"Out?" Janice repeated in surprise. It had been weeks since they'd gone anywhere without Cody. "You sure you two don't mind?" Janice asked Nikki.

"Not at all. Why don't we just keep him for the whole night?" Nikki replied with a wink.

"Think maybe you could put on that little black dress?" Dirk suggested.

"Sure," Janice replied. The last time she'd worn it was their dinner at the Sacajawea. It was also the last full night she and Dirk had spent together. They'd only had stolen opportunities for intimacy since her mother had moved up to Helena. The memory of that night sent a ripple of lust through her. Dirk's expression said he remembered it too.

"You ever gonna tell me what this big secret is?" Janice asked Dirk over dessert at Sir Scott's Oasis, another steak house test-marketing Flying K's American Kobe beef. "Cody looked like he was about to burst when we left tonight."

Dirk chuckled. "He gets that trait from you, not me."

"How is it going between you two?" Janice asked.

Dirk sobered. "He's a great kid, Janice, and a credit to both of us. I just wish to hell I could have been part of his life sooner."

"I do too, but all we can do now is make the most of the time we have."

She deeply regretted that they'd lost all those years that they could have been a family, but there was no point in dwelling on past mistakes when they had a future to build.

"Speaking of building… Mama called this morning to say she and the ol' man found a condo they like in Lake Havasu City. They want to sign the house over to me and remodel the bunkhouse for their summertime use. Which now leads to my big question…" He reached into his coat pocket.

Janice's heart leaped into her throat when he pulled out a small velvet box.

"Is that what I think it is?"

"Yeah. I asked Cody yesterday. Rest assured he has given me his full blessing." Dirk popped the box open. "I know I'm ten years late and it's not as big as I would have liked—"

"It's perfect," she whispered. She licked her lips as her gaze met his.

"Will you marry me?" he asked. "Be my partner and my lover for the rest of my life? I can't promise you much, Red, but I need you. Hell." He laughed. "All I *can* guarantee you as a rancher's wife is a lot of hard work."

"I've never been afraid of hard work, and I want to help you, Dirk. Your dreams are my dreams now. For better or for worse, right?"

His hands shook as he slipped the ring on her finger.

"Yeah, Red, that's one promise I *can* make." He brushed his lips over her face. "For better or for worse, but for damn sure never for granted."

Epilogue

Three months later

Surrounded by close friends and family in the kitchen of the ranch house, a beaming Cody inhaled a lungful of air, puffed out his cheeks, and then squeezed his lids shut on a long, hard gust. When he opened his eyes again, they widened to comic proportions to discover all ten birthday candles still blazing. "I didn't get none of 'em?" he cried in dismay.

"Guess you better try harder," Dirk replied with a mischievous grin.

Janice hadn't known until that instant that Dirk had switched out the birthday candles. His good-natured teasing and growing relationship with Cody warmed her heart, but today was a particular joy.

"You've both done wonders for Dirk," her misty-eyed mother-in-law murmured beside her. "I haven't seen this side of my son in years and didn't think I'd ever see it again."

"They've been good for each other," Janice replied. In the few short weeks since she and Dirk had wed in a private ceremony at the Sacajawea, Cody had come to idolize his "stepfather."

"Yes, they have been," Donna agreed. "He loves that boy, Janice."

"And Cody idolizes him in return. Dirk wants to go

ahead with a legal adoption if Cody agrees. I think he plans to ask Cody later today."

"Adopt his *own* son?" Donna looked aghast. "Aren't you going to tell him the truth?"

"We're not. At least not yet. It was Dirk's decision, not mine," Janice explained. "He said Cody's been through enough. We won't withhold anything he asks about, but we both want him to adjust gradually."

"If you think that's best..." Donna's expression revealed her doubts.

"We believe it's the best way," Janice affirmed and then looked back to Dirk and Cody.

"You better take a bigger breath this time," Dirk coached the boy.

Wade, an obvious co-conspirator, was capturing it all on video as Cody huffed and puffed and then made his second valiant attempt to blow out the candles. This time he kept his eyes open. The candles sputtered only to reignite before his incredulous face.

"Hey! Wait a minute!" He flashed an accusatory look at Dirk and then Janice. "Is this some kinda trick?"

"What do you mean, Cody?" Dirk deadpanned.

Janice covered her mouth in an attempt to suppress the burst of mirth that bubbled in her chest, only to lose the battle when Dirk winked at her. A full-bodied chuckle erupted from her, echoed by Dirk's baritone rumble.

"Hey! It is a joke!" Cody cried. "How do we put these out? I want some of Grandma's chocolate cake."

"Tell you what, partner, why don't we let the women figure that out while we head out to the workshop?"

"What's in the workshop?" Cody asked.

Dirk handed him a jacket. "It's a surprise."

"What is it?" Cody asked, bright-eyed, eagerly thrusting his arms into the new Carhartt jacket he'd wanted—the one just like Dirk's.

"A birthday present," Dirk insisted. "You'll find out what it is when we get out there. Here. You should wear this too." He thrust the black Stetson Wade and Nikki had gifted Cody onto the boy's head.

"What *kind* of present?" Cody cajoled.

"The kind that's a secret. Dang, boy. You're as bad as your mother." Dirk sent a mock glower Janice's way.

"Why don't you go out there too?" Donna suggested to Janice. "You won't want to miss this. Nikki and I can serve up the cake."

"So you know what this surprise is?" Janice asked Donna.

"I do. Justin and Dirk built it together."

"What did they build?" she persisted.

Donna shook her head with a laugh and shooed Janice out the door, tossing her jacket after her. Janice chafed her arms and then pulled it on, following the fresh tracks in the snow to the workshop behind the house. She was only seconds behind the men, arriving just as Dirk instructed Cody to cover his eyes.

"No peeking," Dirk commanded. He and Justin rolled back the workshop's double doors. "OK. You can open now."

The moment Cody's hazel eyes popped open, Dirk swept out his arm. Surrounded by a pile of wood shavings was a bucking barrel, the kind beginner bull riders train on.

"Cody, meet your first bull. Your grandpa and I

named him Twister," Dirk said, "but you can call it anything you like."

"You're really gonna teach me to ride bulls?" Cody's
voice was breathless. His eyes shone.

"Said I would, didn't I? You can start on the barrel
and then when the new calves are big enough, we'll put
you on a few of them."

"Really?"

"Yup. C'mon, partner. We'll go over all the particu-
lars about ropes and rosin later. Right now I know your
teeth are itching to get on this thing. Up you go!"

He hoisted Cody onto the barrel. "Hold out your left
hand. This is your bull rope."

Dirk spent several minutes explaining the bare basics
before wrapping the rope around Cody's hand. "Your
hips and heels are your anchor," he explained.

Dirk positioned the boy's hips forward over his hand
and then pressed Cody's booted heels into the sides of
the barrel. Dirk's ice-blue gaze met and held Janice's.

"The single most important thing I've ever learned
about bull riding is that it's just like life. It's all about
finding your balance."

Read on for an excerpt from the next book in the Hot Cowboy Nights series by Victoria Vane

Sharp Shooter

Mojave Desert, Southern California

LYING ON HIS BELLY BEHIND AN OUTCROPPING OF ROCKS, Reid squinted into the scope of his rifle. He was sweating like a pig in his dirt-encrusted ghillie suit and didn't even want to *think* about how he smelled after three days in hundred-plus temps. He shifted his body. His legs were numb from hours of observation, but he still felt the gravel chewing through the suit and into his skin.

"You got plans after this, *hermano*?" asked his spotter, Rafael Garcia. They'd met during basic eighteen months ago and had done two tours together. Six months after returning, they'd both earned the coveted Scout Sniper hog's tooth they proudly wore around their necks.

"Nothing special," Reid answered. "You?"

"Oh yeah. Big plans, considering this is our final weekend of freedom and the last chance to score some ass. You need to come along this time."

Reid squinted through his riflescope at the village below where the USMC had re-created a near perfect model of their mission theater, complete with hundreds of Arabic speakers who wandered the streets and haggled in the staged marketplace. It was quiet below; maybe too quiet.

"No can do, Raf. I've got phone calls to make and a ton of shit to take care of before we deploy." In truth, he was still licking his wounds.

What pissed him off most wasn't so much getting dumped, as he'd half-expected that, but her chosen method. After two years together, she hadn't even allowed him the satisfaction of tearing up a letter. That's what really sucked. Rather than a letter or even a phone call, she'd sent a Dear John text on New Year's Eve: Can't wait for U anymore. ☹ So sorry Reid. Take care. Tonya.

Five months later, he still wasn't over it. After seeing so many guys dumped during deployments—and now having experienced it himself—he'd banished any thought of women from his mind.

"C'mon, *hermano*," Garcia cajoled. "You've still got all next week to take care of that shit. You gotta get some while the getting is still good. We're looking at eight straight months of *chaqueta*."

"*Chaqueta*? Jacket?" Reid translated with a frown.

"No, man." Garcia grinned, fisting his hand and mimicking jacking off.

"You speak English as well as I do. Why can't you just use it?" Reid asked.

"You're not in Wyoming anymore. You need to learn some Spanish. Hispanics are the fastest growing minority. Especially here in So Cal. Who knows? We may even outnumber you *gringos* before the end of the century. Just think of it as broadening your cultural horizons."

"Yeah? Well, I think my cultural horizons are gonna expand real soon, considering where we're headed."

"And the *hijos de puta madres* over there will kill you for touching their women. Shit, they don't even let you look at them. For the next eight months, we'll all be doing *puñetas*."

Garcia was right. The coming months would be almost monastic. No sex. No booze. A supreme test of both celibacy and abstinence. Most of the grunts would spend the next week drinking till they puked and fucking anything that moved. He didn't judge, but that didn't mean he wanted to be part of it.

"Tell you what, *ése*," Garcia continued, as he raised his binoculars, "if you go this weekend, I'll even take you someplace where your cowboy ass will feel right at home."

"In Southern California?"

"Yeah. We have rednecks in *tejanos* out here too. *Mierda*," Garcia swore softly. "Insurgent sighted at two o'clock. He's got an RPG shouldered."

"Fuck. Can't see him."

This was the final test of a grueling, sleep-deprived seventy-two hours, and he was about to fail. Reid pulled back from his scope to blink the dust out of his eyes, then scanned for his target again. "Sighted," Reid confirmed with relief. "Got the son of a bitch in the crosshairs."

"Too slow, *hombre*. He's already taking cover. Looks like he's going to launch from behind that concrete wall."

"The hell he is." At twelve hundred yards, it was the longest shot Reid had ever attempted, but his bipod supported the deadliest weapon he'd ever fired. The M82A3 with fifty-caliber rounds could certainly handle the distance and even a concrete wall. Hell, it could probably take out a fucking tank from a mile away.

"Wind call?" he asked.

"Steady at seven miles per hour. No cross breeze," Garcia replied.

Reid doped his scope.

"Push it left point two," Garcia instructed.

"You sure about that?" Reid had estimated point three. He was rarely off, but Garcia knew his shit. He'd proven to be the best spotter in their class.

"Yeah, I'm sure. You gotta trust me." Garcia echoed his own thoughts, but Reid was accustomed to relying on his instincts. It was hard to turn that over to someone else. "Tell you what," Garcia continued, "if you miss the mark, you're off the hook. If you hit, you're the designated driver."

To any other guy that kind of bet might provide incentive to miss, but Garcia knew him too well. Reid took pride on *never* missing a shot and had an entire trophy room of big game back in Wyoming to prove it.

"All right by me." Reid made the necessary adjustment and honed in once more on his target, a silhouette behind a concrete wall that stood over half a mile away.

One shot. One kill. The scout sniper mantra. It was time to take it.

Reid inhaled slow and deep. Exhaling, his finger tightened on the trigger. He held the next breath for a three count and then slowly and deliberately squeezed. The recoil rammed his right shoulder. The discharge blasted his ears. Three seconds later, half the concrete wall disintegrated before their eyes.

"*Mierda!*" Garcia lowered his spotting scope with a grin. "That thing's a fucking cannon. So, are we gonna take a taxi or do you wanna drive?"

"I don't know why I let you drag me here. You know as well as I do that I'm gonna hate this place."

Yolanda pouted. "C'mon, *chica*. When was the last time you had any fun? You've had your nose buried in your books for months, and now you're gonna be working all summer in the middle of nowhere. Just give it a chance, OK?"

"There's plenty of other places we could have gone besides a redneck club," Haley groused.

"But this place has the biggest dance floor in California. Four thousand square feet to shake your booty."

"You're the dancer, not me." The club scene wasn't Haley's thing. At all.

"Don't be such a wet blanket. It'll be fun."

Haley cast a disparaging eye over the line of girls in their cowboy boots and ass-squeezing Daisy Dukes. "The place is a bit testosterone-challenged, don't you think?"

Yolanda laughed. "Don't worry about that. In a couple of hours, it's gonna be swarming with horny marines."

"Great." Haley rolled her eyes.

"You're the one who mentioned testosterone," Yolanda said, grinning.

Although they'd been best friends since junior high school, she and Yolanda had vastly different priorities. Haley didn't even try to keep up with her best friend's revolving-door love life.

"Rarely." Yolanda winked at her. "There's a lot more to life than books, Haley, but don't take my word for it. It's time you discover for yourself."

"What's the point?" Haley argued. "I don't have time to date."

"Who says anything about dating?" Yolanda replied. "We're just here to have a good time, right? It doesn't have to lead to anything.

"Look," Yolanda continued, "if you don't want to be accosted by horny marines, just stay out on the floor. You don't even need a partner. They play mainly line dances here, and most of those guys are too macho to line dance."

"I'm just going to make an ass of myself."

"It's why we came early," Yolanda countered. "So you can take advantage of the lessons. If you don't catch on, *no problema*. They'll mix it up later with some freestyle hip-hop. C'mon. At least give it a chance. It'll be fun."

"Yeah, barrels of fun," Haley mumbled.

They moved slowly up the line.

The big, bald, unsmiling bouncer held out his hand. "ID."

"You'd think they'd be a bit friendlier," Haley groused as both girls fished out their wallets.

Yolanda presented her license and promptly received an over-twenty-one bracelet.

"Pay to the right," he said. "Next."

Haley received a scowl when she presented her ID. "Put out both hands."

She complied and got a big black X on the back of each with a Sharpie. Great. If she wanted ink on her body, she'd have gotten a tat.

"We enforce the law," he warned. "Try to drink, and we'll boot your ass. Pay to the right."

She stepped to the counter already feeling like a felon.

"Twenty bucks," the cashier announced without even looking up.

Haley presented her debit card.

The woman shook her head. "Cash only."

"Cash? Who carries cash anymore?"

"No cash. No entry."

"Just a minute. Let me find my friend." Haley searched the crowd for Yolanda, but she'd already gone inside.

"You're holding up the line."

"But I don't have any—"

"I got it." A soft, whiskey-smooth baritone sounded from behind her.

Haley spun around to meet a solid wall of chest. Her gaze tracked north of the button-down Western shirt to meet a pair of sky-blue eyes shadowed by a well-worn Stetson. Built like a rock, with dimples to boot, this tall cowboy stirred interest in places she'd ignored for a very long time. She'd never gone for that type before, but when he gazed down at her with a heart-skipping grin stretching his mouth... *Holy cow...boy*.

He stepped up to the cashier, flipped his wallet open, and handed the woman two twenties.

"I'll pay you back as soon as we get inside," Haley blurted. "I have a friend—"

Blue Eyes shook his head. "It's no big deal. I got it. If it bothers you that much, you can pay me back later on with a dance."

"Thanks for the easy terms, but I'm not much of a

dancer." Haley's mouth stretched into an involuntary smile. He really was hot and a charmer too.

His answering smile morphed into a crooked grin revealing even white teeth. The night was starting to look up. Her gaze tracked to his blue eyes again. Way up.

"That's a bit of a relief actually," he said. "I manage a passable two-step, but that's about the limit of my repertoire." He nodded to the gap that had broadened between them and the door. "Wanna go inside now?"

Haley tensed under the sudden contact of his big, warm palm on her lower back. It was a light touch that still set every nerve ending on alert. Discomposed by her own response, she fought the instinct to pull away. Forcing a breath, she willed herself to relax, and let him guide her toward the door.

Once inside, he offered his hand. "I'm Reid."

She eyeballed him anew. A handshake? Was he for real? "You're not from around here, are you?"

"No, ma'am." His annoyingly disarming grin lingered. She didn't trust how easily she responded to it, to him. "Born and raised in Wyoming."

"Wyoming? So you're the genuine article and not one of those jokers?" She inclined her head to the throng gathered around the mechanical bull.

He shook his head with a scoffing sound. "I earned my spurs on the real thing."

She glanced down at his boots, expecting to see them. He chuckled. "I don't wear 'em unless I'm ridin'."

"So are you going to show them how it's done?"

"I got nothing to prove. Besides, there's no comparison. A mechanical bull can't stomp you into the dirt or plant a horn in your ass."

"Are you working on one of the ranches out here?"

"Nope. I've hung it all up for the U.S. Marine Corps."

"You're a *marine*?" she repeated in dismay.

"Yup. Corporal Reid Everett of the Third Battalion First Marines."

Damn. Damn. Damn. Why did the only guy she'd taken any interest in since God knows when have to be a marine? The revelation instantly snuffed out any flicker of interest. A potential fling with a hot cowboy was one thing, but a jarhead was completely out of consideration.

"Nice meeting you, Reid." She turned away.

He laid a hand on her arm, his brows meeting in a subtle frown. "Not quite the reaction I'd expected…"

"My father was a marine," she explained.

"*Was?*"

"So I'm told," she responded, tight-lipped. "I never knew him. I'm going to find my friend now."

"Wait a minute. Wha'd I say?" He looked confused and maybe even a bit hurt, like she'd locked his wheels up and sent him skidding.

"It's not what you said. It's what you *are*."

Just another whore-mongering marine. They were all just a bunch of horny dogs. Her own father had been one of them—impregnating her mother, never to be heard from again.

The grunts from Camp Pendleton had an especially long and well-earned history. She'd even done a research study on it for one of her college classes. Since the USMC established their base in 1942, the number of illegitimate births within a one-hundred-mile radius of the base had skyrocketed nine months after every major troop deployment. The data was undeniable.

Semper fidelis certainly didn't apply to the women they left behind.

"I'm not into marines, Reid. But don't worry, there are plenty of women here who would be more than eager to give you a memorable pre-deployment send-off."

Not daring to look back, Haley made a brisk retreat.

—◦◦◦—

Reid stared after the petite blond in consternation. Although he'd arrived without the slightest interest in getting laid, that was before he'd eyed her. She seemed so different from all the rest. Reserved. Almost aloof. Dressed in a pale yellow sundress with a long, loose braid down her back, she'd stuck out like a sore thumb compared to the others in their belly shirts, miniskirts, and booty shorts.

He'd wondered what all that gold silk would look like loose and kissing the dimples of her ass. He shook his head in mild disappointment. Guess he'd never find out.

"*Ay! Cabrón!*" Garcia appeared at Reid's side with two bottles of Dos Equis and a shit-eating grin. He offered one of the long necks. "Who was that hot little *rubia*?"

"Dunno." Reid accepted the beer with a grimace. "Never got her name." He still couldn't figure her abrupt about-face. She'd begun to soften toward him, only to turn frigid as ice in the blink of an eye. "I gathered she's not partial to jarheads."

"Then best cut your losses, 'cause you sure as shit aren't going to score there. Maybe you should try a *Chicana*? Just pick one and ask her to slow dance. There're plenty of hot little *mamasitas* on that floor who'd go for that six-three frame and pretty boy face."

Reid took a swig of beer. The dance lessons had finished with a manic performance of "Cotton-Eye Joe." The lines broke up with dancers dispersing toward the various bars.

"Here's your chance, bro. All you gotta do is offer her a drink. I'll even teach you to say it in Spanish: *Quiero comer tu coño*."

Reid eyed Garcia with suspicion. "I thought *comer* was 'to eat.'"

"Eat, drink." Garcia shrugged. "It's all the same in Spanish."

"I'm not falling for it, Garcia. I've been around you long enough to have a pretty good notion of what *coño* means."

"Hey, man." Garcia raised his hands. "Just doing you a favor. That phrase is sure to come in handy for you one day."

"I appreciate your concern for my dick, *amigo*, but I'm really not interested in chasing tail. Blond or *Chicana*. I'm perfectly happy to leave the field open, chill with a couple of beers, and shoot some pool."

"Suit yourself, *cabrón*. But the only balls I'm interested in are right here." He cupped his crotch with a smirk.

The blare of hip-hop music drew their attention back to the floor. Couples were already pairing for some up-close freak and grind, while a few girls were twerking in groups.

"*Mira ese culo*! Look at that ass, man." Garcia gestured to a curvy brunette. He up-ended his bottle, emptied it in one long swallow, and then handed it to Reid. "Target sighted, *hermano*. Time to engage."

—ᴍ—

Haley didn't know why she'd let Yolanda drag her to the club. She didn't have time for guys. She was far too busy with work and school even to think about them. Or had been. Until the cowboy. He'd definitely made her *think*, but her budding infatuation died a premature death the moment he'd declared himself a leatherneck. Maybe she wasn't being fair, but the deck was firmly stacked against him.

She already wanted to leave, but Yolanda had driven. Unless her friend chose someone else to take her home tonight, she'd be stuck here until closing. Haley looked around the club with increasing dismay. She hated dancing and was surrounded by marines.

She scouted the dance floor and spotted Yolanda holding up her hair and doing a body roll, sandwiched between two guys. Maybe she'd be driving herself after all. By the look of things, Yo was gonna get a ride of *some* kind.

Yolanda spotted her and waved frantically, beckoning Haley to join her and the two guys. Haley answered with a sharp head shake. If she was going to be stuck here all night, she really needed a drink. She formed a fist with her thumb raised to her lips, the universal drink sign. Yolanda nodded acknowledgment and then ground her booty into her new partner.

Haley considered the acetone wipes Yolanda had shoved into her purse. A few minutes of scrubbing in the bathroom would erase the black marks on her hands. She weighed the consequences. If she got caught, she'd get tossed out on her ass. It was definitely worth the risk.

Moments later, Haley exited the restroom, hands thoroughly cleansed of black marker. She then discovered an ATM at the back of the club and whipped out her debit card. After collecting her cash, she headed for the nearest bar, only to be intercepted by four different guys sporting buzz cuts. She rolled her eyes. More marines. It wasn't too hard to brush them off *yet*, but the night was early and they weren't fully tanked.

She could really use that drink, but the bartenders would ask to see her bracelet before taking an order. With her friend on the floor, her only option was to ask one of the grunts to buy the drink for her. Opting for the devil she knew, the cowboy, Haley scouted the bar. At least she had the excuse of paying him back. She had enough cash to cover her debt and still buy a couple of cocktails. She found him a few minutes later shooting pool with a cadre of his leatherneck buddies.

"Hey, cowboy. I have something for you." She slapped the twenty on the table where he was setting up his first shot.

Her unintended innuendo was met with silence as his baby blues darted up from the table to meet her gaze. The rest of the group eyeballed her up and down with open interest, making her feel like she'd entered a wolf's den.

She bit her lip, wishing she'd said something else. "I-I mean I found an ATM. I can pay you back now."

His tawny brows met. "Said I didn't care about that." He pushed the twenty across the table and turned his attention back to the cue.

That was it? A brush off? Haley's hackles rose. Was this his idea of payback for her earlier snub? *I don't think so, cowboy.*

"All right then." She parked her hip on the edge of the table, blocking his view of the balls. "If you won't take it from me, play me for it."

He stepped back from the table, his gaze sweeping over her with open cynicism. "You want me to play you?"

His partner at the table sniggered. "If the cowboy won't take you up on it, I will. I'll play you like a sonata, baby."

Straightening to his full height, the cowboy shot his buddy a dangerous look. She guessed he was a few inches over six feet and wondered how much of that was the boots. Probably only an inch or so. Without them, he'd still tower at least a foot above her five foot two inches.

She dropped another twenty. "Double or nothing? Eight ball, nine ball, nine ball kiss, Chicago, Chinese, Rotation 61," she rattled off the game variations.

A buff marine in a muscle shirt flashed a lecherous grin. "I'll rotate you sixty-nine, sweetheart." No doubt about it, they were already halfway to shit-faced.

Haley ignored him. "Slop shot, call shot. Your choice, cowboy. Loser buys the drinks."

———∞———

Reid considered the blond who'd brushed him off like a fly from shit less than an hour ago. When he'd paid her cover he hadn't expected anything in return except maybe a dance, but now she'd positioned herself squarely in his crosshairs.

"So you think you're a player, eh?" Reid eyed her with renewed speculation, wondering what game she was really playing.

"Only pool," she answered as if reading his mind. "A better question would be what kind of *player* are you?" She slid off the table, letting the double entendre hang.

"Guess you'll just have to find out for yourself. Mind if the lady steps in?" he asked the cluster of marines. The request was purely rhetorical. They all knew he was staking his claim, but he'd still sweeten the deal. "Tell you what, give us some space, and I'll buy you all a round."

"Go on," she urged the grunts as if shooing chickens, adding with a grin, "I'm sure Corporal Everett doesn't want any witnesses when he gets his ass handed to him."

The marines dispersed toward the bar with muffled guffaws.

His interest ramped another notch, Reid propped his cue against the table and cocked his head to study all five-foot-nothin' of her. She was probably no more than a buck ten soaking wet, yet had the balls to go toe-to-toe with him. "You sure talk big for such a puny little thing."

"I laid my money down, didn't I? What are we play-ing?" she asked.

"Let's just keep it a simple game of eight ball." He offered her a cue. "Ladies first?"

"No. Lag for break. I play by the rules." She set up two balls for the shot.

He came up beside her and leaned over the table, his cue poised. "Always?" He was close enough to smell her, fresh and sweet like ripe strawberries. "Sometimes it's more fun to break 'em."

She snorted and chalked her cue. "Says the guy whose entire life is dictated by the USMC for what, the next four years?"

"Six more. I signed on for eight."

"*Eight?*" She pulled back with a surprised look. "What kind of idiocy is that?"

He stiffened. She had no qualms about speaking her mind, for damn sure. Lucky she was an attractive female. Good-looking women could just about get away with murder. Hell, many had. It was an injustice, or maybe God's idea of a joke, but facts were facts. Men had a long history of making life and death decisions guided by their dicks. His was already exerting a great deal of influence.

"Back home we have another word for it. It's called *patriotism*."

"Don't get your feathers all ruffled," she came back. "I just don't understand anyone's desire for that kind of life."

"The military creates order out of chaos. That often applies as much to the individual as to the mission."

"That may be, but there are plenty of other ways than the military to 'find yourself.'"

"I s'pose so," he replied. "But look how many people waste years of their lives in college only to end up flipping burgers."

She tossed her head. "And killing skills are so much more practical in life?" Her voice and eyes challenged. Taunted. But he wasn't about to take her bait.

"The Marines teach more than killing. Look…er… Hell, I still don't even know your name."

"Haley," she answered softly. "Haley Cooper."

"Look, Miz Cooper, we obviously don't see eye to eye on this issue, so let's just drop it and play."

They completed the lag shot, both balls bouncing off

the table to return to the head rail. Reid's ball was closest, a millimeter from touching the rail. He considered the table. "Looks like it's gonna be ladies first after all."

"You sure you want me to break?" She flashed him a smug smile. "You might live to regret that decision, cowboy."

Reid stood a couple of steps behind and slightly to the right, perfectly positioned to scope her out as she set up her shot. Every movement was too damned distracting. Her dress clung to her ass, riding up as she bent over the table, but not as far as he'd like. He guessed she was a distance runner by the look of her lean and shapely legs. He found his gaze caught in a loop, tracking up and down between her legs and ass.

She broke, and then straightened, tugging her skirt back down over her legs. "You haven't said what your job is, Corporal Everett."

"Scout sniper." He flushed, knowing what was coming next. She'd try to put him on the defensive.

"You're a *sniper*?" Her eyes widened. "Isn't that the same as an *assassin*?"

He felt his color deepen another shade, but was careful to keep his expression and voice neutral. "A scout sniper's primary function is to conduct close reconnaissance and surveillance in order to gain intelligence on the enemy and terrain. By necessity, he must be skilled in long-range marksmanship from concealed locations in order to support combat operations."

"Wow. That was a mouthful. Did you quote all that from some soldier manual?"

"A U.S. Marine isn't a *soldier*."

"What's the difference? You both make war, don't

you?" She studied him as if she knew she'd ventured onto treacherous ground but was still determined to see how far he'd let her tread.

"The Marine Corps' primary mission isn't to *make* war but to *protect* this country and those who can't protect themselves, Miz Cooper." He continued unapologetically, "Unfortunately, sometimes that does mean war and killing." She was intentionally pushing his hot buttons, but he was accustomed to maintaining rigid self-control.

"So you actually think some people *deserve* to die?" Her face was flushed, and her green eyes blazed.

"Some do," he answered levelly. There was no way to win once an argument got emotional. "I'm a peaceful man who believes in minding my own pastures, but I also believe in good and evil. There are a lot of very bad people in this world. Certainly the ones who fly airplanes through skyscrapers. When that kind of thing happens, I believe in doing whatever it takes to protect our own."

He could see her getting more worked up by the minute, and damned if he wasn't also—just not in the same way. She'd been baiting him from the start, spewing arguments that usually just pissed him off, but in this case, it was turning him on.

His gaze locked on her mouth. Her tongue darted out as if she read his thoughts. She drew a breath as if to formulate another rebuttal, but he'd had enough. Before her lips could spout off anymore of the Pacifist Tree Hugger's Manifesto, he pulled her into his arms and silenced her with his.

━━〰━━

The kiss came without warning, and Haley was too stunned at first to react. He began gently enough, his lips sliding over hers, hands cupping her face, thumbs stroking her jaw, and then he grew more insistent, his tongue probing the seal of her lips. His callused hands were simultaneously firm and gentle, and his lips paradoxically soft and commanding.

Mere seconds had her head spinning and stomach fluttering. She was slipping fast and not about to let him pull her in any deeper. Part of her wanted to give into it, to see where it might lead, but the other half resented his audacity. Her pride won out. She resisted the urge to soften, to open to him, then stiffened, pressing her hands against his chest.

He released her instantly.

She stepped back, knees weak and pulse racing. "I didn't come here looking to hook up."

"Neither did I. But sometimes unexpected things happen." His gaze locked with hers, a look of speculation gleaming in his eyes. "When they do, it's best to just go with your gut instinct."

"That so? Well all my instincts scream 'no marines,' so don't let it *happen* again."

Suddenly remembering the cue in her hand, Haley turned back to the table. It took all of her will to focus back on the game. She could hardly believe how he'd nearly unraveled her with a single kiss. Then again, no one had *ever* kissed her like that. She made her break, pocketing the one, and then moved methodically around the table, calling each shot as she sank every solid. Only the eight ball remained, but it was trapped behind two stripes.

Reid's lips curved with smug certainty. "Looks like I'll get my turn after all."

"Don't count your chickens, cowboy." She laid down her cue and searched the wall behind her for a shorter one. "Jump cue," she answered his silent question.

"You're kidding right?"

"Nope." Approaching the table, she angled for her shot. She could almost feel his eyes on her ass. She glanced over her shoulder. Sure enough. He was leaning against the wall with both arms crossed over his broad chest, his gaze zeroed in on her behind.

"Enjoying the view?"

"Sure am," he confessed, unabashed.

He was sadly mistaken if he thought he'd unnerve her. Keeping him in her peripheral vision, she widened her stance and stretched out over the table. All sign of smugness evaporated from his face. He tugged on his jeans.

Haley grinned, reveling in her small victory, and then prepared for a bigger one. "Eight ball, side pocket," she declared with confidence. On a three count she took the shot, jumping the stripes to pocket the eight. "Yeah baby!" She threw down the cue and fisted the air, gloating in her triumph.